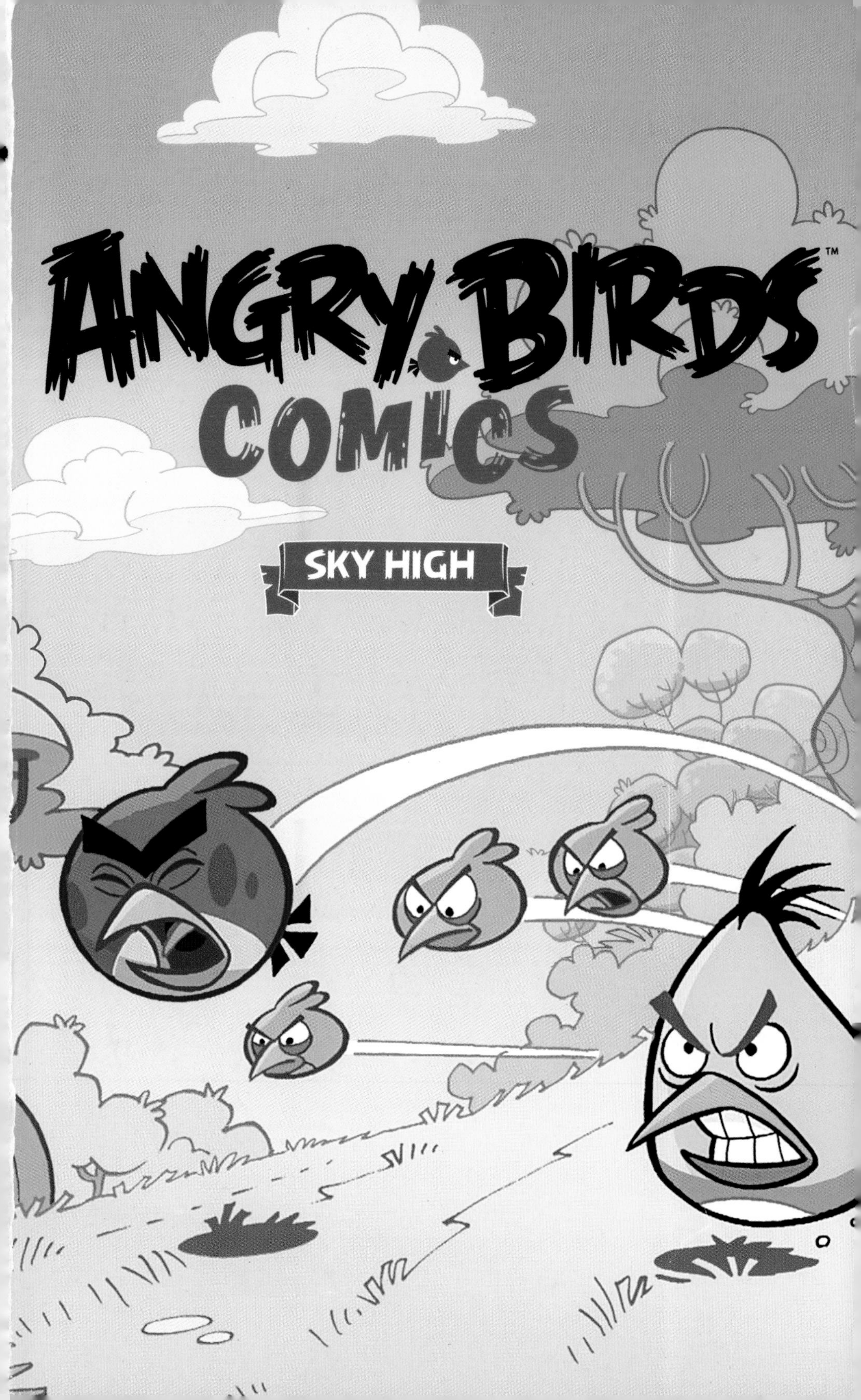
ANGRY BIRDS™
COMICS
SKY HIGH

COVER ARTWORK BY: CIRO CANGIALOSI

ORIGINAL SERIES EDITS BY: DAVID HEDGECOCK
COLLECTION EDITS BY: JUSTIN EISINGER & ALONZO SIMON
COLLECTION PRODUCTION BY: CLAUDIA CHONG

ROVIO BOOKS

Laura Nevanlinna, Publishing Director
Jukka Heiskanen, Editor-in-Chief, Comics
Juha Mäkinen, Editor, Comics
Jan Schulte-Tigges, Art Director, Comics
Henri Sarimo, Graphic Designer
Nathan Cosby, Freelance Editor

Thanks to Jukka Heiskanen, Juha Mäkinen, and the Rovio team for their hard work and invaluable assistance.

ISBN: 978-1-63140-368-2

18 17 16 15 1 2 3 4

IDW
www.IDWPUBLISHING.com
IDW founded by Ted Adams, Alex Garner, Kris Oprisko, and Robbie Robbins

Ted Adams, CEO & Publisher
Greg Goldstein, President & COO
Robbie Robbins, EVP/Sr. Graphic Artist
Chris Ryall, Chief Creative Officer/Editor-in-Chief
Matthew Ruzicka, CPA, Chief Financial Officer
Alan Payne, VP of Sales
Dirk Wood, VP of Marketing
Lorelei Bunjes, VP of Digital Services
Jeff Webber, VP of Digital Publishing & Business Development

Facebook: facebook.com/idwpublishing
Twitter: @idwpublishing
YouTube: youtube.com/idwpublishing
Instagram: instagram.com/idwpublishing
deviantART: idwpublishing.deviantart.com
Pinterest: pinterest.com/idwpublishing/idw-staff-faves

Originally published in ANGRY BIRDS COMICS issues #9–12.

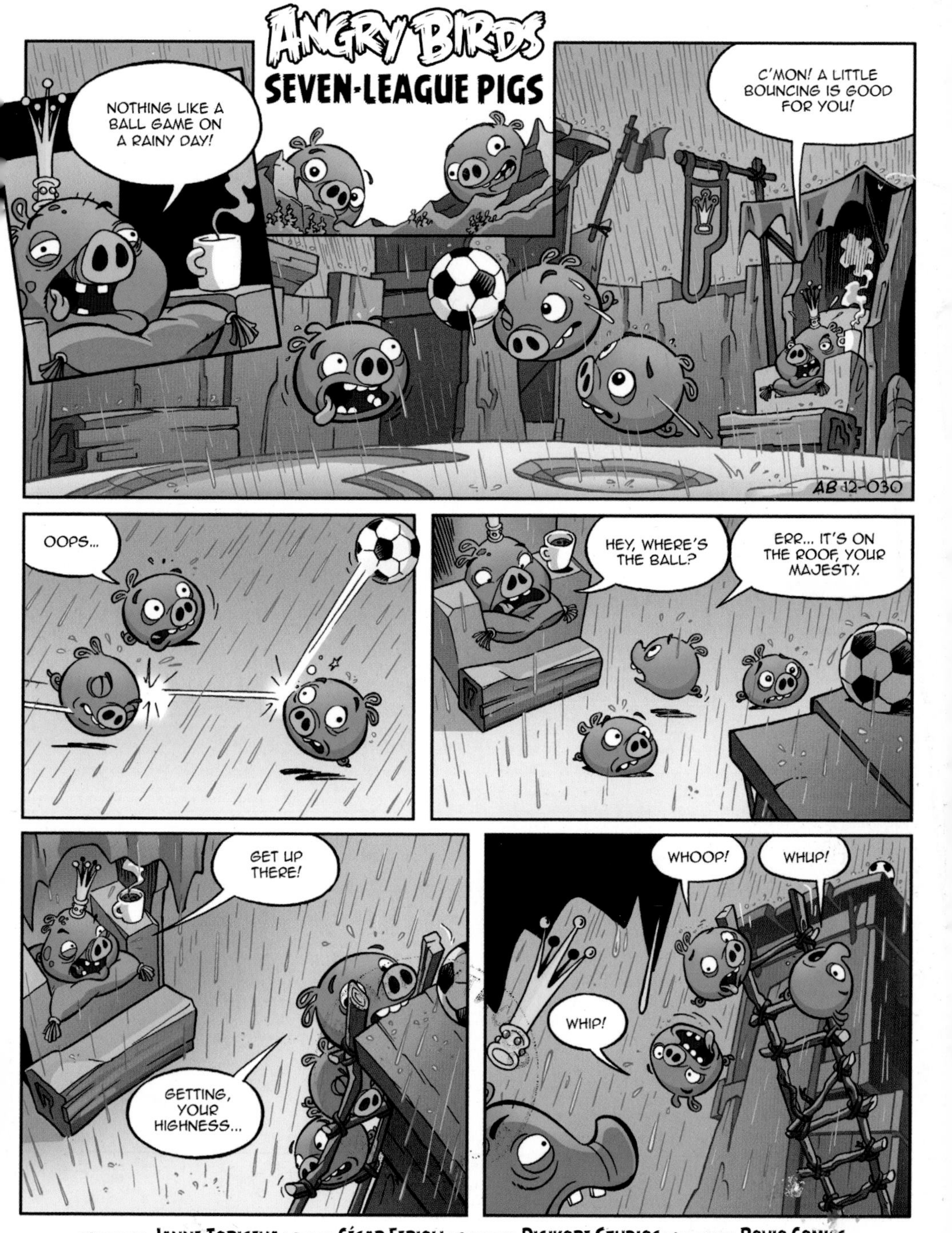
ANGRY BIRDS
SEVEN-LEAGUE PIGS
NOTHING LIKE A BALL GAME ON A RAINY DAY!
C'MON! A LITTLE BOUNCING IS GOOD FOR YOU!
AB 12-030
OOPS...
HEY, WHERE'S THE BALL?
ERR... IT'S ON THE ROOF, YOUR MAJESTY.
GET UP THERE!
GETTING, YOUR HIGHNESS...
WHOOP!
WHUP!
WHIP!

WRITTEN BY: JANNE TORISEVA • ART BY: CÉSAR FERIOLI • COLORS BY: DIGIKORE STUDIOS • LETTERS BY: ROVIO COMICS

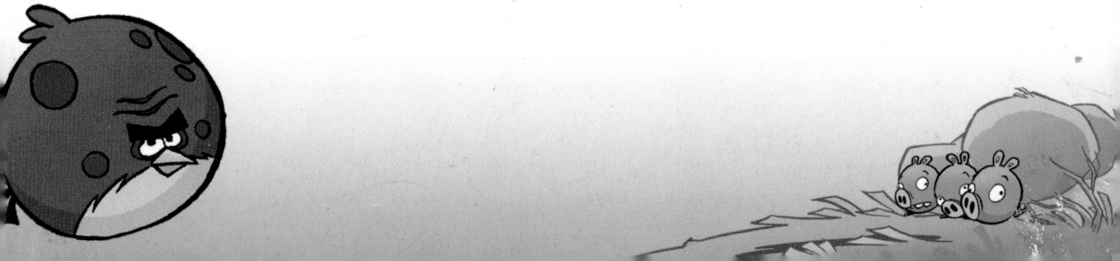

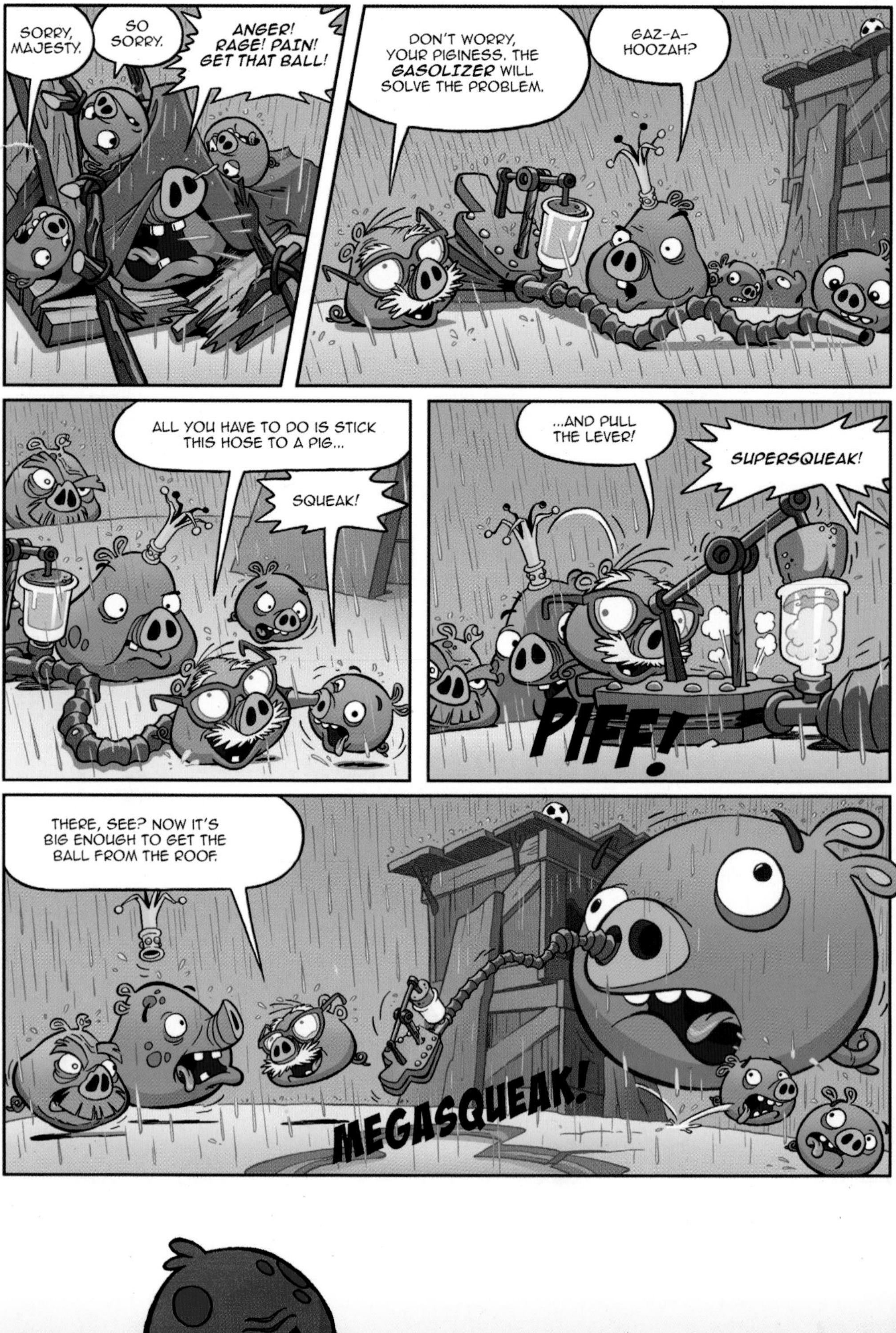
SORRY, MAJESTY.
SO SORRY.
ANGER! RAGE! PAIN! GET THAT BALL!
DON'T WORRY, YOUR PIGINESS. THE GASOLIZER WILL SOLVE THE PROBLEM.
GAZ-A-HOOZAH?
ALL YOU HAVE TO DO IS STICK THIS HOSE TO A PIG...
SQUEAK!
...AND PULL THE LEVER!
SUPERSQUEAK!
PIFF!
THERE, SEE? NOW IT'S BIG ENOUGH TO GET THE BALL FROM THE ROOF.
MEGASQUEAK!

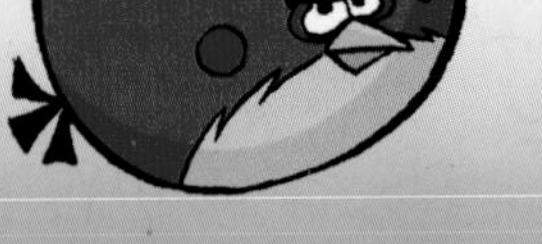

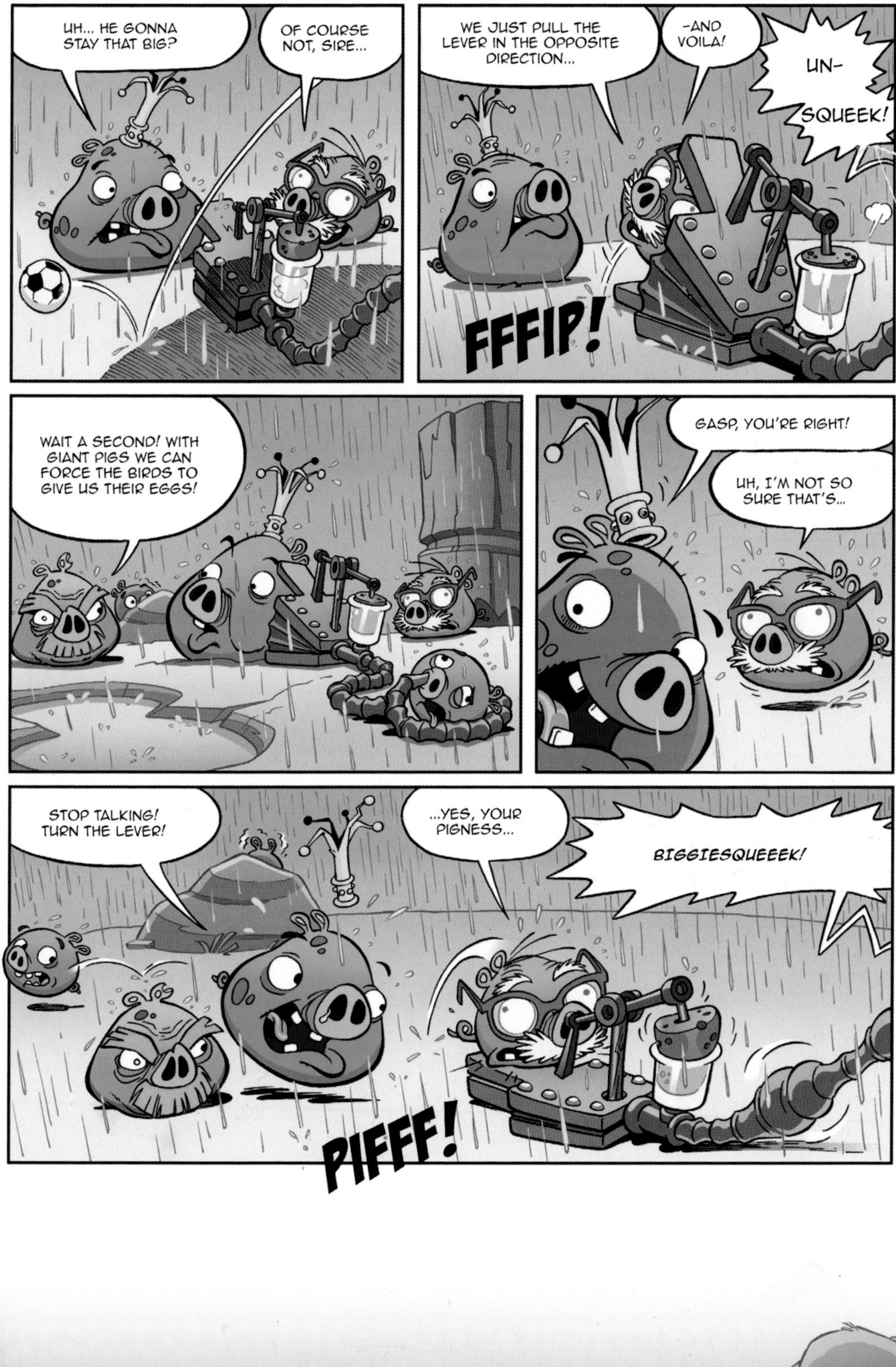
UH... HE GONNA STAY THAT BIG?
OF COURSE NOT, SIRE...
WE JUST PULL THE LEVER IN THE OPPOSITE DIRECTION...
-AND VOILA!
UN-SQUEEK!
FFFIP!
WAIT A SECOND! WITH GIANT PIGS WE CAN FORCE THE BIRDS TO GIVE US THEIR EGGS!
GASP, YOU'RE RIGHT!
UH, I'M NOT SO SURE THAT'S...
STOP TALKING! TURN THE LEVER!
...YES, YOUR PIGNESS...
BIGGIESQUEEEK!
PIFFF!
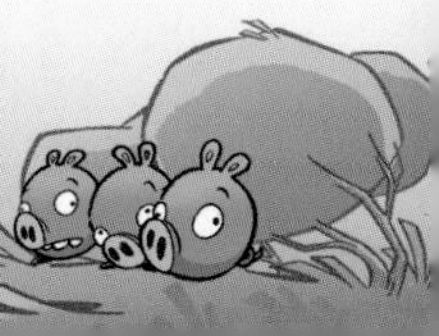

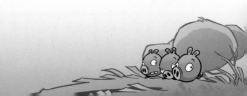

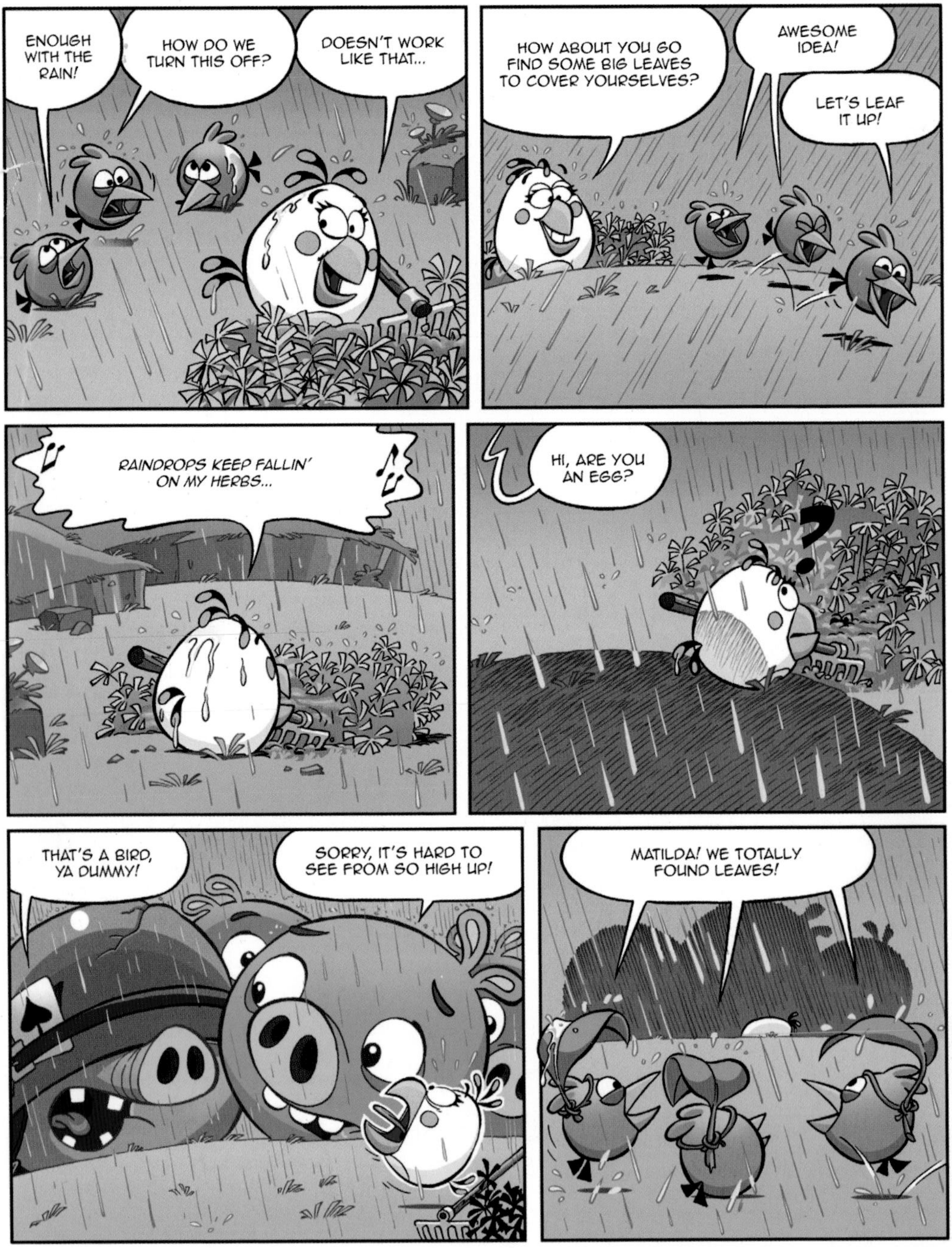
ENOUGH WITH THE RAIN!
HOW DO WE TURN THIS OFF?
DOESN'T WORK LIKE THAT...
HOW ABOUT YOU GO FIND SOME BIG LEAVES TO COVER YOURSELVES?
AWESOME IDEA!
LET'S LEAF IT UP!
RAINDROPS KEEP FALLIN' ON MY HERBS...
HI, ARE YOU AN EGG?
THAT'S A BIRD, YA DUMMY!
SORRY, IT'S HARD TO SEE FROM SO HIGH UP!
MATILDA! WE TOTALLY FOUND LEAVES!

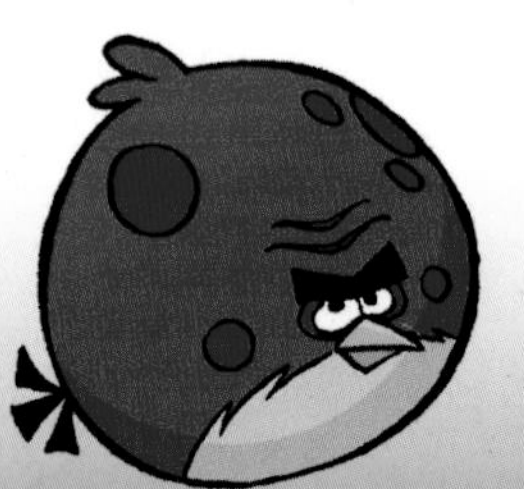

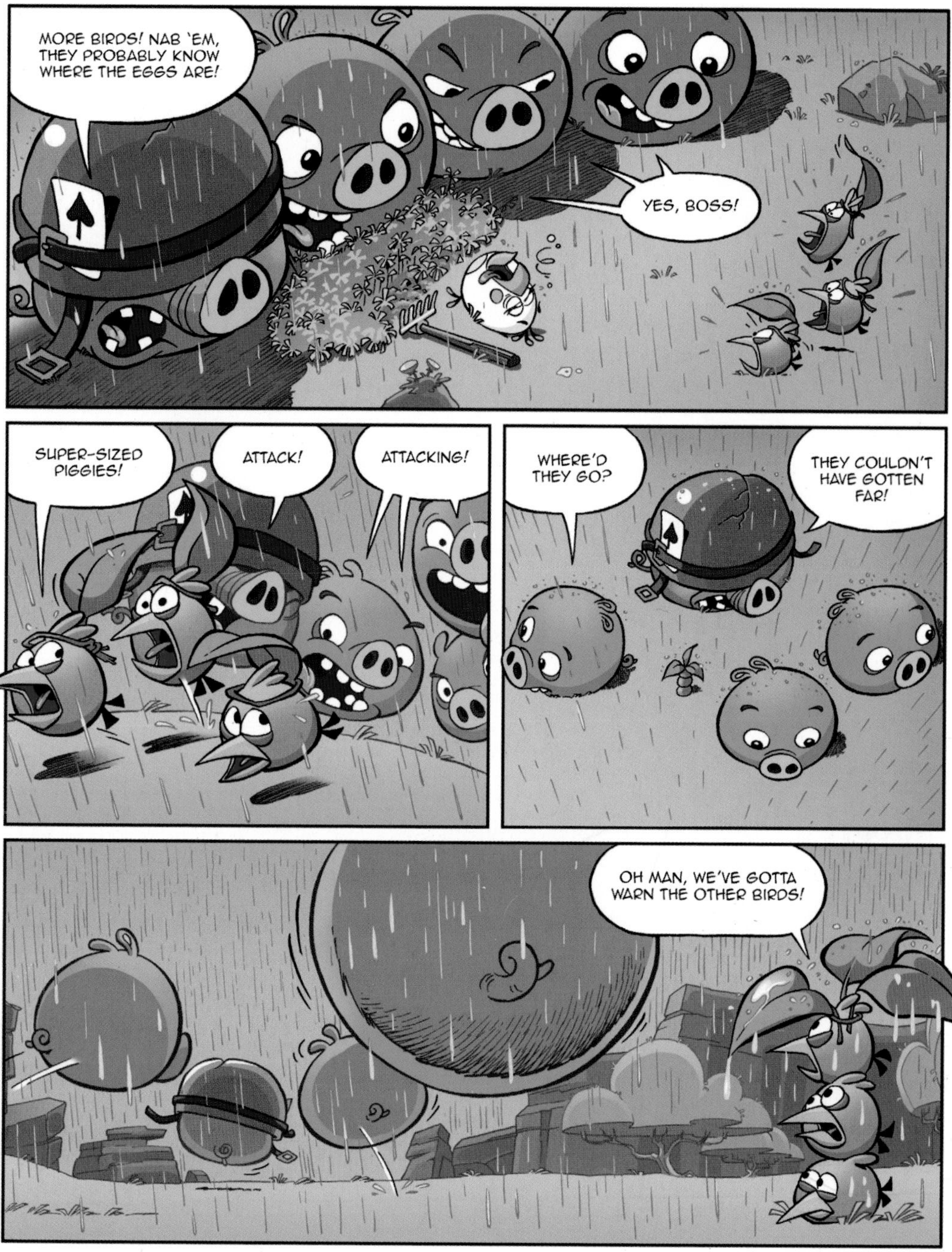
MORE BIRDS! NAB 'EM, THEY PROBABLY KNOW WHERE THE EGGS ARE!
YES, BOSS!
SUPER-SIZED PIGGIES!
ATTACK!
ATTACKING!
WHERE'D THEY GO?
THEY COULDN'T HAVE GOTTEN FAR!
OH MAN, WE'VE GOTTA WARN THE OTHER BIRDS!

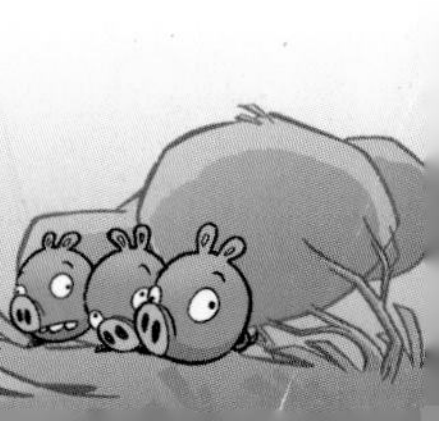

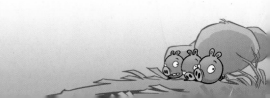

GRRR!

"TRY PAINTING", MATILDA SAYS.

"IT'S GOOD FOR YOUR NERVES!"

CALM DOWN, BOMB, BEFORE...

SPLA- BOOM!

DANG IT, BOMB...

BIG PIGS BIG PIGS BIG PIGS!

CALM DOWN! WHAT'S UP?

THEY'RE HUGE!

AND THEY WANT THE EGGS!

I HEAR CHIRPS!

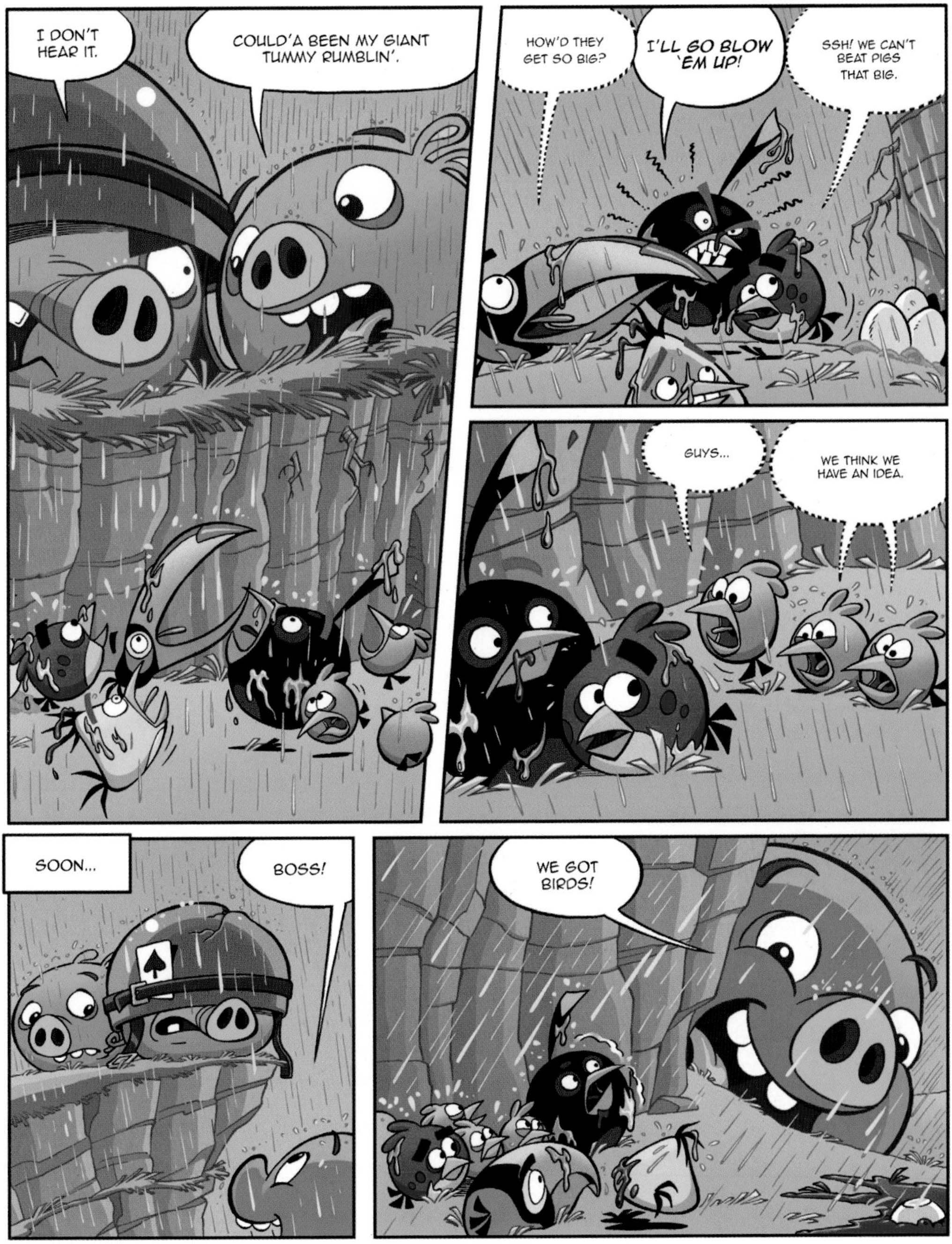
I DON'T HEAR IT.
COULD'A BEEN MY GIANT TUMMY RUMBLIN'.
HOW'D THEY GET SO BIG?
I'LL GO BLOW 'EM UP!
SSH! WE CAN'T BEAT PIGS THAT BIG.
GUYS...
WE THINK WE HAVE AN IDEA.
SOON...
BOSS!
WE GOT BIRDS!

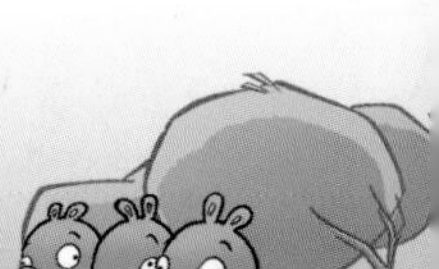

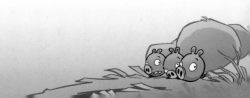

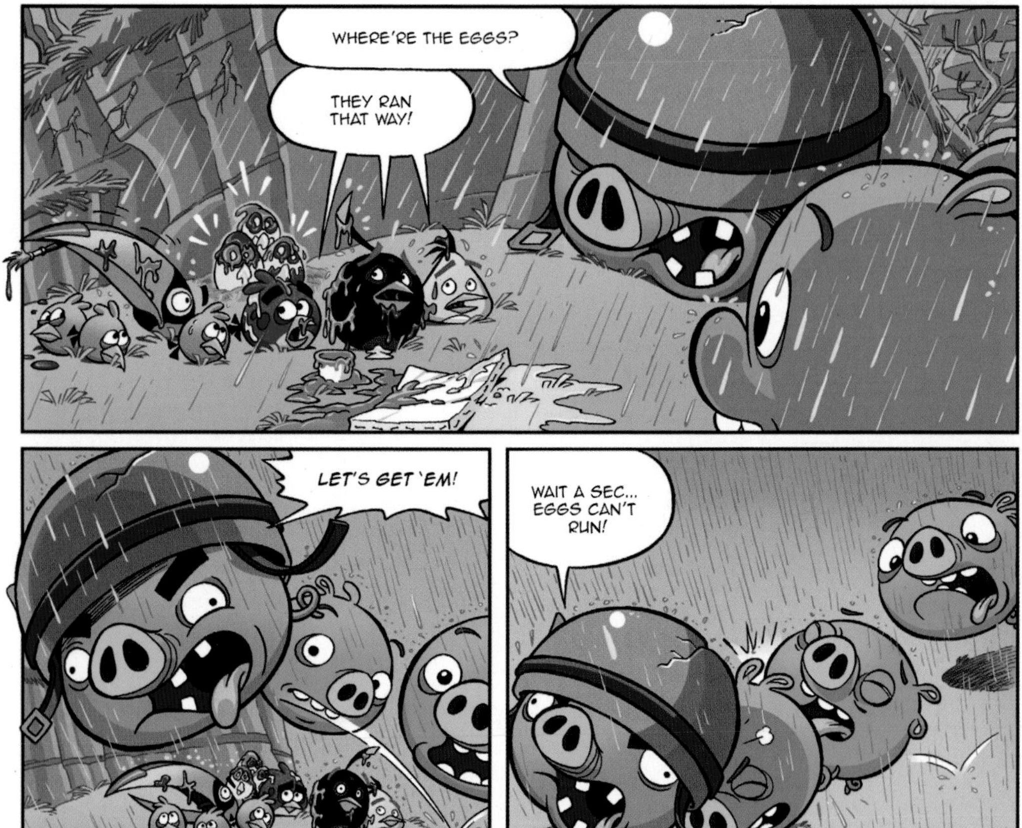
WHERE'RE THE EGGS?
THEY RAN THAT WAY!
LET'S GET 'EM!
WAIT A SEC... EGGS CAN'T RUN!
BACK TO THE BIRDS!
WHERE'D THEY...?

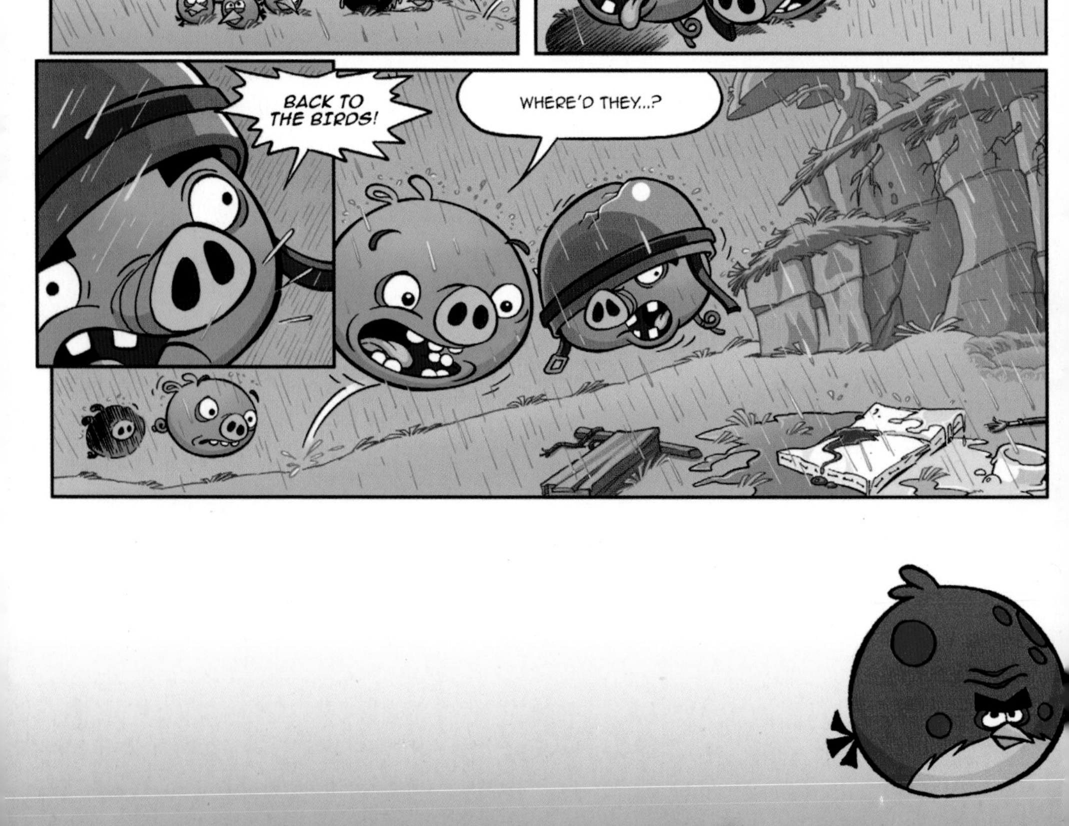

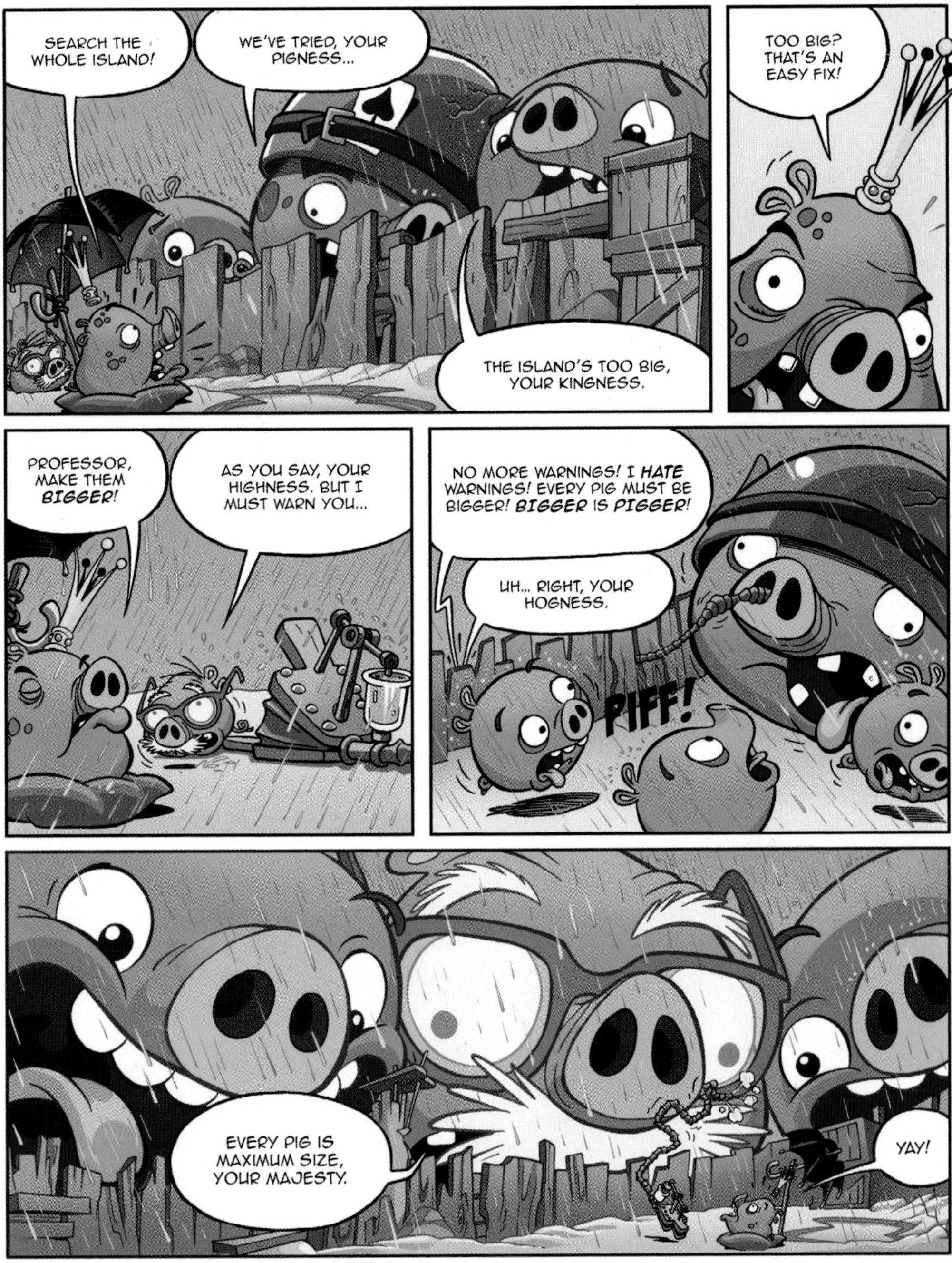
SEARCH THE WHOLE ISLAND!
WE'VE TRIED, YOUR PIGNESS...
THE ISLAND'S TOO BIG, YOUR KINGNESS.
TOO BIG? THAT'S AN EASY FIX!
PROFESSOR, MAKE THEM **BIGGER**!
AS YOU SAY, YOUR HIGHNESS. BUT I MUST WARN YOU...
NO MORE WARNINGS! I ***HATE*** WARNINGS! EVERY PIG MUST BE BIGGER! **BIGGER** IS **PIGGER**!
UH... RIGHT, YOUR HOGNESS.
PIFF!
EVERY PIG IS MAXIMUM SIZE, YOUR MAJESTY.
YAY!

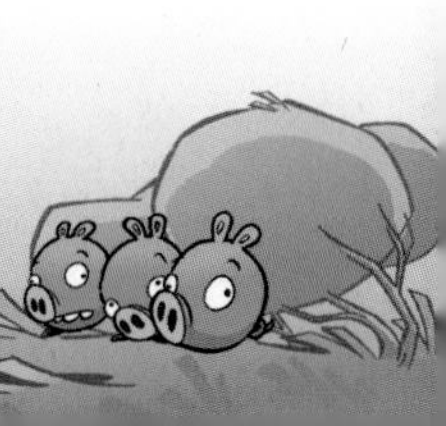

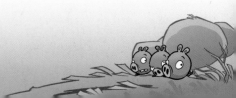

AND YOUR KING WILL BE THE BIGGEST!
PIFF!
CAREFUL, SIRE! THE MACHINE IS OVERHEATING...
THE GASOLIZER! YOU EXPLODED IT, YOUR HIGHNESS!
LESS TALK, MORE FINDING EGGS!
POF!
ACHOO! THIS IS AWFUL!
I'LL MAKE YOU SOME HERB SOUP LATER!
NO WAY ARE THE BIG PIGS GONNA FIND US NOW!
IT'S GETTING DARK...
HOW CAN YOU TELL IN THIS AWFUL STORM?
EGGGS!

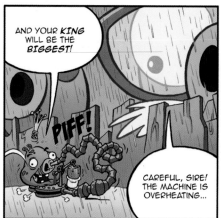

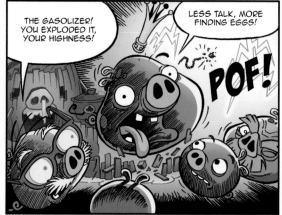

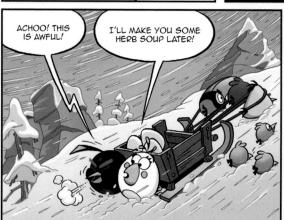

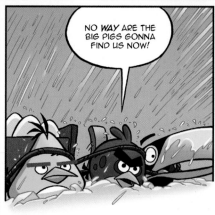

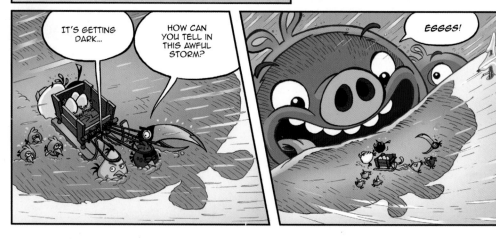

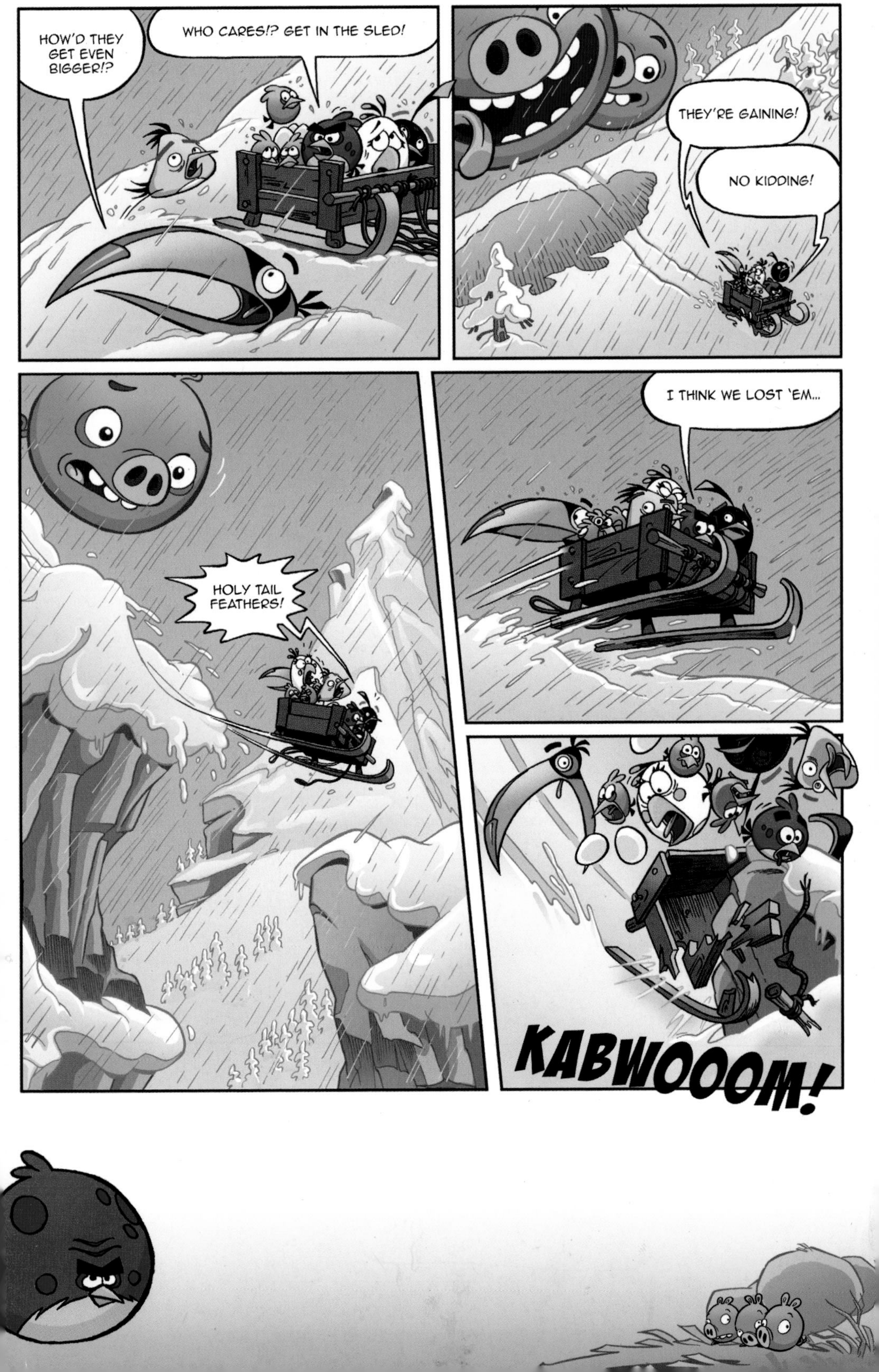
HOW'D THEY GET EVEN BIGGER!?
WHO CARES!? GET IN THE SLED!
THEY'RE GAINING!
NO KIDDING!
HOLY TAIL FEATHERS!
I THINK WE LOST 'EM...
KABWOOOM!

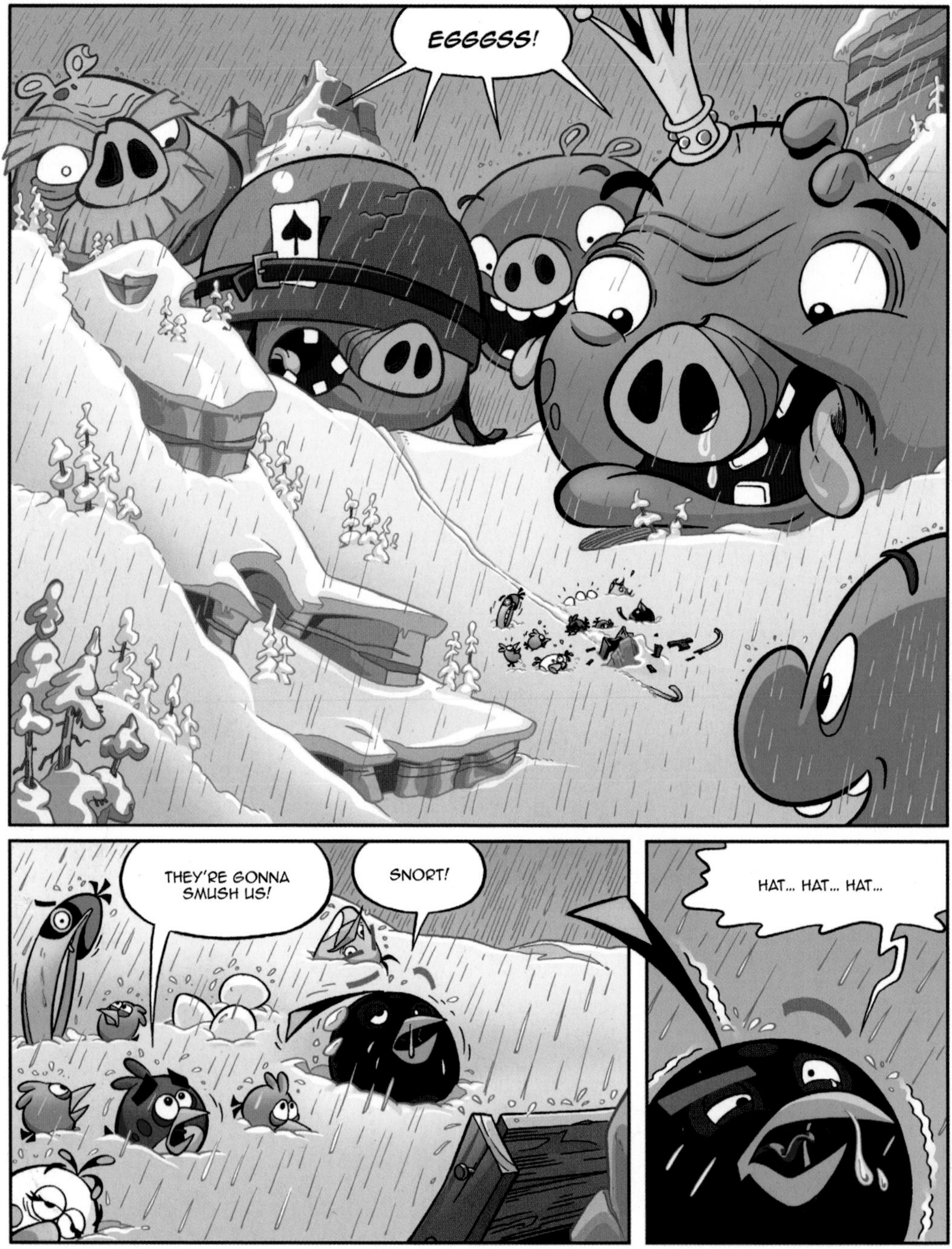
EGGGSS!
THEY'RE GONNA SMUSH US!
SNORT!
HAT... HAT... HAT...

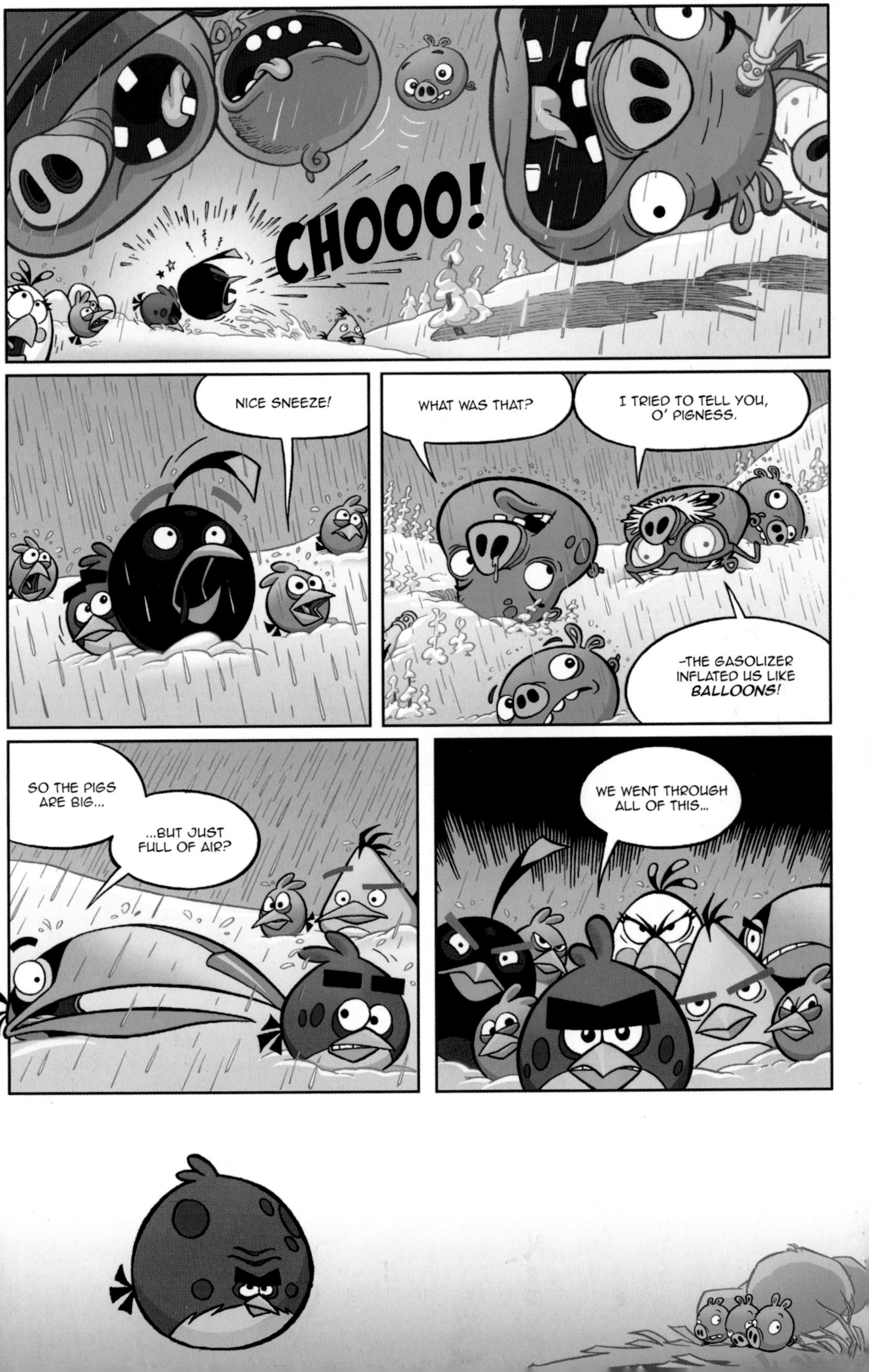
CHOOO!
NICE SNEEZE!
WHAT WAS THAT?
I TRIED TO TELL YOU, O' PIGNESS.
-THE GASOLIZER INFLATED US LIKE *BALLOONS*!
SO THE PIGS ARE BIG...
...BUT JUST FULL OF AIR?
WE WENT THROUGH ALL OF THIS...

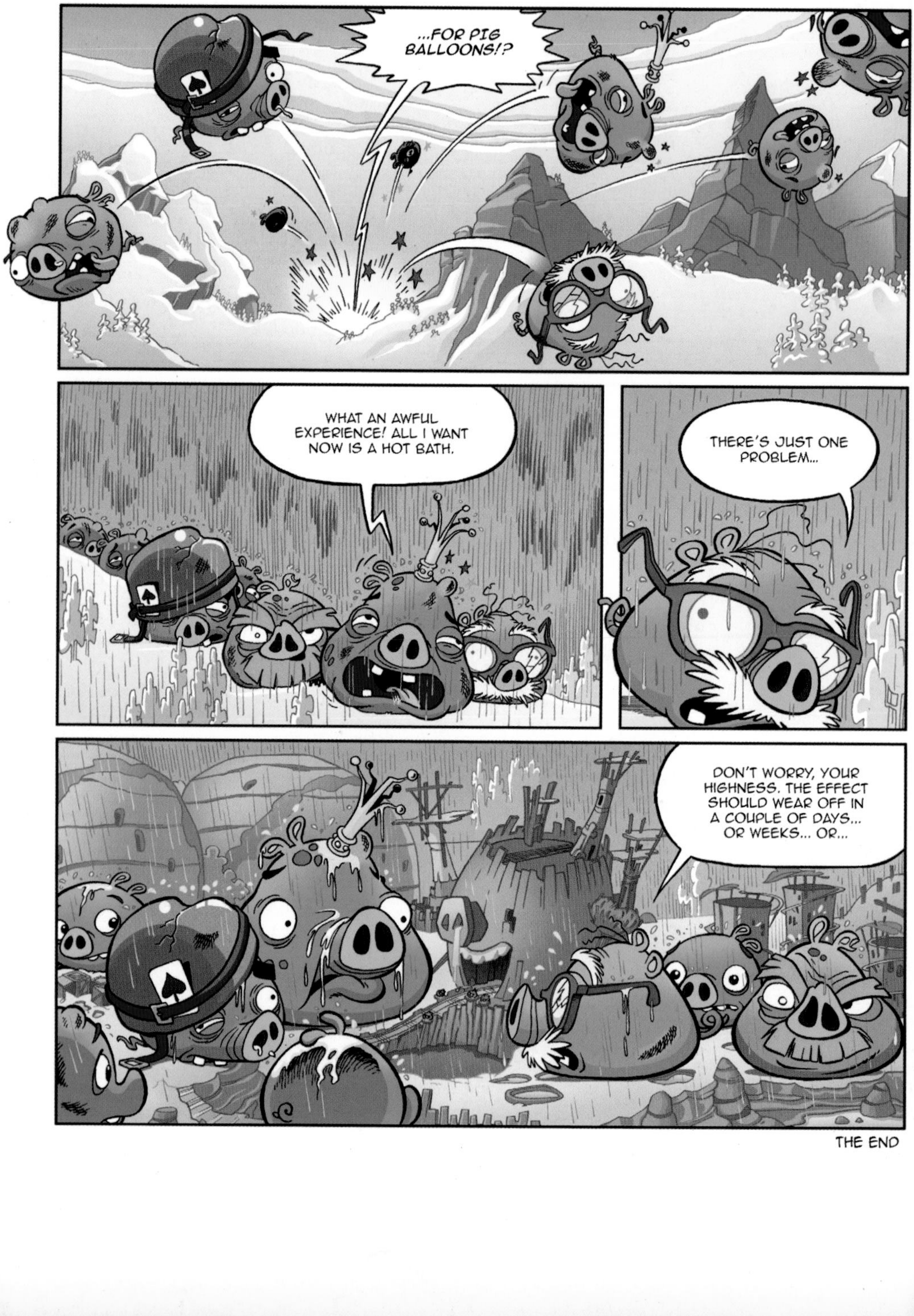
...FOR PIG BALLOONS!?
WHAT AN AWFUL EXPERIENCE! ALL I WANT NOW IS A HOT BATH.
THERE'S JUST ONE PROBLEM...
DON'T WORRY, YOUR HIGHNESS. THE EFFECT SHOULD WEAR OFF IN A COUPLE OF DAYS... OR WEEKS... OR...

THE END

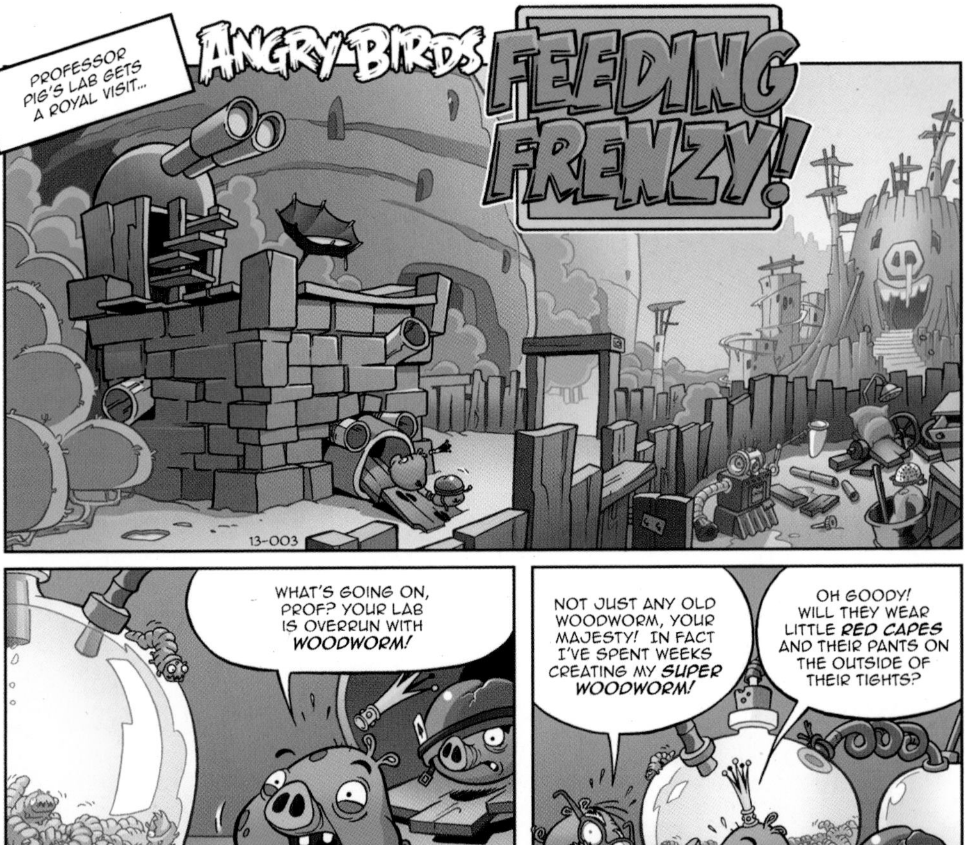
PROFESSOR PIG'S LAB GETS A ROYAL VISIT...
ANGRY BIRDS
FEEDING FRENZY!
13-003
WHAT'S GOING ON, PROF? YOUR LAB IS OVERRUN WITH *WOODWORM!*
NOT JUST ANY OLD WOODWORM, YOUR MAJESTY! IN FACT I'VE SPENT WEEKS CREATING MY *SUPER WOODWORM!*
OH GOODY! WILL THEY WEAR LITTLE *RED CAPES* AND THEIR PANTS ON THE OUTSIDE OF THEIR TIGHTS?
MORE TO THE POINT, YOU CRAZY OLD COOT... WHAT DID YOU INVENT THEM *FOR?*
THEY'RE MY LITTLE *HELPERS...* THEY CUT THROUGH WOOD AND HELP ME MAKE MANY OF MY INVENTIONS!
I LIKE THEM!
REALLY? BETTER NOT LET THEM TOO NEAR YOUR *HEAD,* COLONEL!

WRITTEN BY: GLENN DAKIN • ART BY: CÉSAR FERIOLI • COLORS BY: DIGIKORE STUDIOS • LETTERS BY: ROVIO COMICS

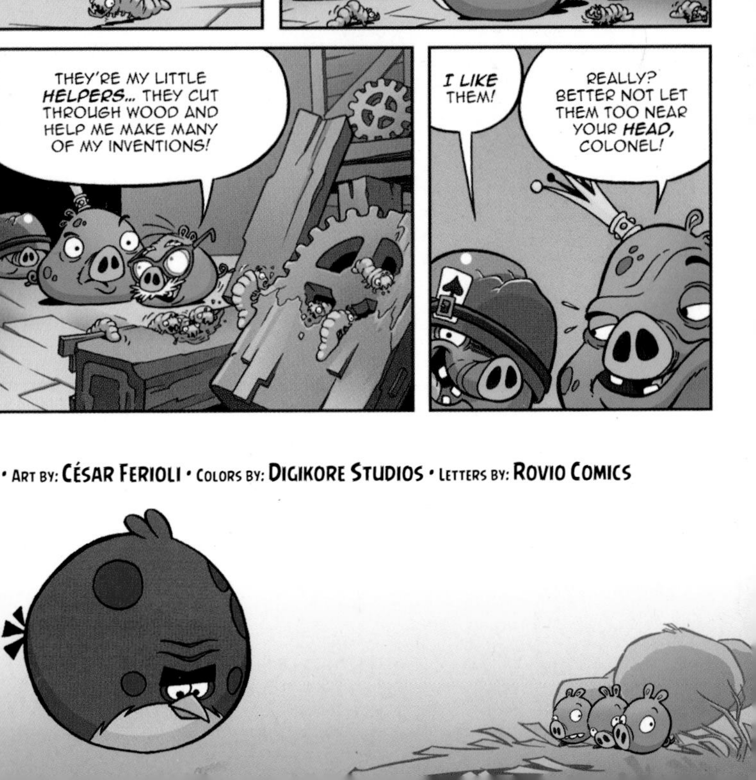

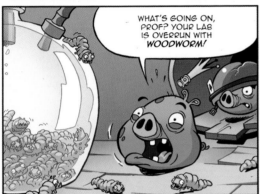

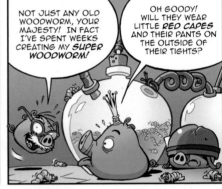

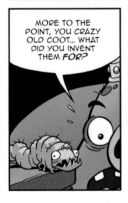

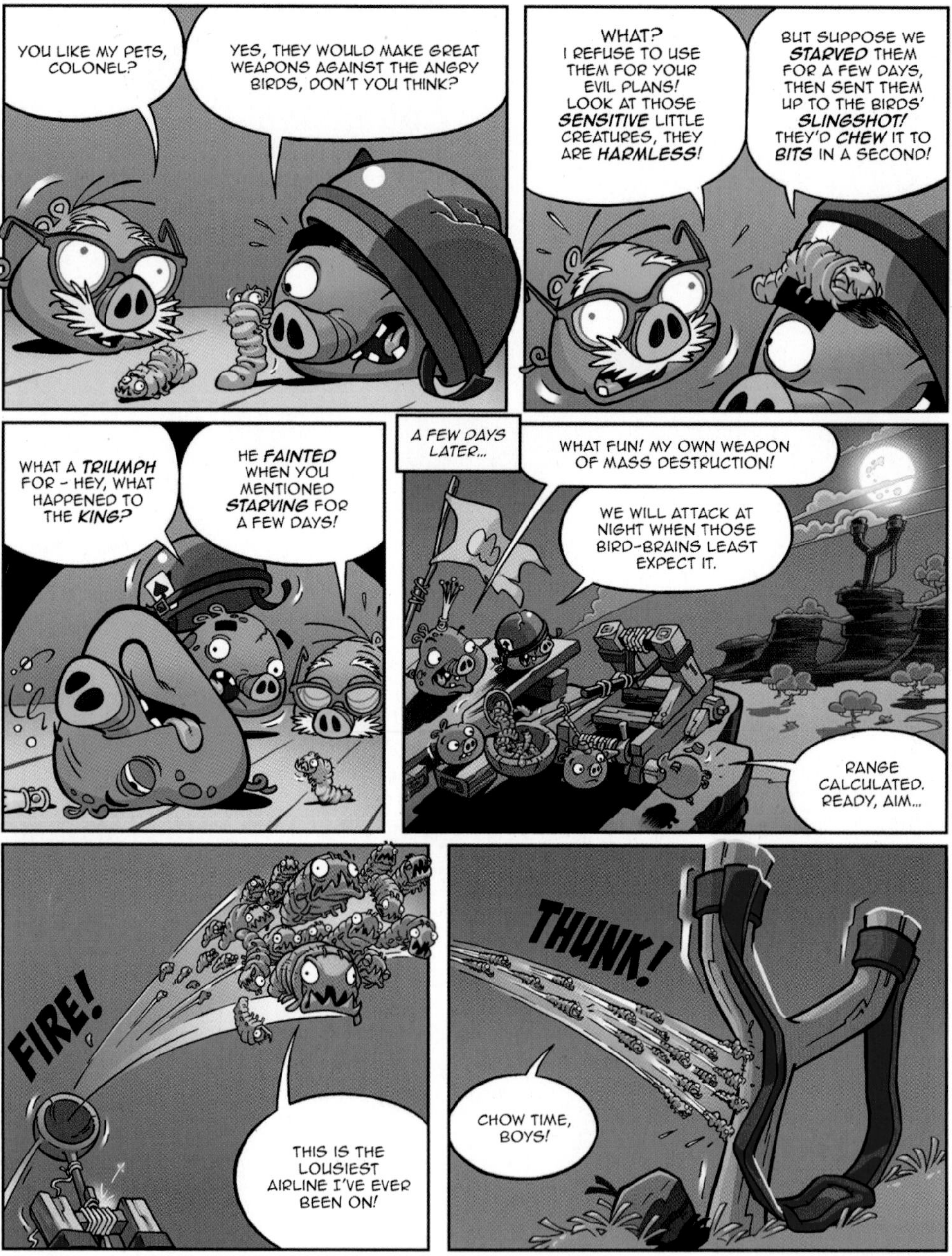
YOU LIKE MY PETS, COLONEL?
YES, THEY WOULD MAKE GREAT WEAPONS AGAINST THE ANGRY BIRDS, DON'T YOU THINK?
WHAT? I REFUSE TO USE THEM FOR YOUR EVIL PLANS! LOOK AT THOSE SENSITIVE LITTLE CREATURES, THEY ARE HARMLESS!
BUT SUPPOSE WE STARVED THEM FOR A FEW DAYS, THEN SENT THEM UP TO THE BIRDS' SLINGSHOT! THEY'D CHEW IT TO BITS IN A SECOND!
WHAT A TRIUMPH FOR - HEY, WHAT HAPPENED TO THE KING?
HE FAINTED WHEN YOU MENTIONED STARVING FOR A FEW DAYS!
A FEW DAYS LATER...
WHAT FUN! MY OWN WEAPON OF MASS DESTRUCTION!
WE WILL ATTACK AT NIGHT WHEN THOSE BIRD-BRAINS LEAST EXPECT IT.
RANGE CALCULATED. READY, AIM...
FIRE!
THIS IS THE LOUSIEST AIRLINE I'VE EVER BEEN ON!
THUNK!
CHOW TIME, BOYS!

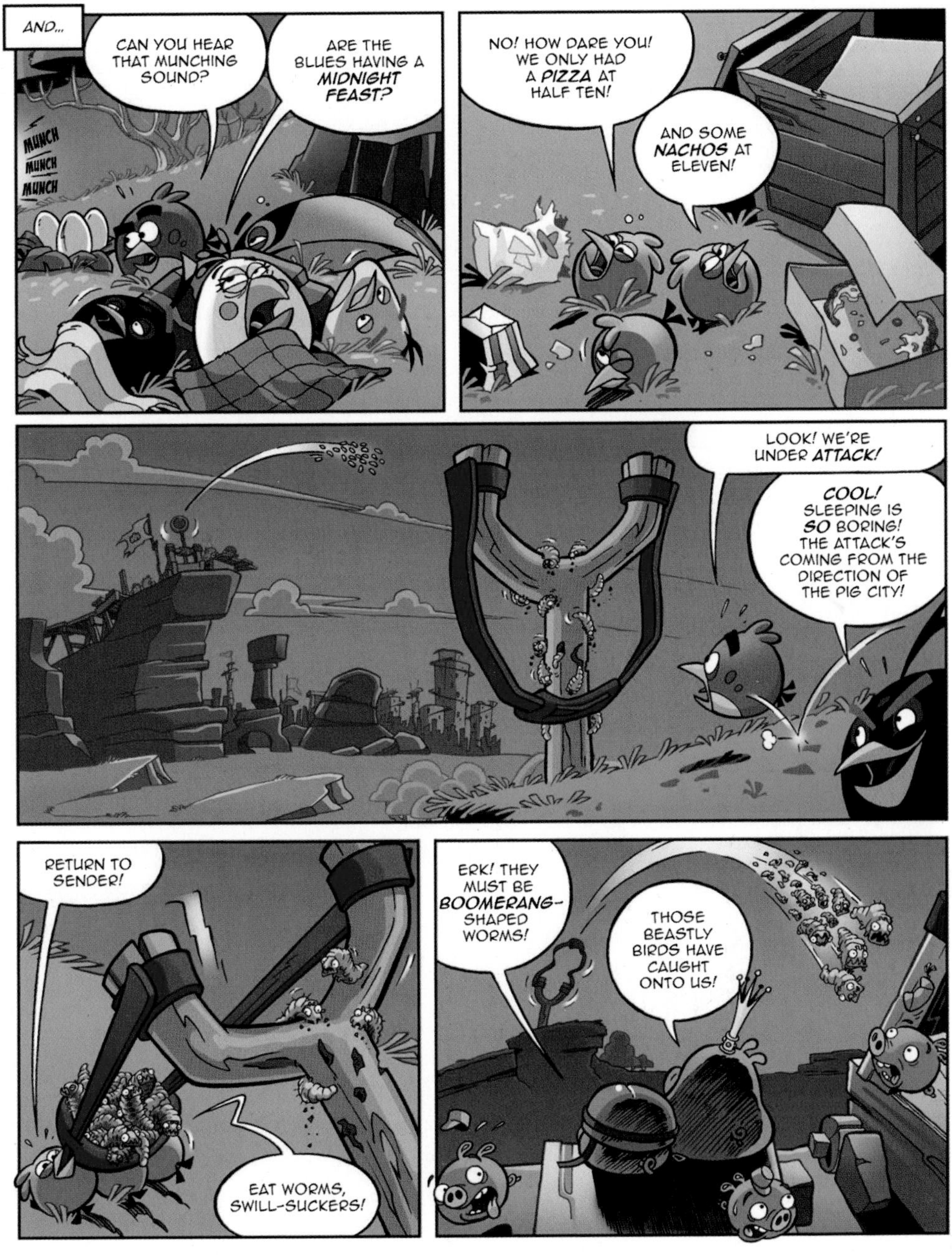
AND...
CAN YOU HEAR THAT MUNCHING SOUND?
MUNCH
MUNCH
MUNCH
ARE THE BLUES HAVING A MIDNIGHT FEAST?
NO! HOW DARE YOU! WE ONLY HAD A PIZZA AT HALF TEN!
AND SOME NACHOS AT ELEVEN!
LOOK! WE'RE UNDER ATTACK!
COOL! SLEEPING IS SO BORING! THE ATTACK'S COMING FROM THE DIRECTION OF THE PIG CITY!
RETURN TO SENDER!
EAT WORMS, SWILL-SUCKERS!
ERK! THEY MUST BE BOOMERANG-SHAPED WORMS!
THOSE BEASTLY BIRDS HAVE CAUGHT ONTO US!

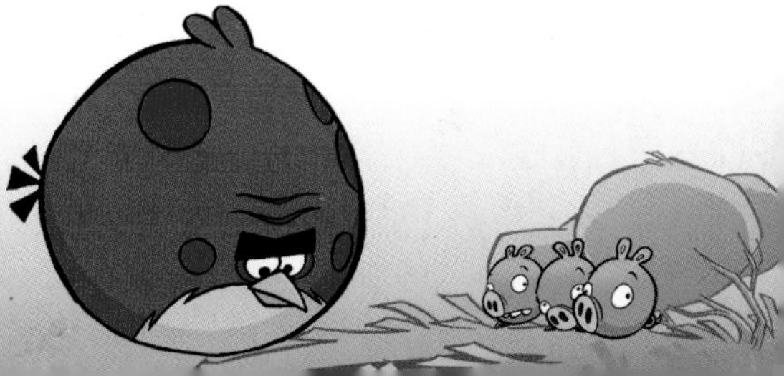

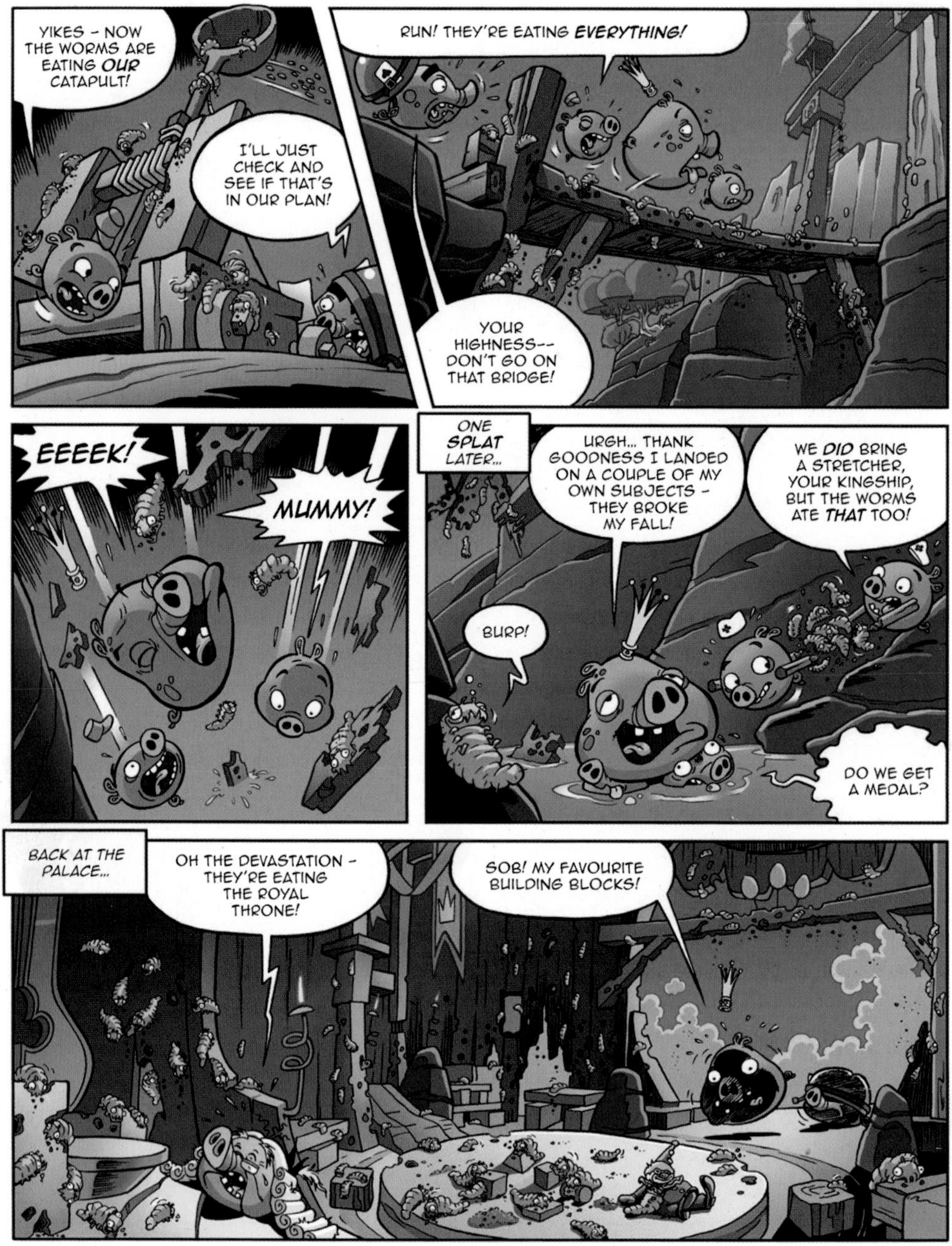
YIKES - NOW THE WORMS ARE EATING OUR CATAPULT!
I'LL JUST CHECK AND SEE IF THAT'S IN OUR PLAN!
RUN! THEY'RE EATING EVERYTHING!
YOUR HIGHNESS-- DON'T GO ON THAT BRIDGE!
EEEEK!
MUMMY!
ONE SPLAT LATER...
URGH... THANK GOODNESS I LANDED ON A COUPLE OF MY OWN SUBJECTS - THEY BROKE MY FALL!
WE DID BRING A STRETCHER, YOUR KINGSHIP, BUT THE WORMS ATE THAT TOO!
BURP!
DO WE GET A MEDAL?
BACK AT THE PALACE...
OH THE DEVASTATION - THEY'RE EATING THE ROYAL THRONE!
SOB! MY FAVOURITE BUILDING BLOCKS!

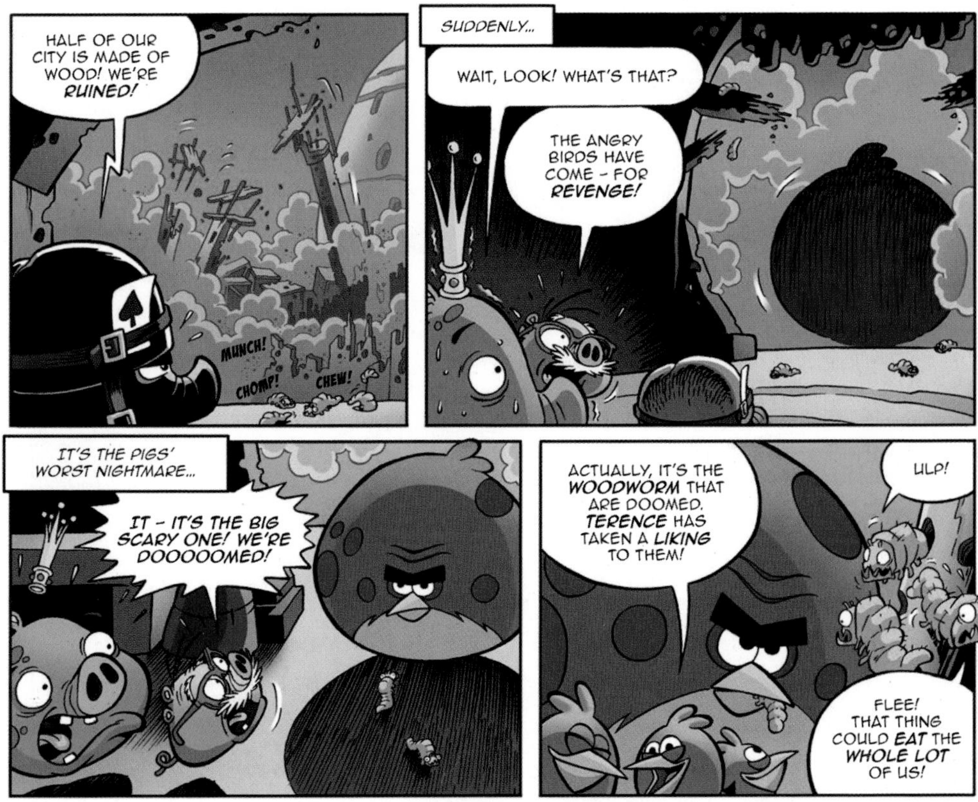

HALF OF OUR CITY IS MADE OF WOOD! WE'RE RUINED!
MUNCH!
CHOMP!
CHEW!
SUDDENLY...
WAIT, LOOK! WHAT'S THAT?
THE ANGRY BIRDS HAVE COME – FOR REVENGE!
IT'S THE PIGS' WORST NIGHTMARE...
IT – IT'S THE BIG SCARY ONE! WE'RE DOOOOOMED!
ACTUALLY, IT'S THE WOODWORM THAT ARE DOOMED. TERENCE HAS TAKEN A LIKING TO THEM!
ULP!
FLEE! THAT THING COULD EAT THE WHOLE LOT OF US!
ALL'S WELL THAT ENDS WELL, YOUR MAJESTY!
BAH! I HAVEN'T FORGOTTEN THIS WAS YOUR IDEA, COLONEL! I KNEW YOUR HEAD WAS MADE OF WOOD!
THE END!

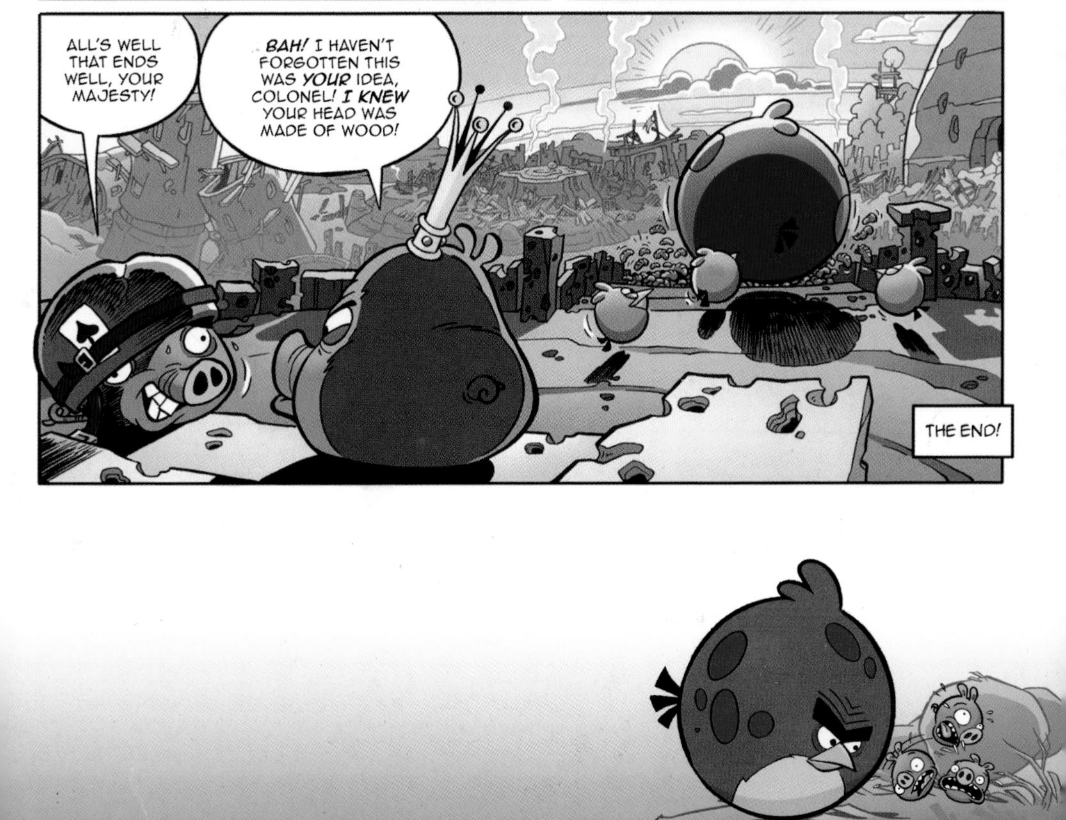

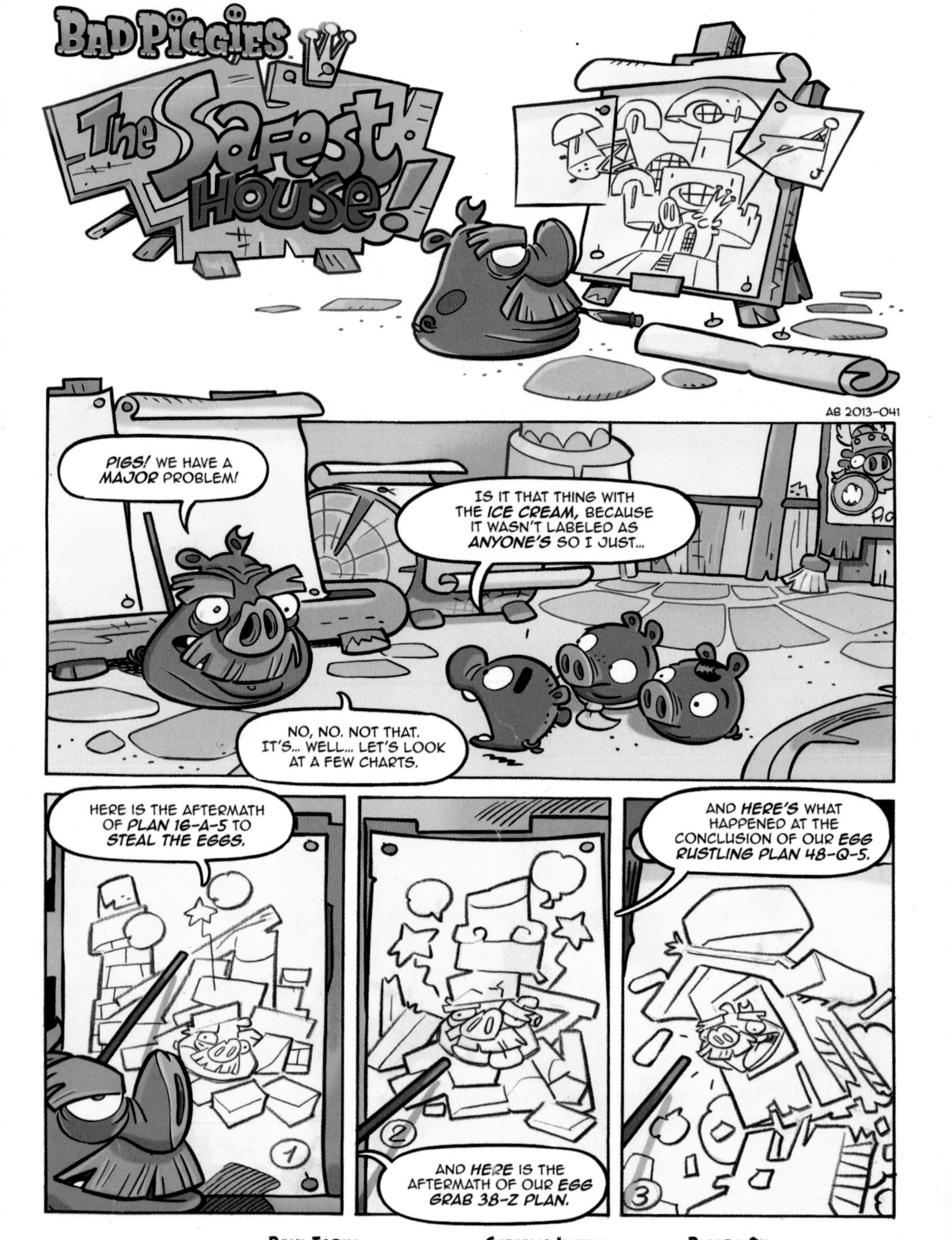
BAD PIGGIES
The Safest HOUSE!
AB 2013-041
PIGS! WE HAVE A MAJOR PROBLEM!
IS IT THAT THING WITH THE ICE CREAM, BECAUSE IT WASN'T LABELED AS ANYONE'S SO I JUST...
NO, NO. NOT THAT. IT'S... WELL... LET'S LOOK AT A FEW CHARTS.
HERE IS THE AFTERMATH OF PLAN 16-A-5 TO STEAL THE EGGS.
AND HERE IS THE AFTERMATH OF OUR EGG GRAB 38-Z PLAN.
AND HERE'S WHAT HAPPENED AT THE CONCLUSION OF OUR EGG RUSTLING PLAN 48-Q-5.

WRITTEN BY: PAUL TOBIN • ART AND COLORS BY: STEFANO INTINI • LETTERS BY: PISARA OY

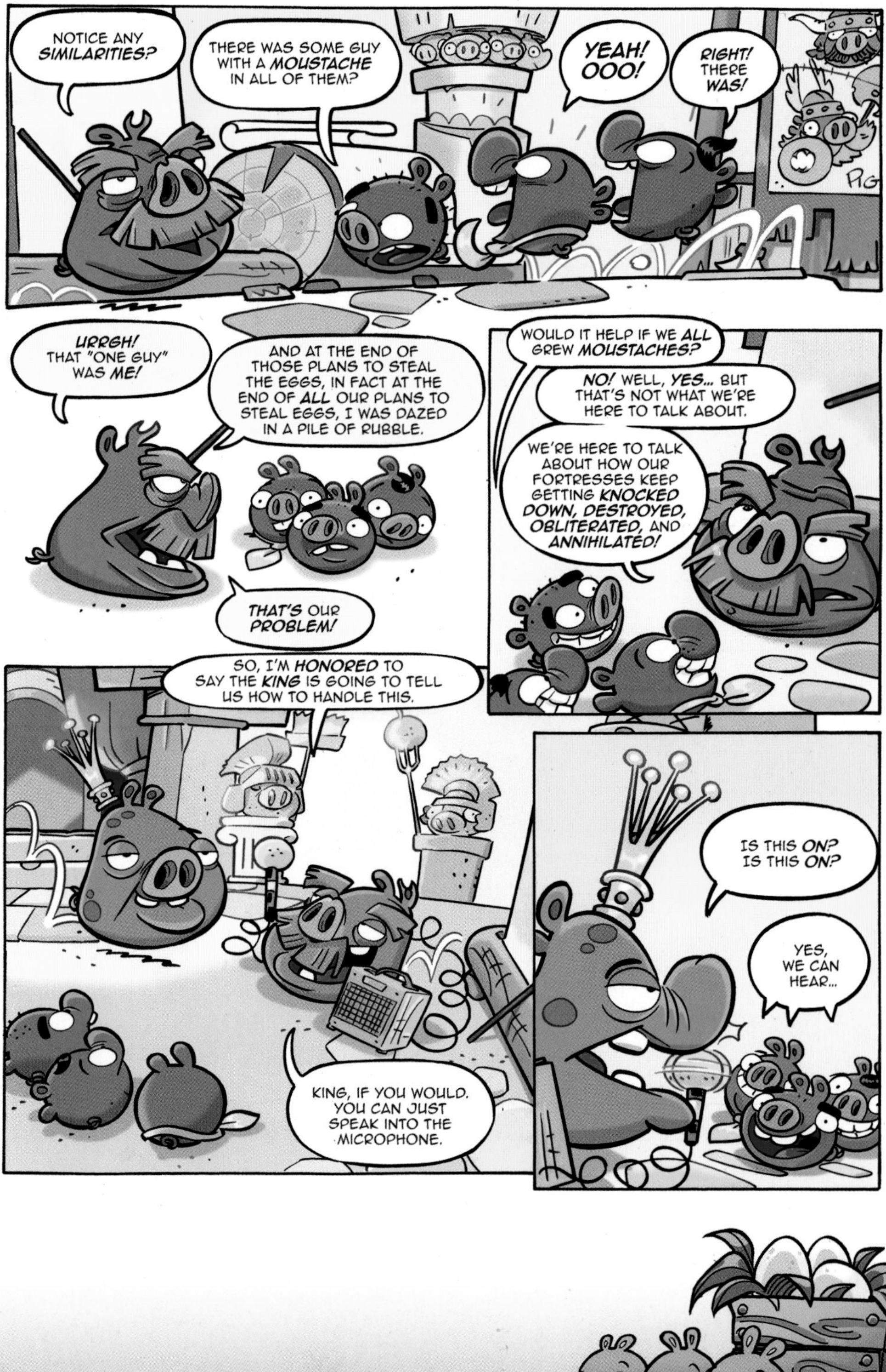
NOTICE ANY SIMILARITIES?
THERE WAS SOME GUY WITH A MOUSTACHE IN ALL OF THEM?
YEAH! OOO!
RIGHT! THERE WAS!
URRGH! THAT "ONE GUY" WAS ME!
AND AT THE END OF THOSE PLANS TO STEAL THE EGGS, IN FACT AT THE END OF ALL OUR PLANS TO STEAL EGGS, I WAS DAZED IN A PILE OF RUBBLE.
THAT'S OUR PROBLEM!
WOULD IT HELP IF WE ALL GREW MOUSTACHES?
NO! WELL, YES... BUT THAT'S NOT WHAT WE'RE HERE TO TALK ABOUT.
WE'RE HERE TO TALK ABOUT HOW OUR FORTRESSES KEEP GETTING KNOCKED DOWN, DESTROYED, OBLITERATED, AND ANNIHILATED!
SO, I'M HONORED TO SAY THE KING IS GOING TO TELL US HOW TO HANDLE THIS.
KING, IF YOU WOULD. YOU CAN JUST SPEAK INTO THE MICROPHONE.
IS THIS ON? IS THIS ON?
YES, WE CAN HEAR...

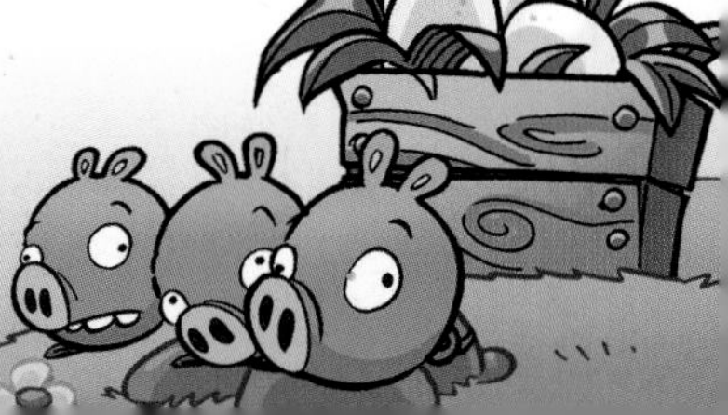

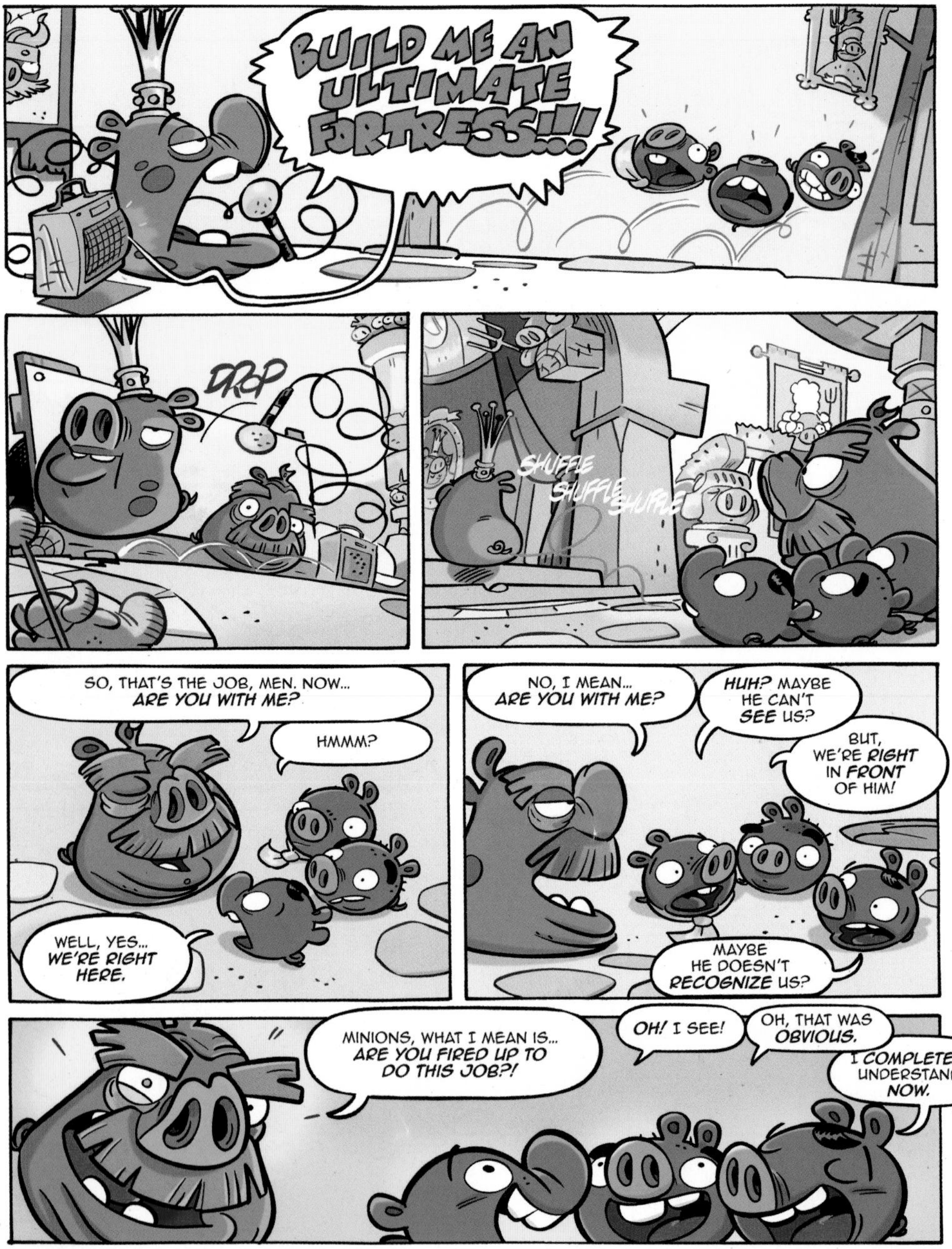
BUILD ME AN ULTIMATE FORTRESS...!!!
DROP
SHUFFLE SHUFFLE SHUFFLE
SO, THAT'S THE JOB, MEN. NOW... ARE YOU WITH ME?
HMMM?
WELL, YES... WE'RE RIGHT HERE.
NO, I MEAN... ARE YOU WITH ME?
HUH? MAYBE HE CAN'T SEE US?
BUT, WE'RE RIGHT IN FRONT OF HIM!
MAYBE HE DOESN'T RECOGNIZE US?
MINIONS, WHAT I MEAN IS... ARE YOU FIRED UP TO DO THIS JOB?!
OH! I SEE!
OH, THAT WAS OBVIOUS.
I COMPLETELY UNDERSTAND NOW.

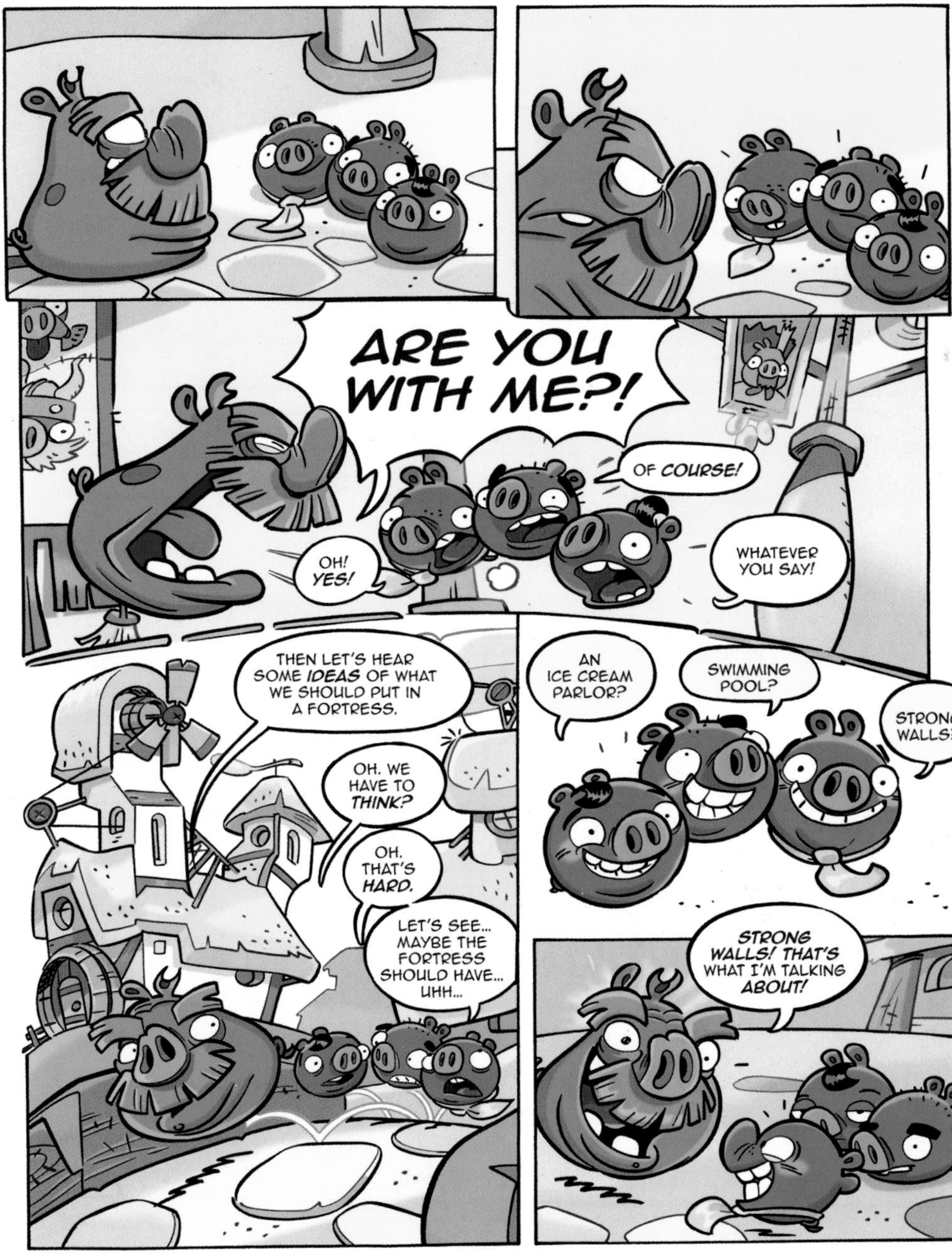
ARE YOU WITH ME?!
OF COURSE!
OH! YES!
WHATEVER YOU SAY!
THEN LET'S HEAR SOME IDEAS OF WHAT WE SHOULD PUT IN A FORTRESS.
OH. WE HAVE TO THINK?
OH. THAT'S HARD.
LET'S SEE... MAYBE THE FORTRESS SHOULD HAVE... UHH...
AN ICE CREAM PARLOR?
SWIMMING POOL?
STRONG WALLS?
STRONG WALLS! THAT'S WHAT I'M TALKING ABOUT!

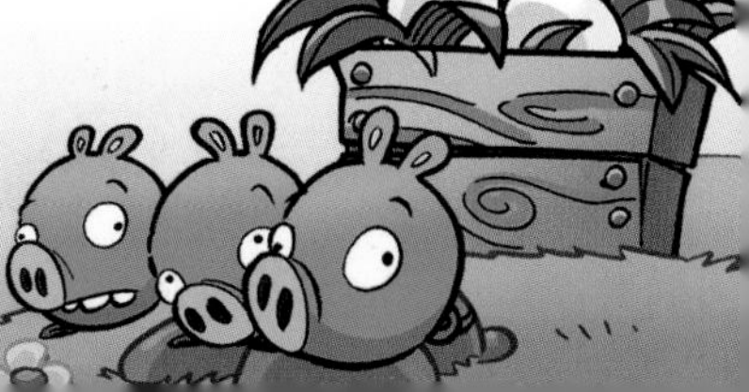

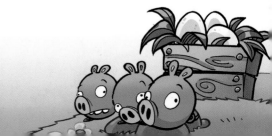

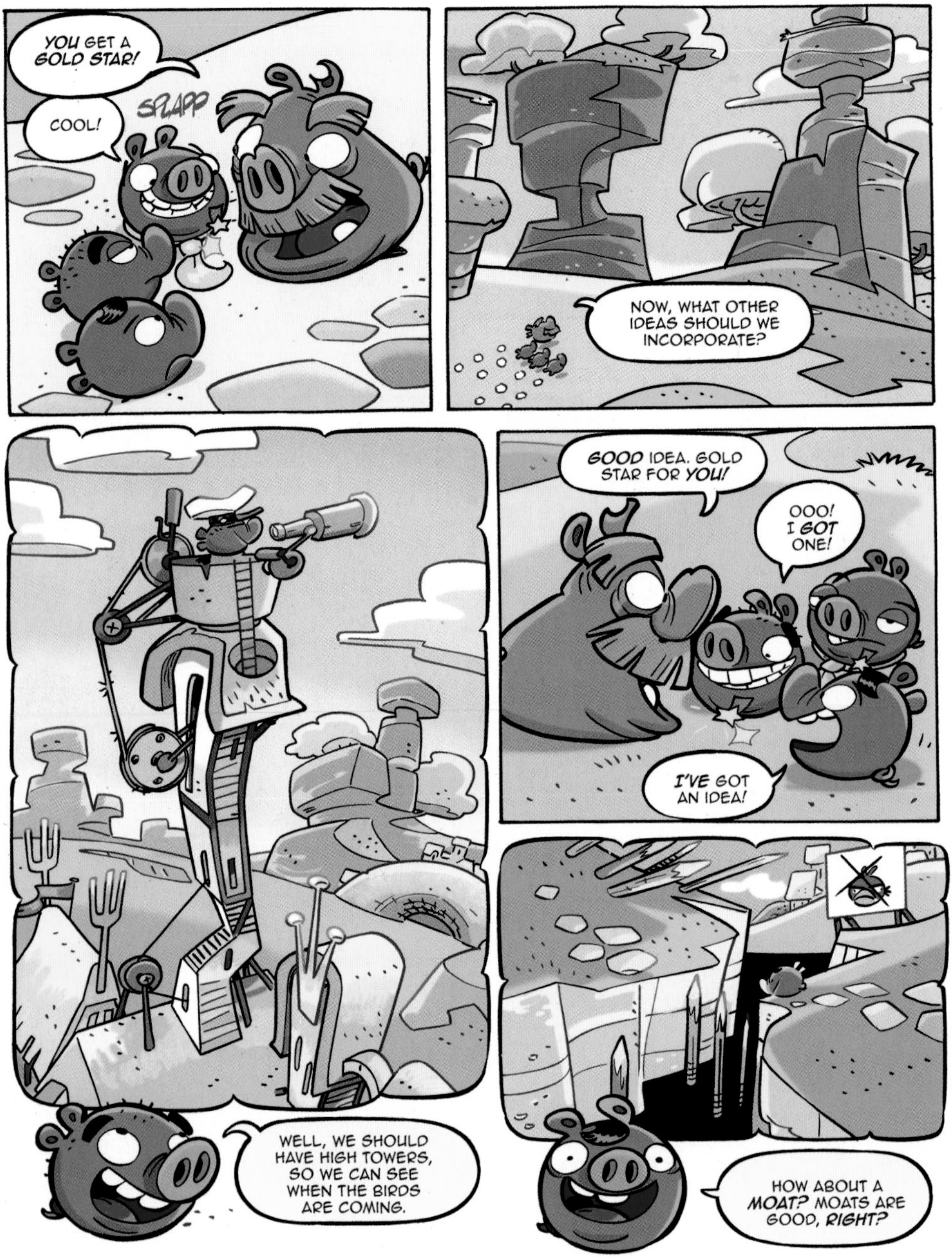
YOU GET A GOLD STAR!
SPLAPP
COOL!
NOW, WHAT OTHER IDEAS SHOULD WE INCORPORATE?
WELL, WE SHOULD HAVE HIGH TOWERS, SO WE CAN SEE WHEN THE BIRDS ARE COMING.
GOOD IDEA. GOLD STAR FOR YOU!
OOO! I GOT ONE!
I'VE GOT AN IDEA!
HOW ABOUT A MOAT? MOATS ARE GOOD, RIGHT?

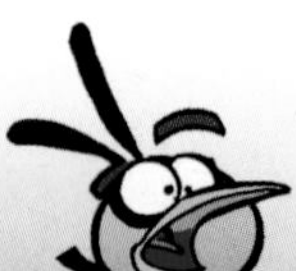

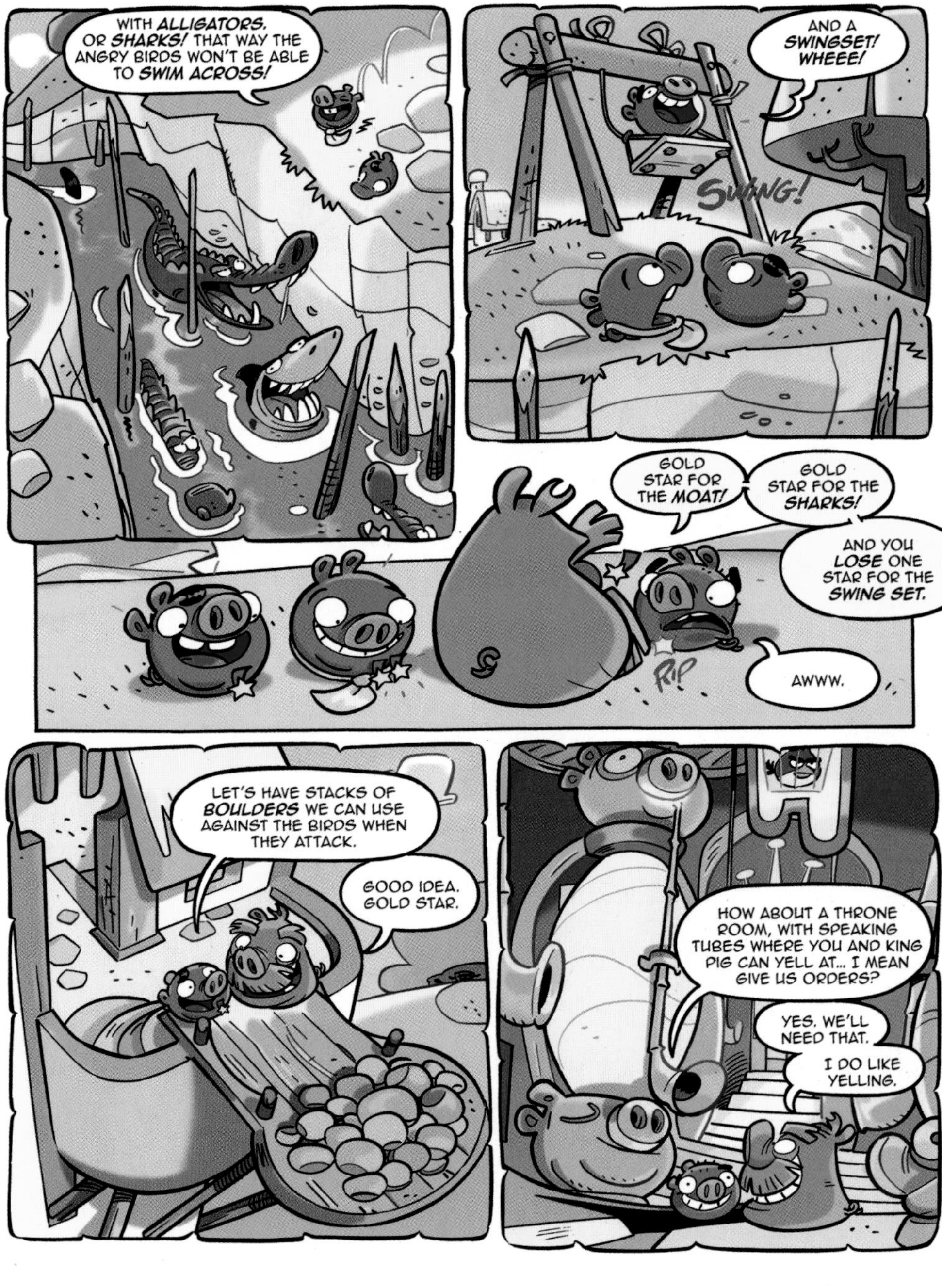
WITH ALLIGATORS. OR SHARKS! THAT WAY THE ANGRY BIRDS WON'T BE ABLE TO SWIM ACROSS!
AND A SWINGSET! WHEEE!
SWING!
GOLD STAR FOR THE MOAT!
GOLD STAR FOR THE SHARKS!
AND YOU LOSE ONE STAR FOR THE SWING SET.
RIP
AWWW.
LET'S HAVE STACKS OF BOULDERS WE CAN USE AGAINST THE BIRDS WHEN THEY ATTACK.
GOOD IDEA. GOLD STAR.
HOW ABOUT A THRONE ROOM, WITH SPEAKING TUBES WHERE YOU AND KING PIG CAN YELL AT... I MEAN GIVE US ORDERS?
YES. WE'LL NEED THAT.
I DO LIKE YELLING.

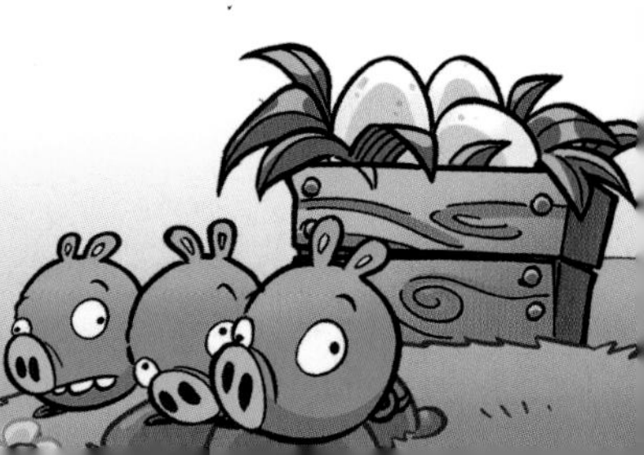

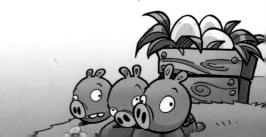

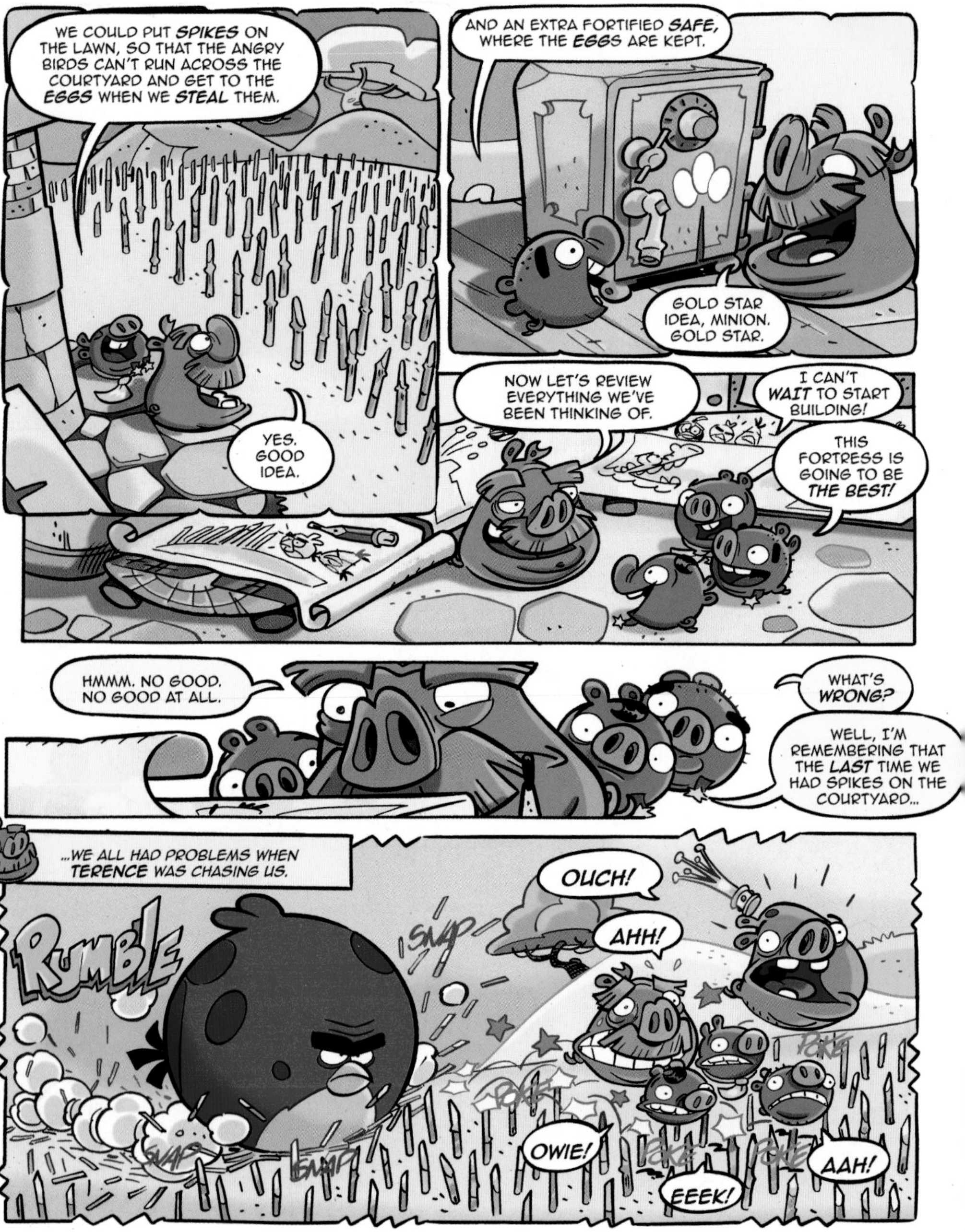
WE COULD PUT SPIKES ON THE LAWN, SO THAT THE ANGRY BIRDS CAN'T RUN ACROSS THE COURTYARD AND GET TO THE EGGS WHEN WE STEAL THEM.
YES. GOOD IDEA.
AND AN EXTRA FORTIFIED SAFE, WHERE THE EGGS ARE KEPT.
GOLD STAR IDEA, MINION. GOLD STAR.
NOW LET'S REVIEW EVERYTHING WE'VE BEEN THINKING OF.
I CAN'T WAIT TO START BUILDING!
THIS FORTRESS IS GOING TO BE THE BEST!
HMMM. NO GOOD. NO GOOD AT ALL.
WHAT'S WRONG?
WELL, I'M REMEMBERING THAT THE LAST TIME WE HAD SPIKES ON THE COURTYARD...
...WE ALL HAD PROBLEMS WHEN TERENCE WAS CHASING US.
RUMBLE
SNAP
OUCH!
AHH!
POKE
SNAP
SNAP
POKE
OWIE!
POKE
POKE
EEEK!
AAH!

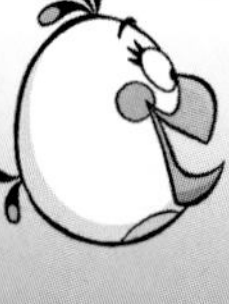

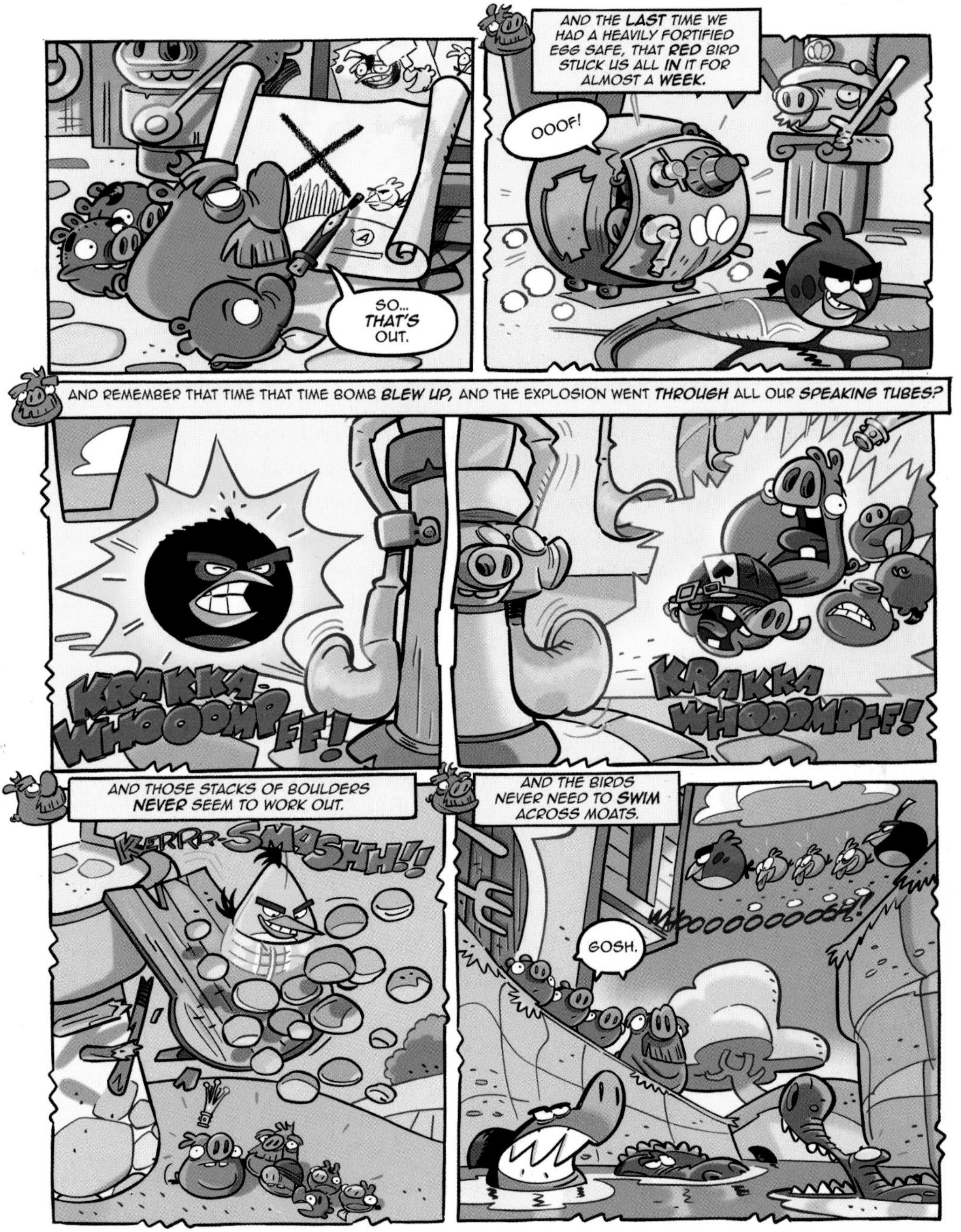
SO... THAT'S OUT.
AND THE LAST TIME WE HAD A HEAVILY FORTIFIED EGG SAFE, THAT RED BIRD STUCK US ALL IN IT FOR ALMOST A WEEK.
OOOF!
AND REMEMBER THAT TIME THAT TIME BOMB BLEW UP, AND THE EXPLOSION WENT THROUGH ALL OUR SPEAKING TUBES?
KRAKKA-WHOOOMPFF!
KRAKKA WHOOOMPFF!
AND THOSE STACKS OF BOULDERS NEVER SEEM TO WORK OUT.
KERRR-SMASHH!!
AND THE BIRDS NEVER NEED TO SWIM ACROSS MOATS.
WHOOOOOOOOOOSH!
GOSH.

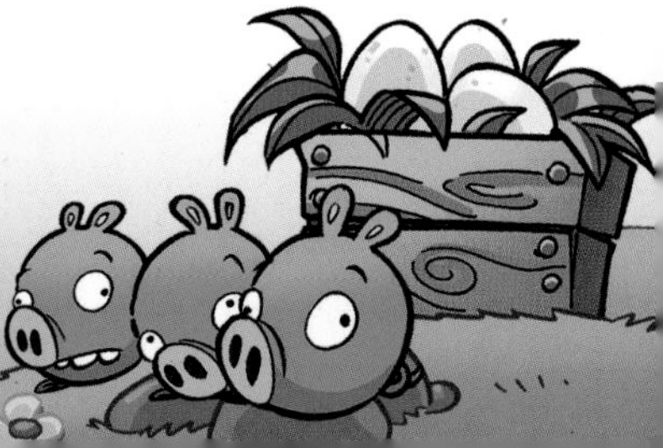

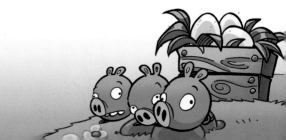

AND THE HIGH TOWERS ALWAYS BACKFIRE.
AHHHHHH!
AHHHH!
AHHHH!
AHHHH!
AHHHHHH!!!
AHHHHHH!!!
AHHHHHHHHH!
?

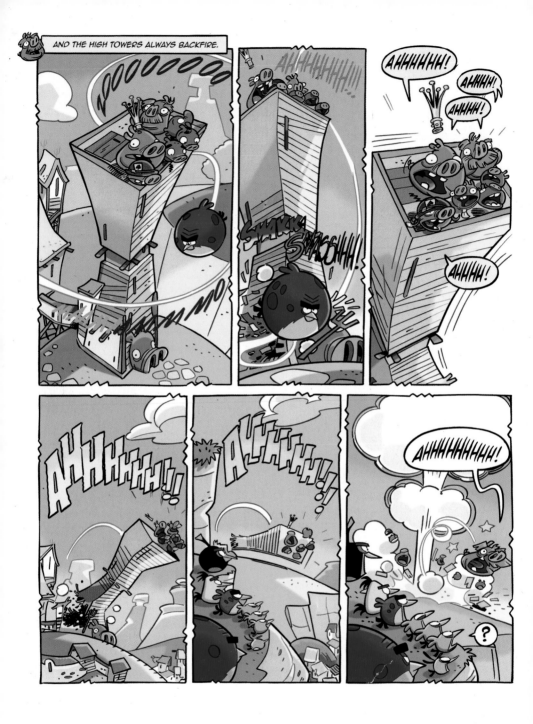

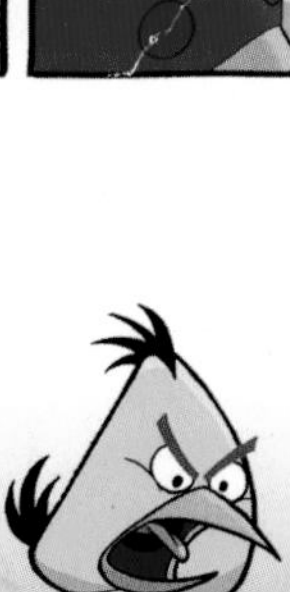

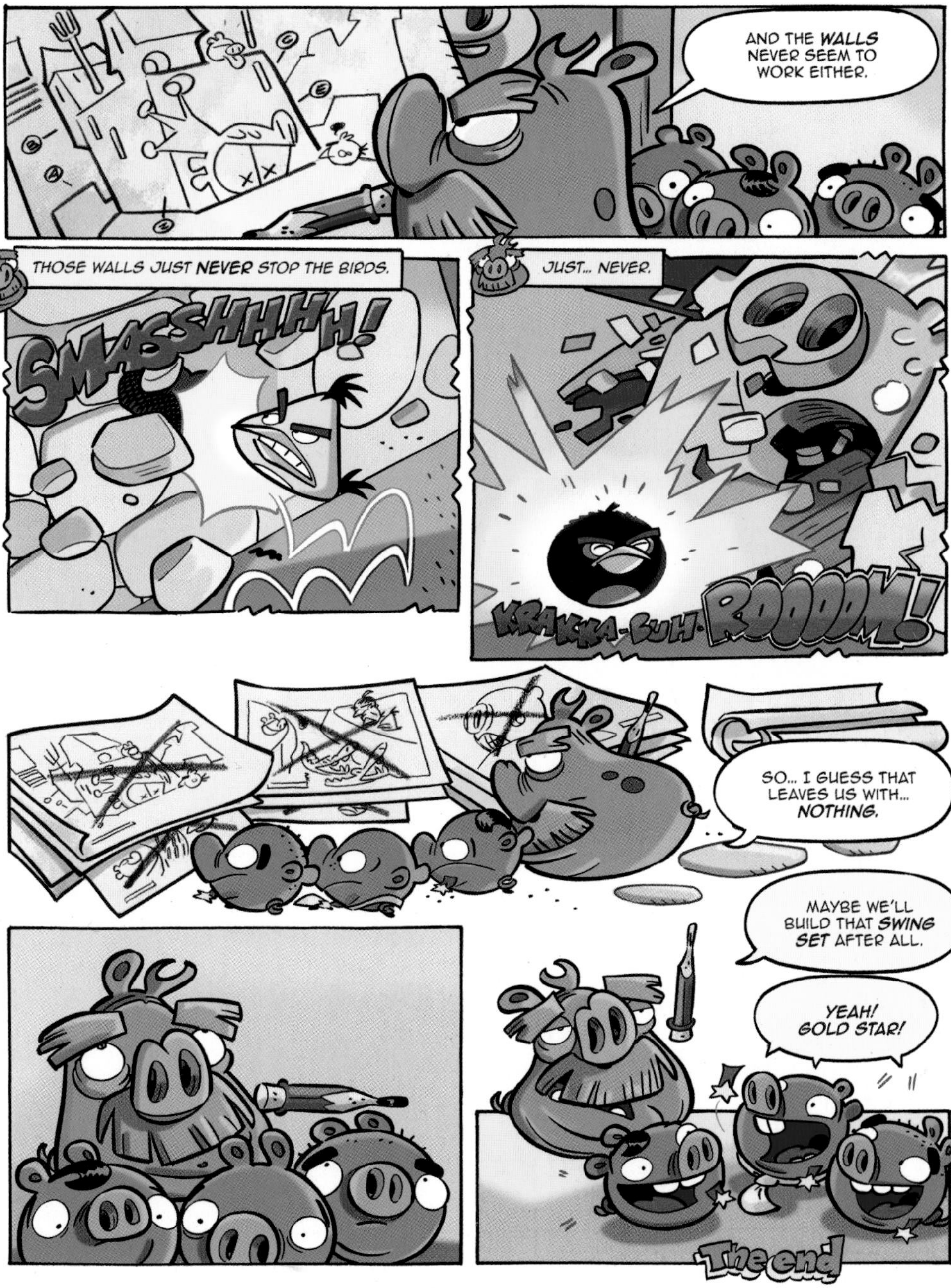
AND THE *WALLS* NEVER SEEM TO WORK EITHER.
THOSE WALLS JUST **NEVER** STOP THE BIRDS.
SMASHHHHH!
JUST... NEVER.
KRAKKA-BUH-ROOOOM!
SO... I GUESS THAT LEAVES US WITH... *NOTHING.*
MAYBE WE'LL BUILD THAT *SWING SET* AFTER ALL.
YEAH! GOLD STAR!
The end

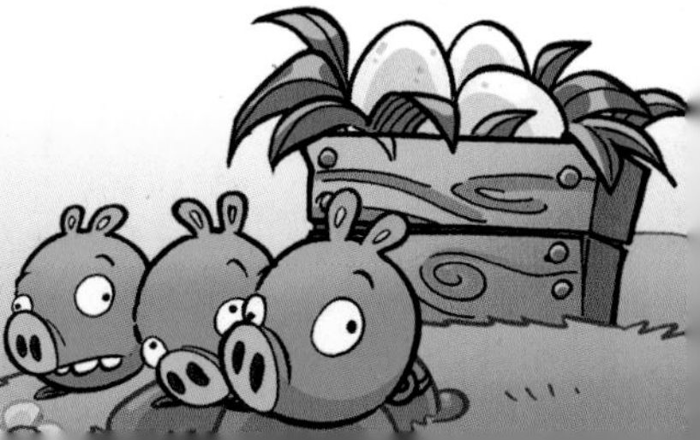

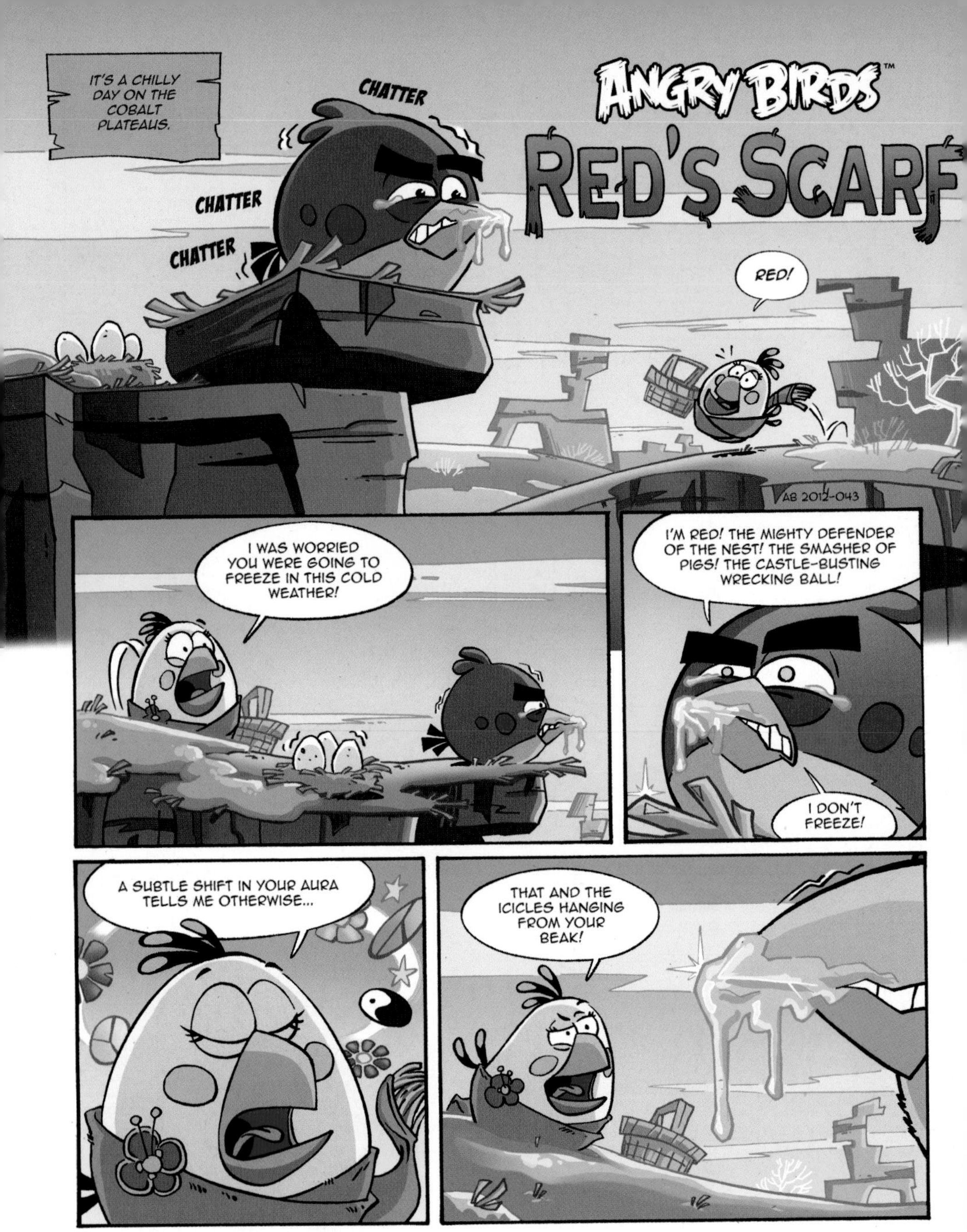
ANGRY BIRDS™
RED'S SCARF
IT'S A CHILLY DAY ON THE COBALT PLATEAUS.
CHATTER
CHATTER
CHATTER
RED!
AB 2012-043
I WAS WORRIED YOU WERE GOING TO FREEZE IN THIS COLD WEATHER!
I'M RED! THE MIGHTY DEFENDER OF THE NEST! THE SMASHER OF PIGS! THE CASTLE-BUSTING WRECKING BALL!
I DON'T FREEZE!
A SUBTLE SHIFT IN YOUR AURA TELLS ME OTHERWISE...
THAT AND THE ICICLES HANGING FROM YOUR BEAK!

WRITTEN BY: IAN CARNEY • ART BY: JEAN-MICHEL BOESCH • COLORS BY: DIGIKORE STUDIOS • LETTERS BY: PISARA OY

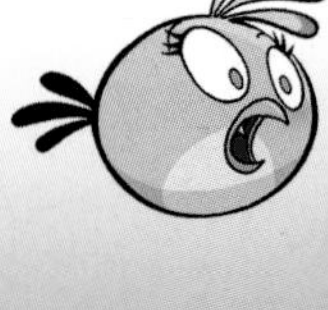

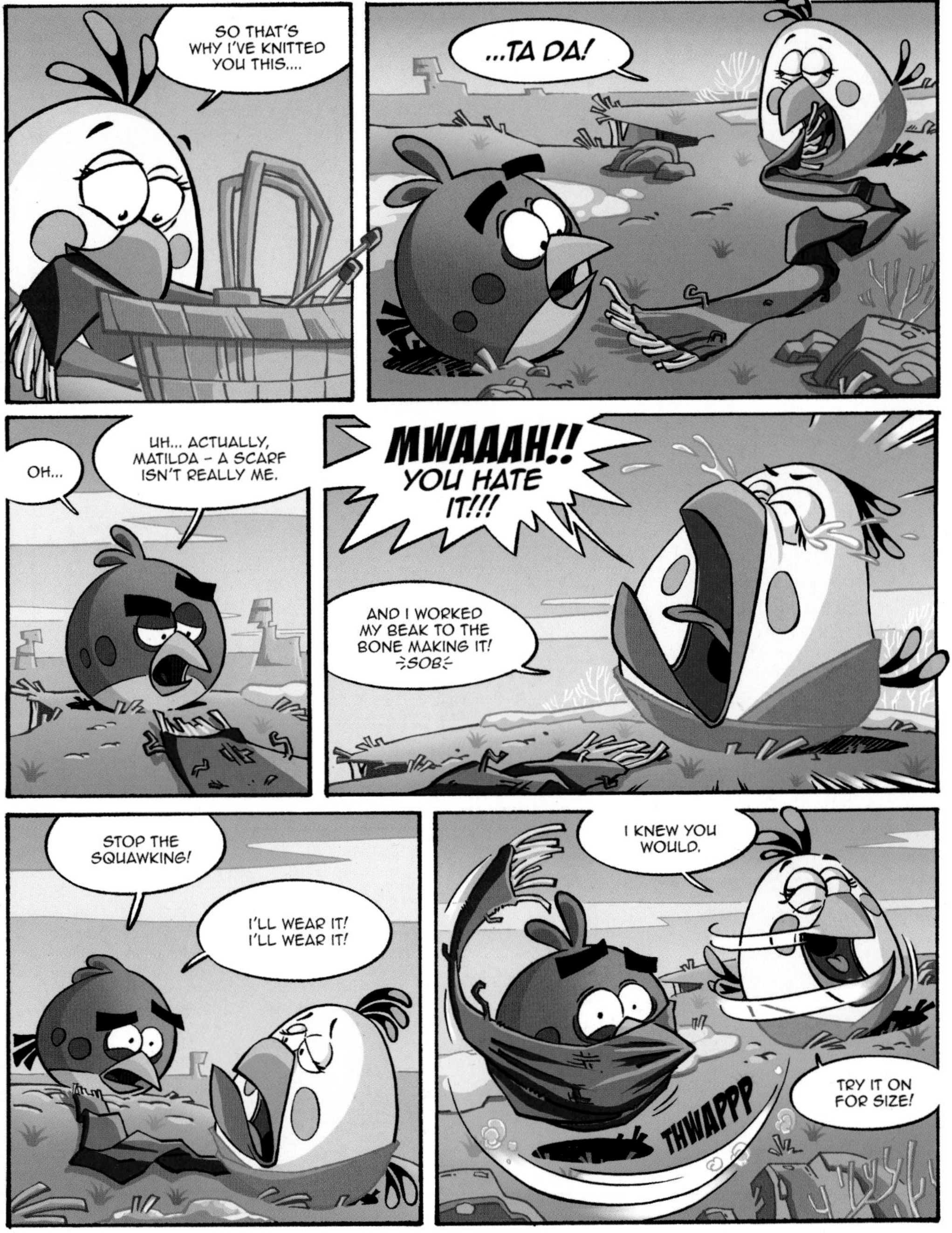
SO THAT'S WHY I'VE KNITTED YOU THIS....
...TA DA!
OH...
UH... ACTUALLY, MATILDA – A SCARF ISN'T REALLY ME.
MWAAAH!! YOU HATE IT!!!
AND I WORKED MY BEAK TO THE BONE MAKING IT! -SOB-
STOP THE SQUAWKING!
I'LL WEAR IT! I'LL WEAR IT!
I KNEW YOU WOULD.
TRY IT ON FOR SIZE!
THWAPPP

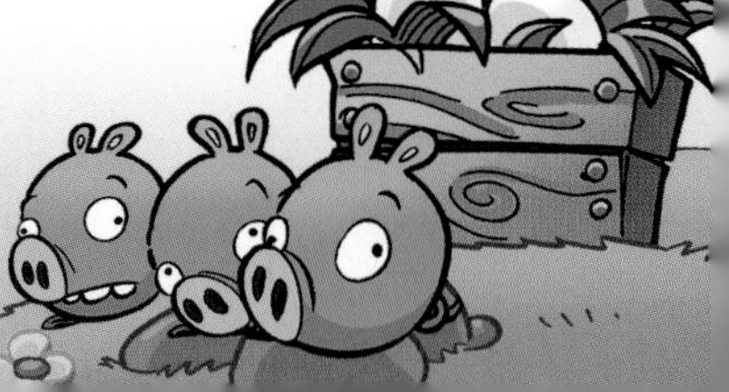

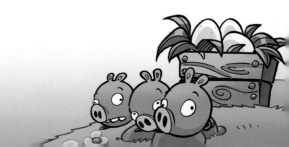

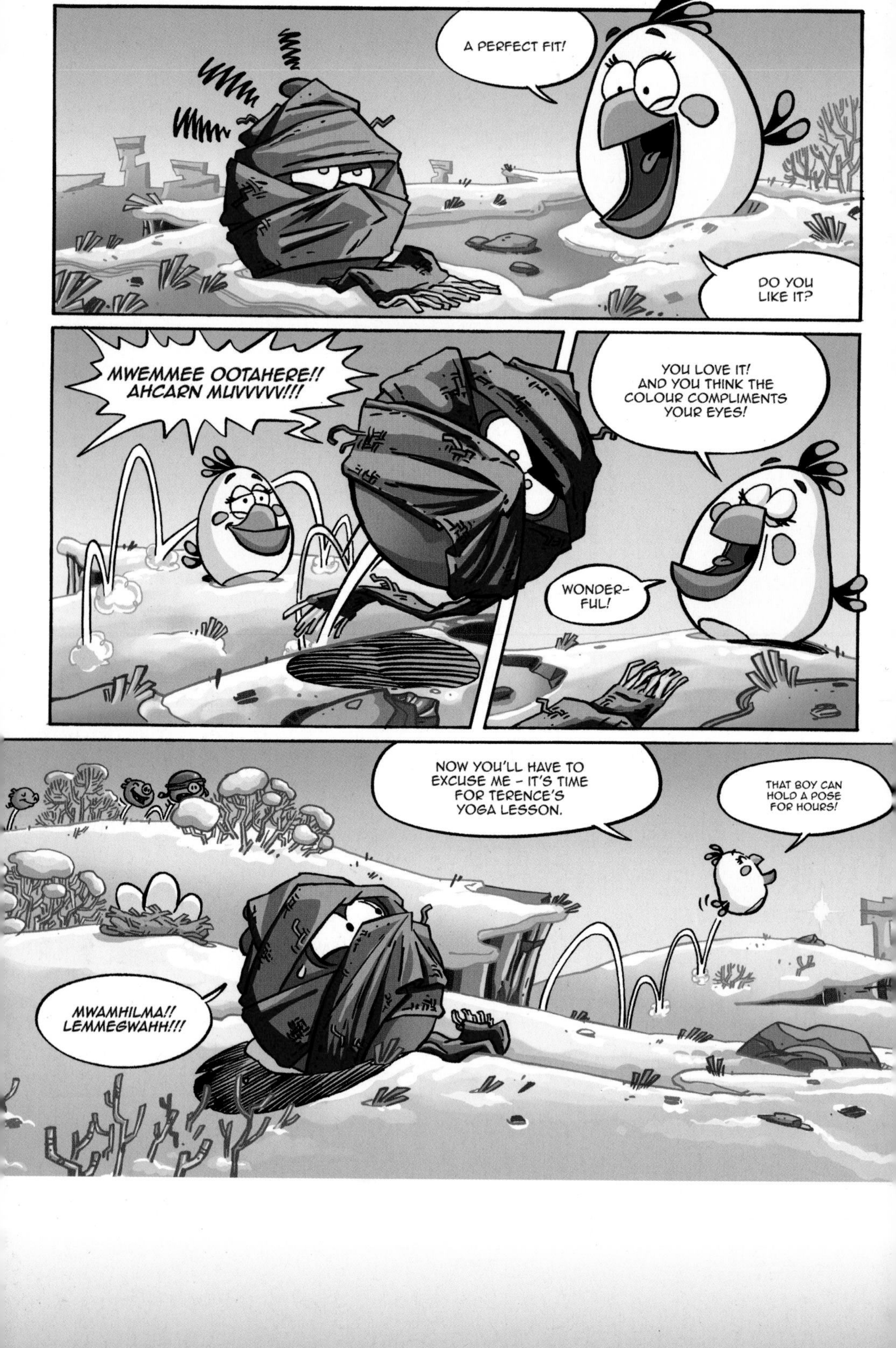
A PERFECT FIT!
DO YOU LIKE IT?
MWEMMEE OOTAHERE!! AHCARN MUVVVVV!!!
YOU LOVE IT! AND YOU THINK THE COLOUR COMPLIMENTS YOUR EYES!
WONDER-FUL!
NOW YOU'LL HAVE TO EXCUSE ME – IT'S TIME FOR TERENCE'S YOGA LESSON.
THAT BOY CAN HOLD A POSE FOR HOURS!
MWAMHILMA!! LEMMEGWAHH!!!

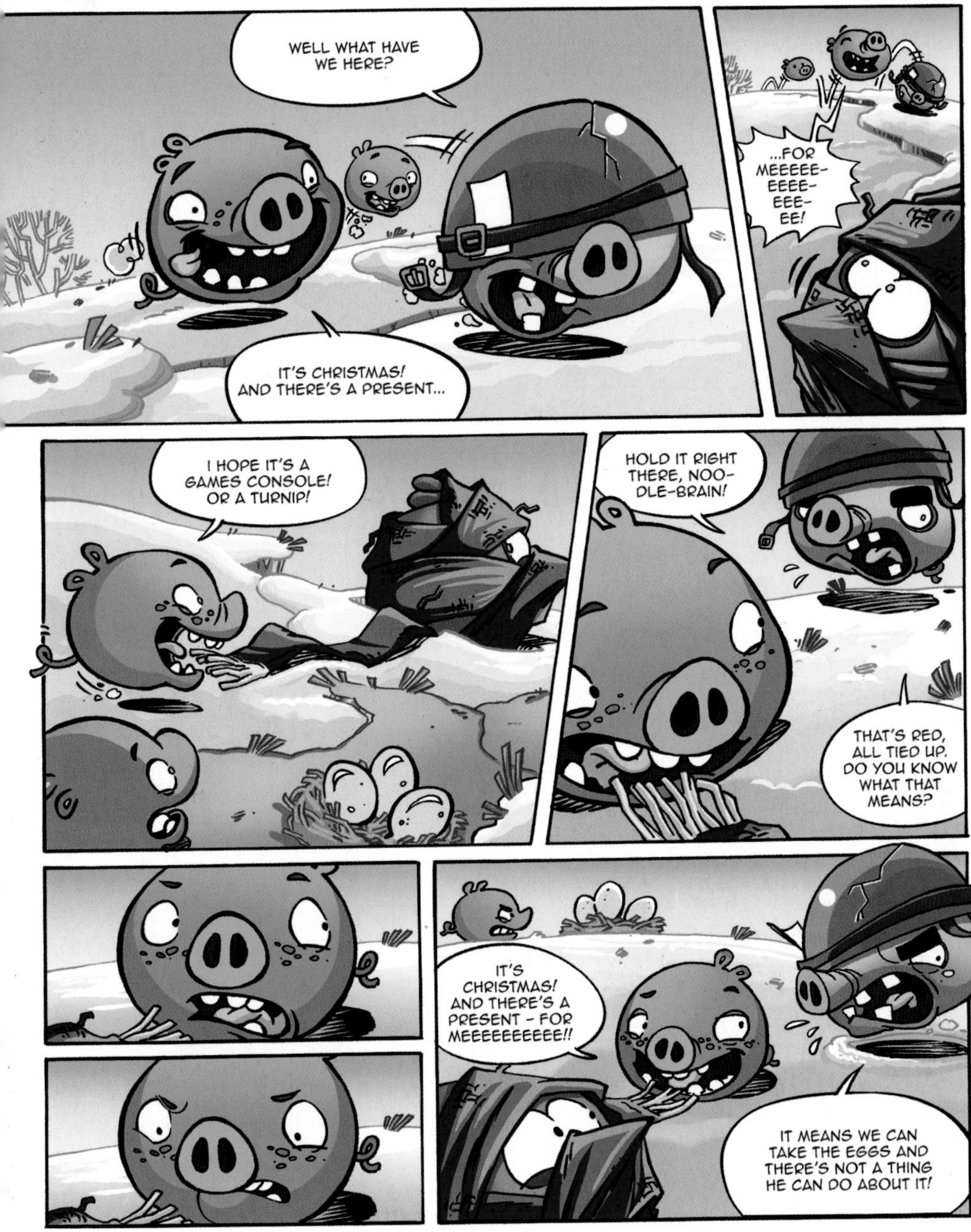
WELL WHAT HAVE WE HERE?
IT'S CHRISTMAS! AND THERE'S A PRESENT...
...FOR MEEEEE-EEEE-EEE-EE!
I HOPE IT'S A GAMES CONSOLE! OR A TURNIP!
HOLD IT RIGHT THERE, NOO-DLE-BRAIN!
THAT'S RED, ALL TIED UP. DO YOU KNOW WHAT THAT MEANS?
IT'S CHRISTMAS! AND THERE'S A PRESENT - FOR MEEEEEEEEEE!!
IT MEANS WE CAN TAKE THE EGGS AND THERE'S NOT A THING HE CAN DO ABOUT IT!

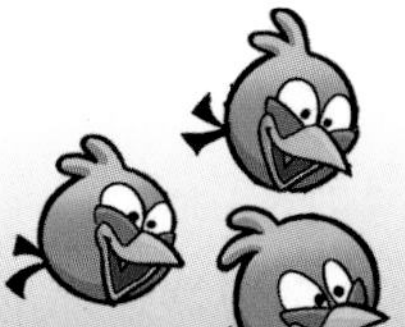

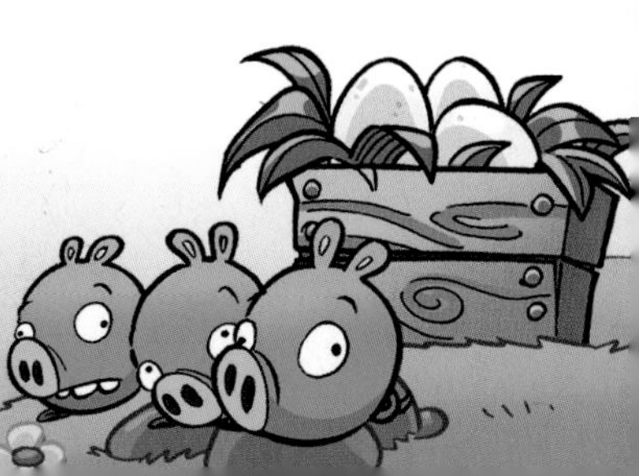

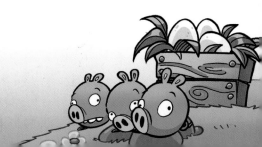

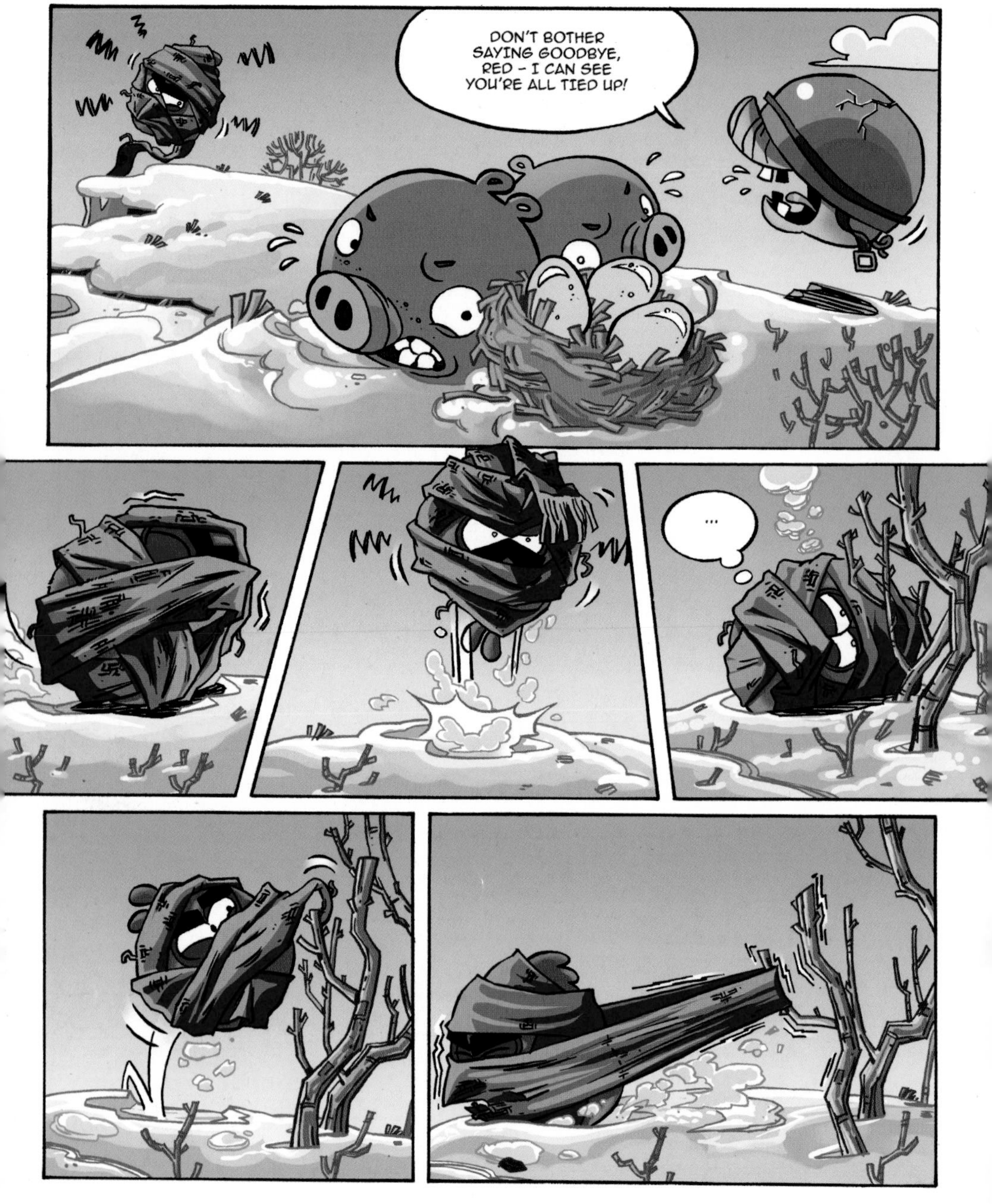
DON'T BOTHER SAYING GOODBYE, RED – I CAN SEE YOU'RE ALL TIED UP!
...

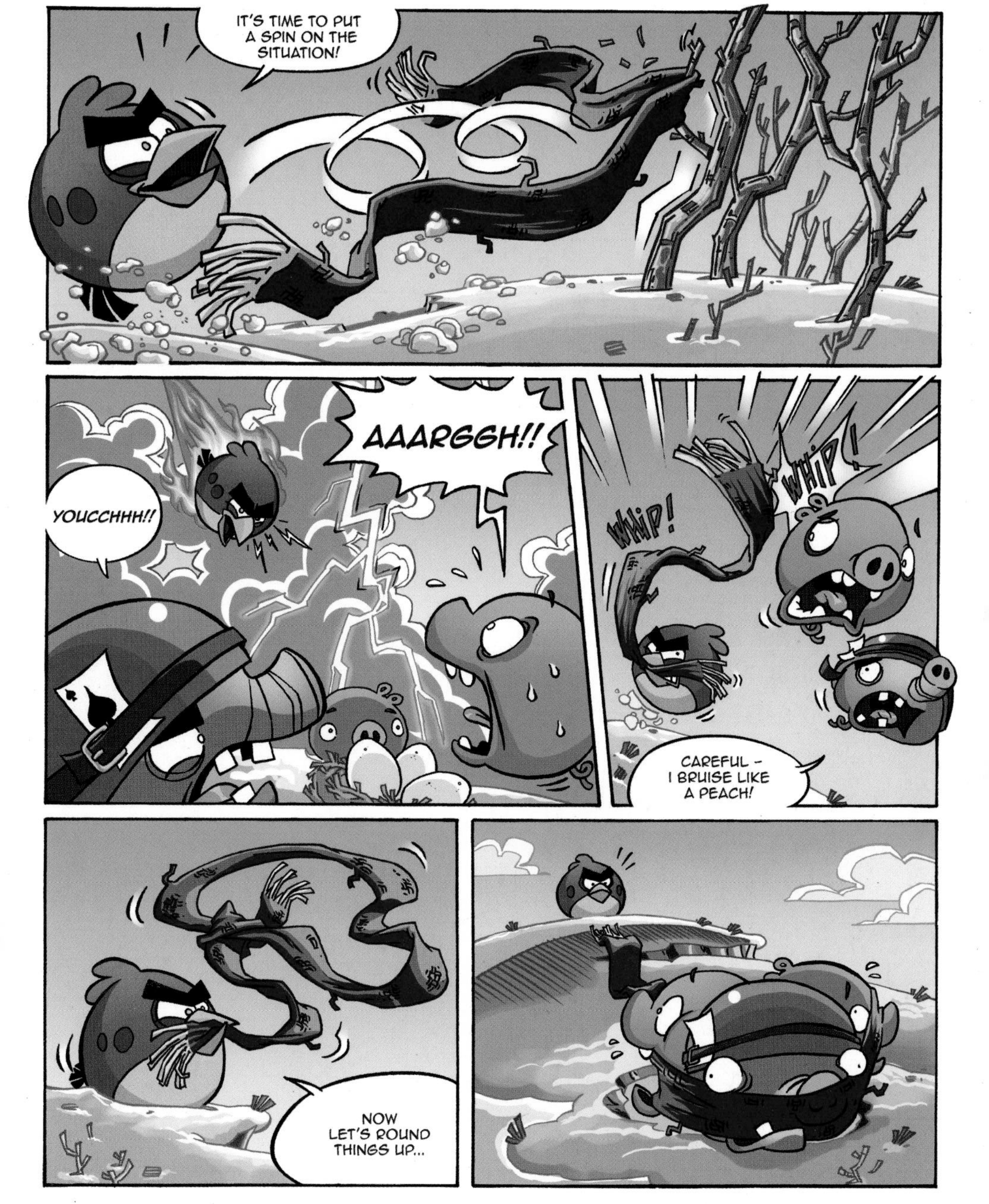
IT'S TIME TO PUT A SPIN ON THE SITUATION!
AAARGGH!!
YOUCCHHH!!
WHIP!
WHIP!
CAREFUL – I BRUISE LIKE A PEACH!
NOW LET'S ROUND THINGS UP...

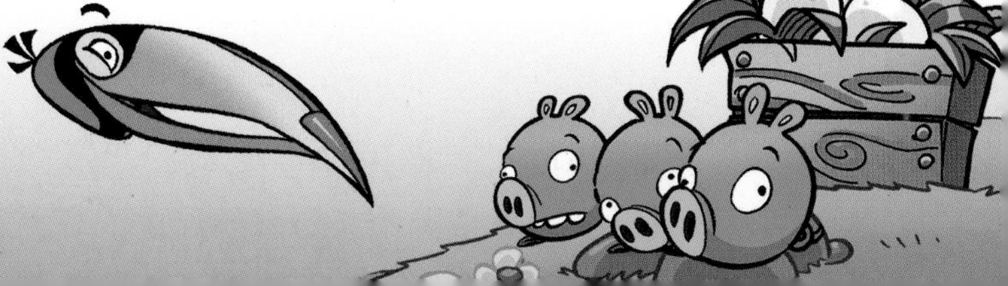

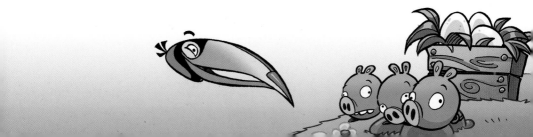

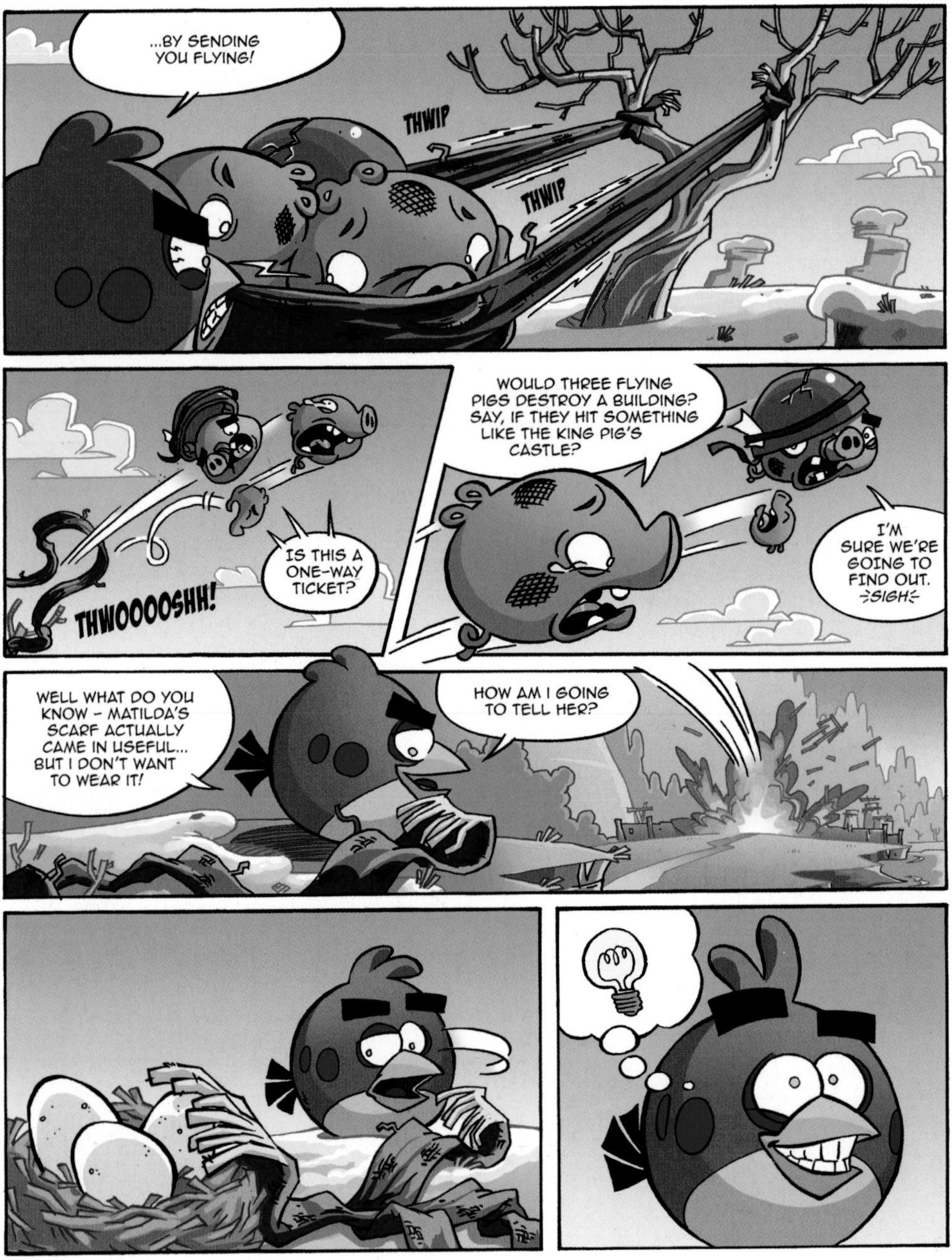
...BY SENDING YOU FLYING!
THWIP
THWIP
THWOOOOSHH!
IS THIS A ONE-WAY TICKET?
WOULD THREE FLYING PIGS DESTROY A BUILDING? SAY, IF THEY HIT SOMETHING LIKE THE KING PIG'S CASTLE?
I'M SURE WE'RE GOING TO FIND OUT. ⪢SIGH⪡
WELL WHAT DO YOU KNOW - MATILDA'S SCARF ACTUALLY CAME IN USEFUL... BUT I DON'T WANT TO WEAR IT!
HOW AM I GOING TO TELL HER?

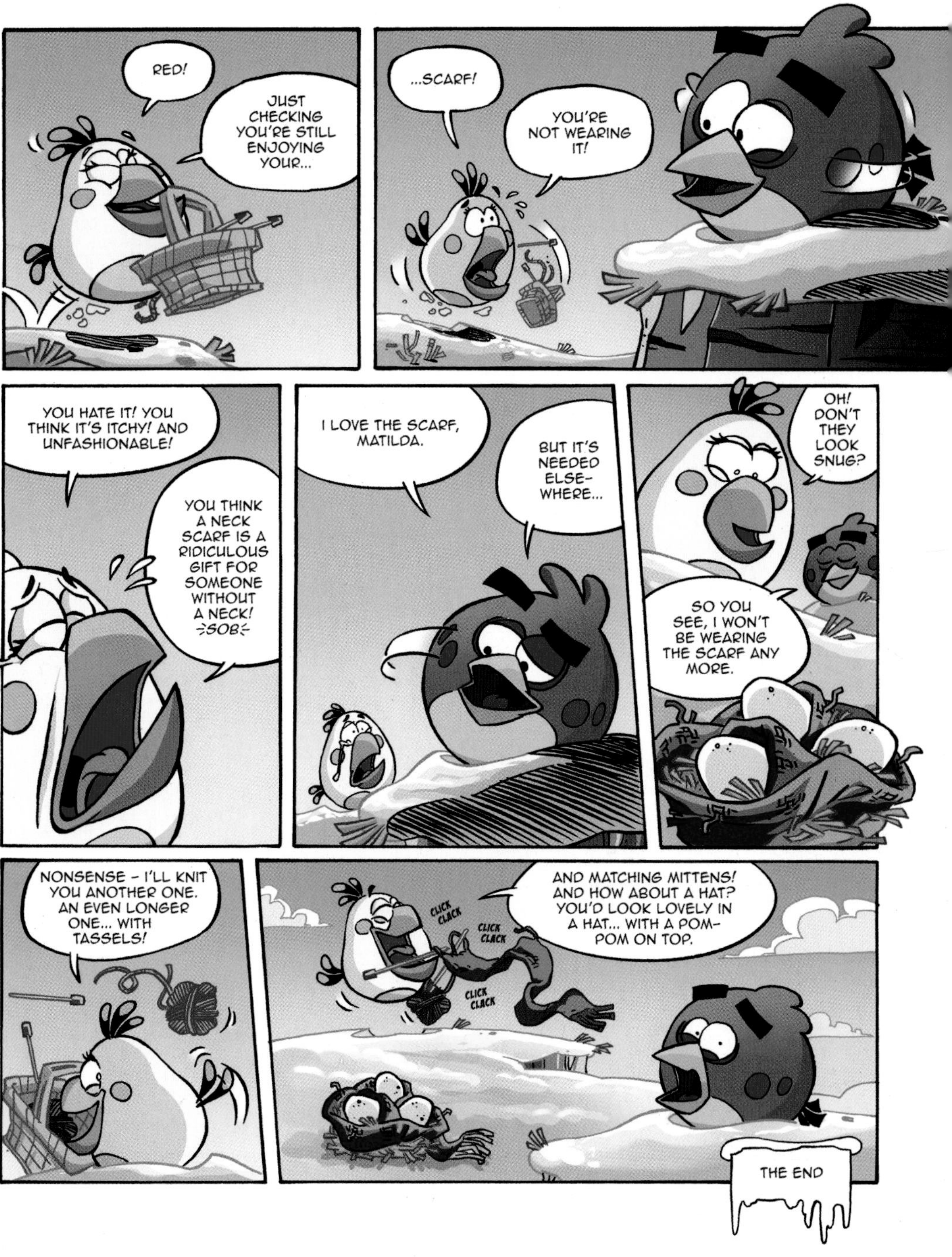
RED!
JUST CHECKING YOU'RE STILL ENJOYING YOUR...
...SCARF!
YOU'RE NOT WEARING IT!
YOU HATE IT! YOU THINK IT'S ITCHY! AND UNFASHIONABLE!
YOU THINK A NECK SCARF IS A RIDICULOUS GIFT FOR SOMEONE WITHOUT A NECK! SOB
I LOVE THE SCARF, MATILDA.
BUT IT'S NEEDED ELSE-WHERE...
OH! DON'T THEY LOOK SNUG?
SO YOU SEE, I WON'T BE WEARING THE SCARF ANY MORE.
NONSENSE – I'LL KNIT YOU ANOTHER ONE. AN EVEN LONGER ONE... WITH TASSELS!
CLICK CLACK
CLICK CLACK
CLICK CLACK
AND MATCHING MITTENS! AND HOW ABOUT A HAT? YOU'D LOOK LOVELY IN A HAT... WITH A POM-POM ON TOP.
THE END

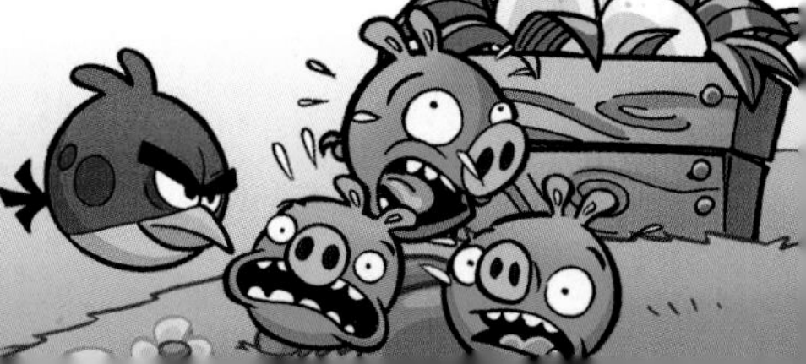

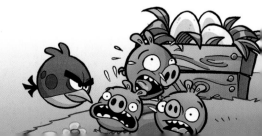

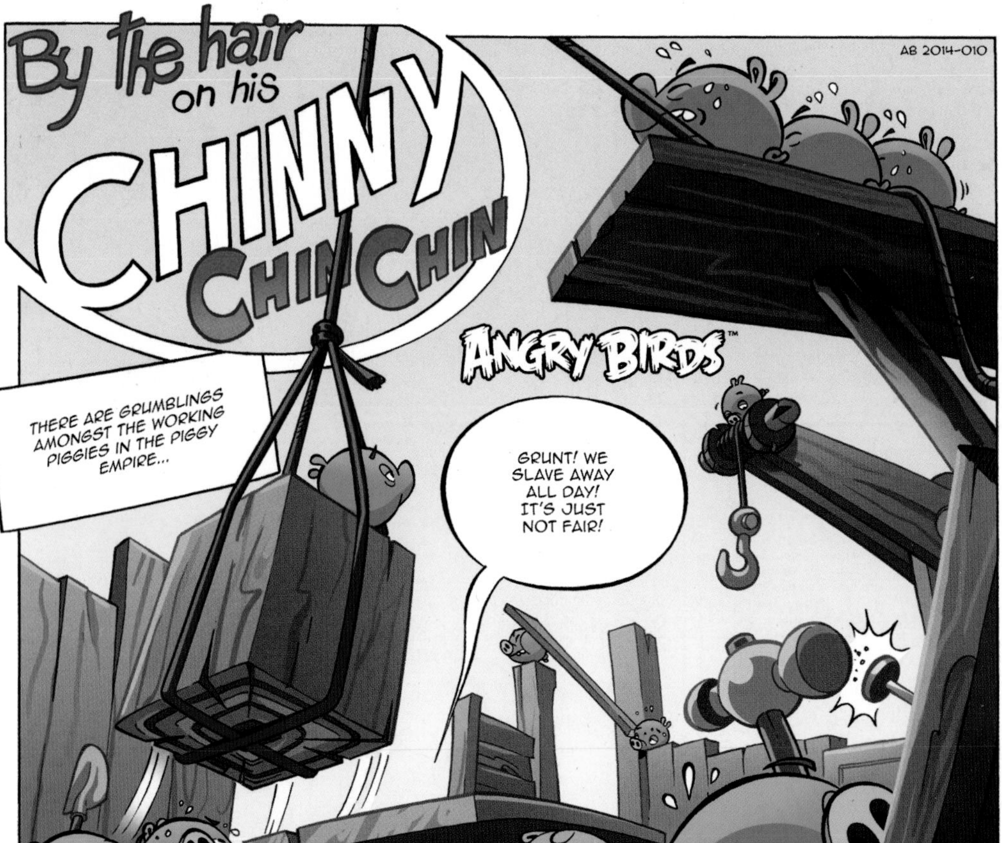
By the hair on his CHINNY CHIN CHIN
AB 2014-010
ANGRY BIRDS
THERE ARE GRUMBLINGS AMONGST THE WORKING PIGGIES IN THE PIGGY EMPIRE...
GRUNT! WE SLAVE AWAY ALL DAY! IT'S JUST NOT FAIR!
"EVERYONE HAS TO DO THEIR BIT!" THE KING SAYS!
NOT *EVERYONE!*
WHEN'S THE LAST TIME YOU SAW MOUSTACHE PIG BREAK INTO A SWEAT?

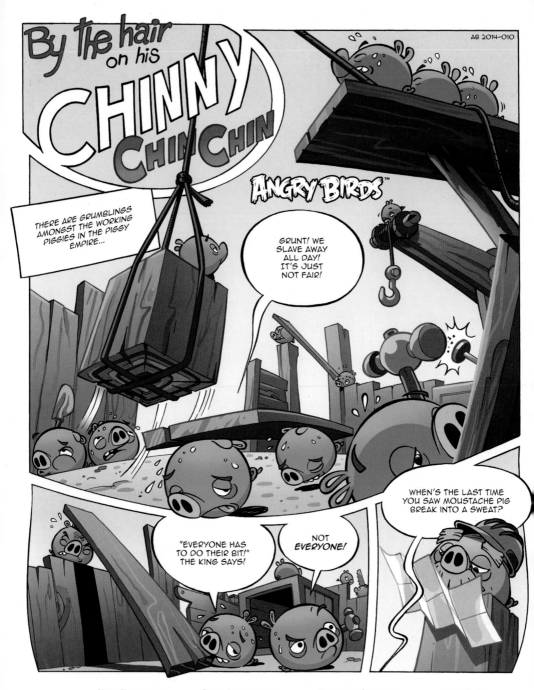

WRITTEN BY: KARI KORHONEN • ART BY: PACO RODRIQUES • COLORS BY: DIGIKORE STUDIOS • LETTERS BY: PISARA OY

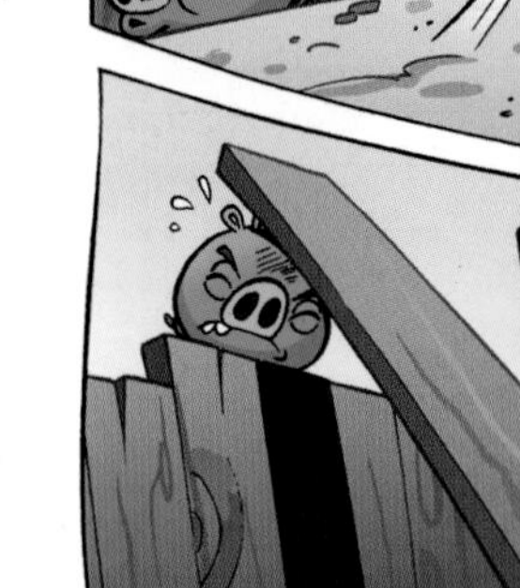

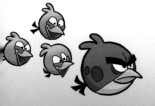

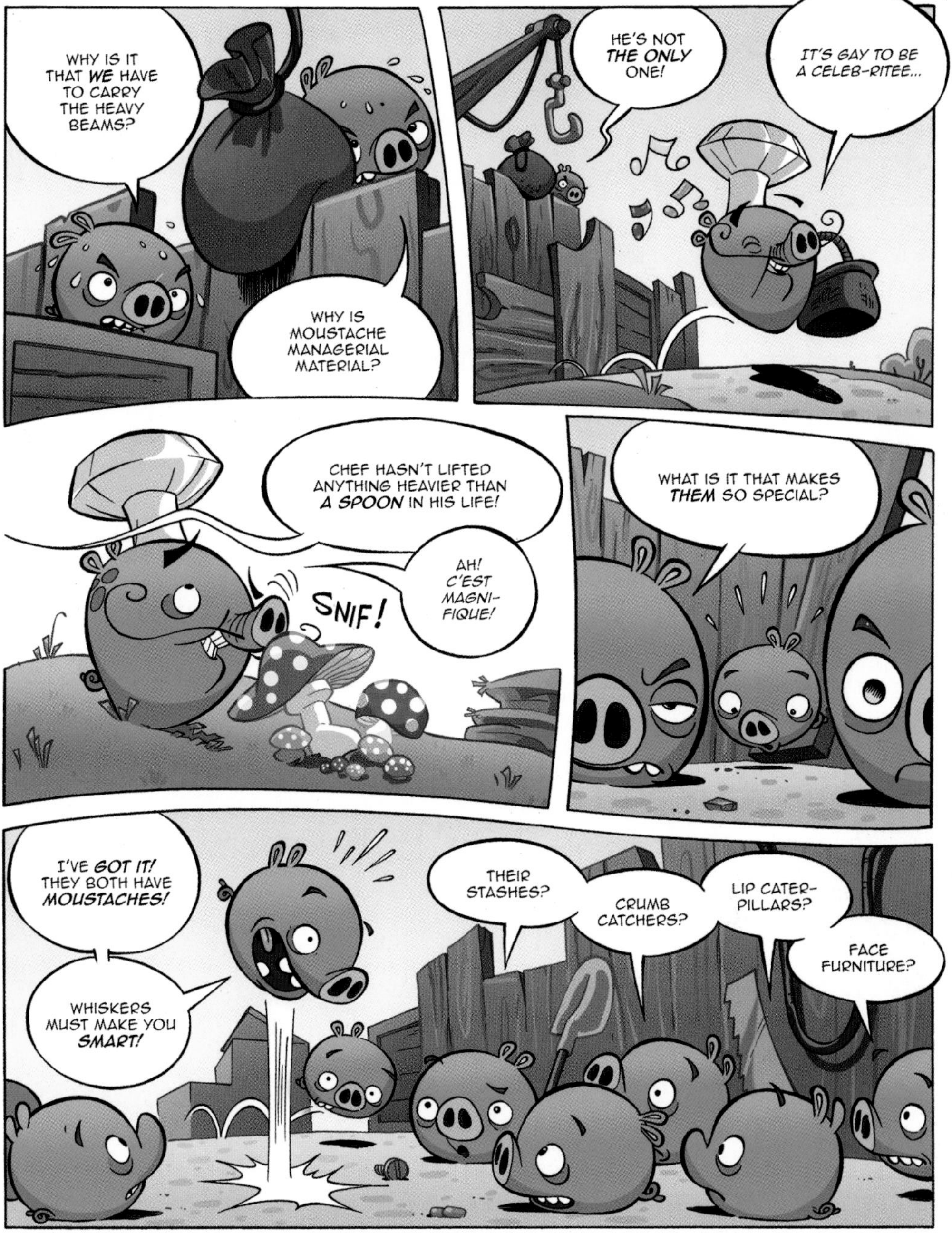
WHY IS IT THAT WE HAVE TO CARRY THE HEAVY BEAMS?
WHY IS MOUSTACHE MANAGERIAL MATERIAL?
HE'S NOT THE ONLY ONE!
IT'S GAY TO BE A CELEB-RITEE...
CHEF HASN'T LIFTED ANYTHING HEAVIER THAN A SPOON IN HIS LIFE!
SNIF!
AH! C'EST MAGNI-FIQUE!
WHAT IS IT THAT MAKES THEM SO SPECIAL?
I'VE GOT IT! THEY BOTH HAVE MOUSTACHES!
WHISKERS MUST MAKE YOU SMART!
THEIR STASHES?
CRUMB CATCHERS?
LIP CATER-PILLARS?
FACE FURNITURE?

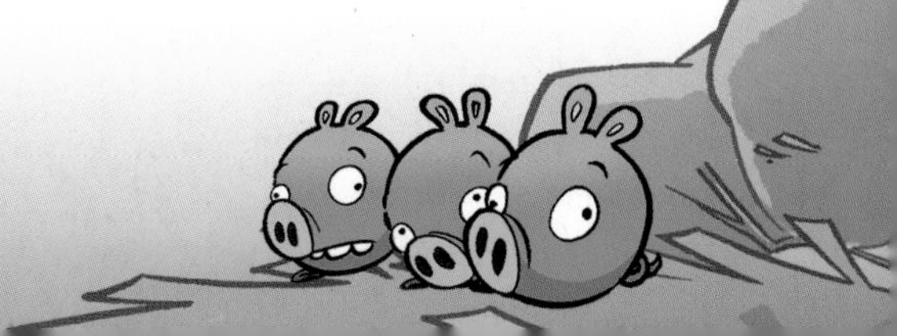

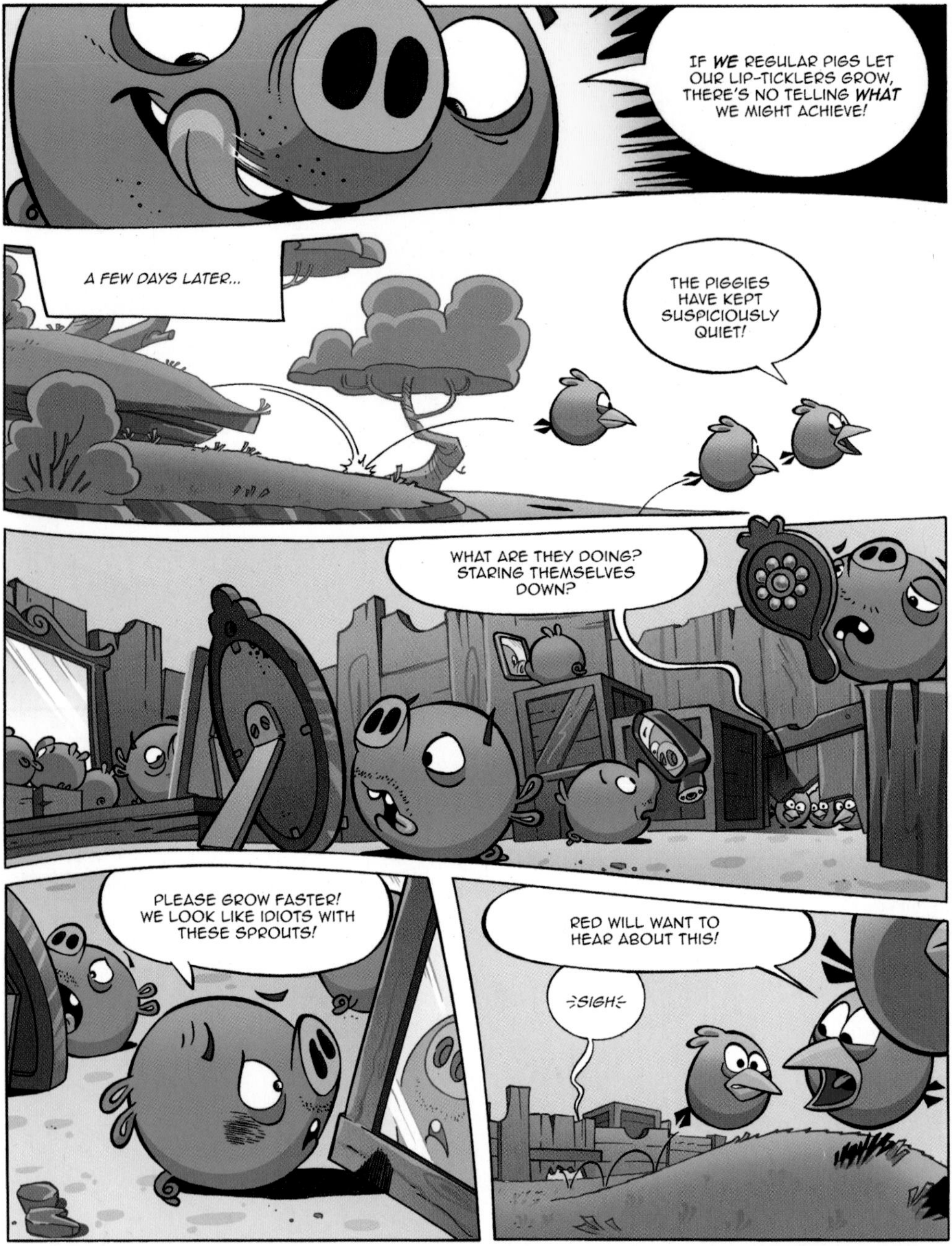
IF WE REGULAR PIGS LET OUR LIP-TICKLERS GROW, THERE'S NO TELLING WHAT WE MIGHT ACHIEVE!
A FEW DAYS LATER...
THE PIGGIES HAVE KEPT SUSPICIOUSLY QUIET!
WHAT ARE THEY DOING? STARING THEMSELVES DOWN?
PLEASE GROW FASTER! WE LOOK LIKE IDIOTS WITH THESE SPROUTS!
RED WILL WANT TO HEAR ABOUT THIS!
SIGH

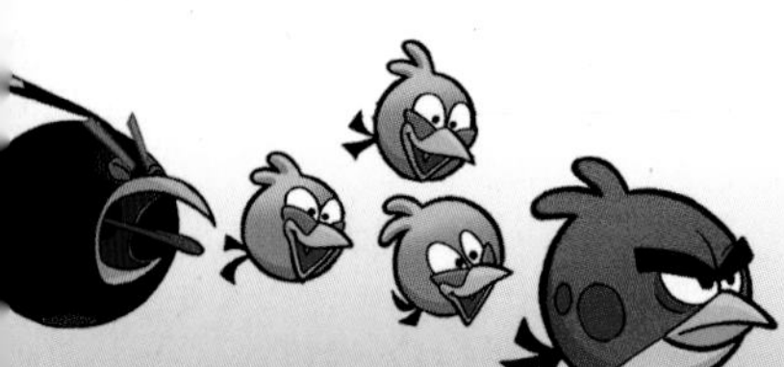

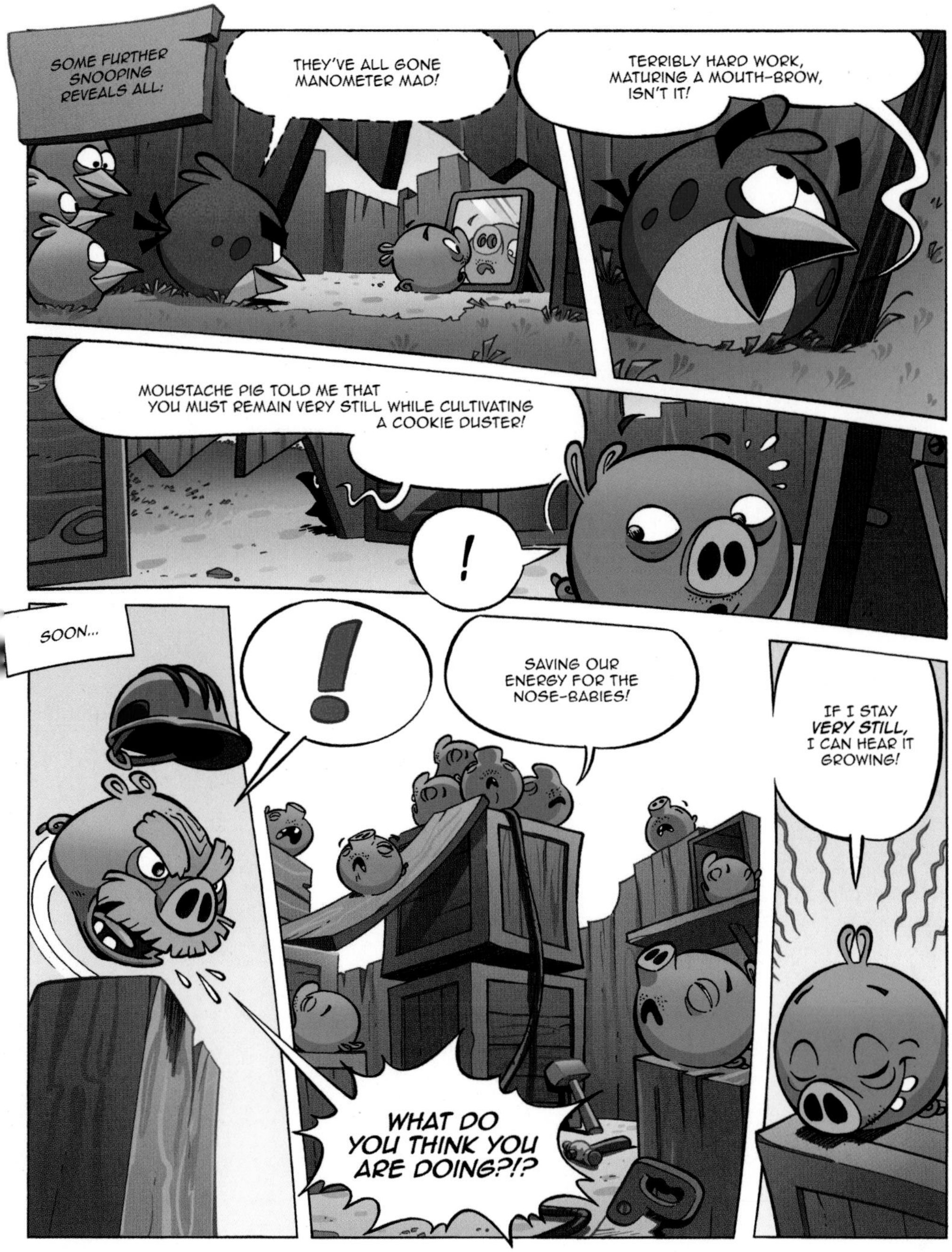
SOME FURTHER SNOOPING REVEALS ALL:
THEY'VE ALL GONE MANOMETER MAD!
TERRIBLY HARD WORK, MATURING A MOUTH-BROW, ISN'T IT!
MOUSTACHE PIG TOLD ME THAT YOU MUST REMAIN VERY STILL WHILE CULTIVATING A COOKIE DUSTER!
!
SOON...
!
SAVING OUR ENERGY FOR THE NOSE-BABIES!
IF I STAY VERY STILL, I CAN HEAR IT GROWING!
WHAT DO YOU THINK YOU ARE DOING?!?

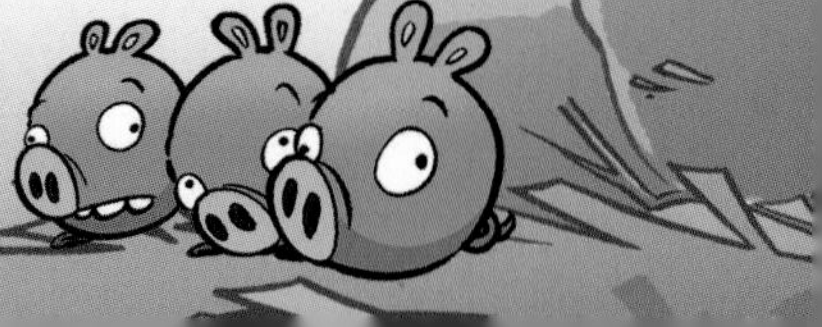

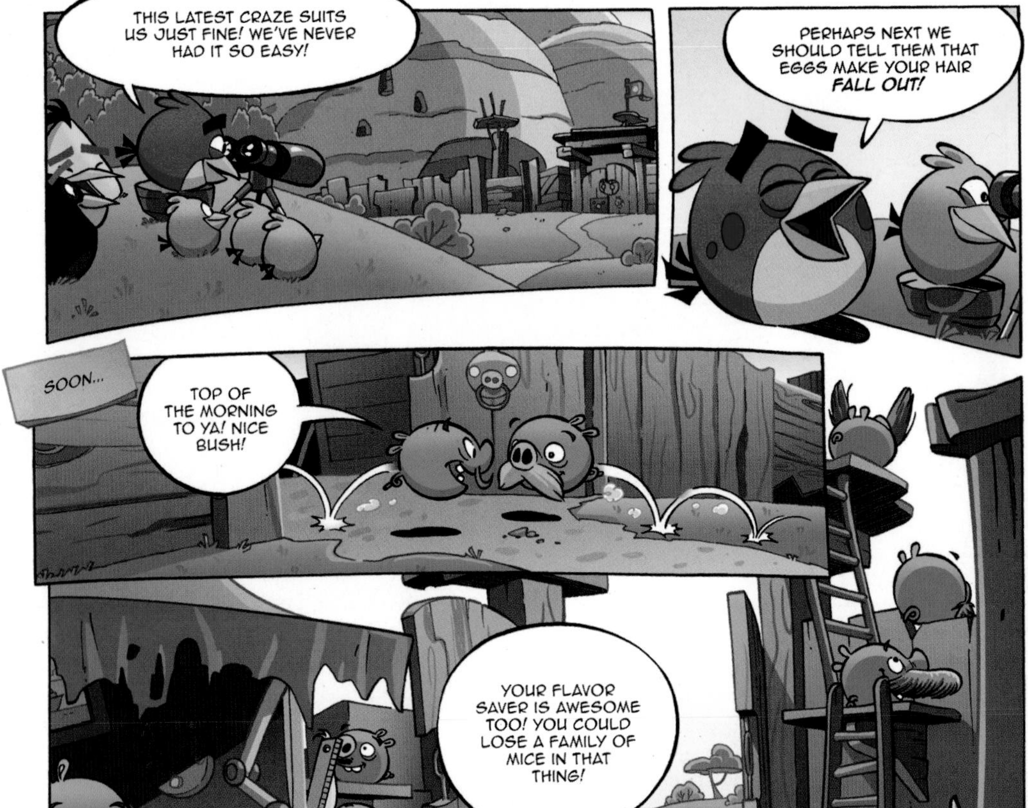
THIS LATEST CRAZE SUITS US JUST FINE! WE'VE NEVER HAD IT SO EASY!
PERHAPS NEXT WE SHOULD TELL THEM THAT EGGS MAKE YOUR HAIR *FALL OUT!*
SOON...
TOP OF THE MORNING TO YA! NICE BUSH!
YOUR FLAVOR SAVER IS AWESOME TOO! YOU COULD LOSE A FAMILY OF MICE IN THAT THING!

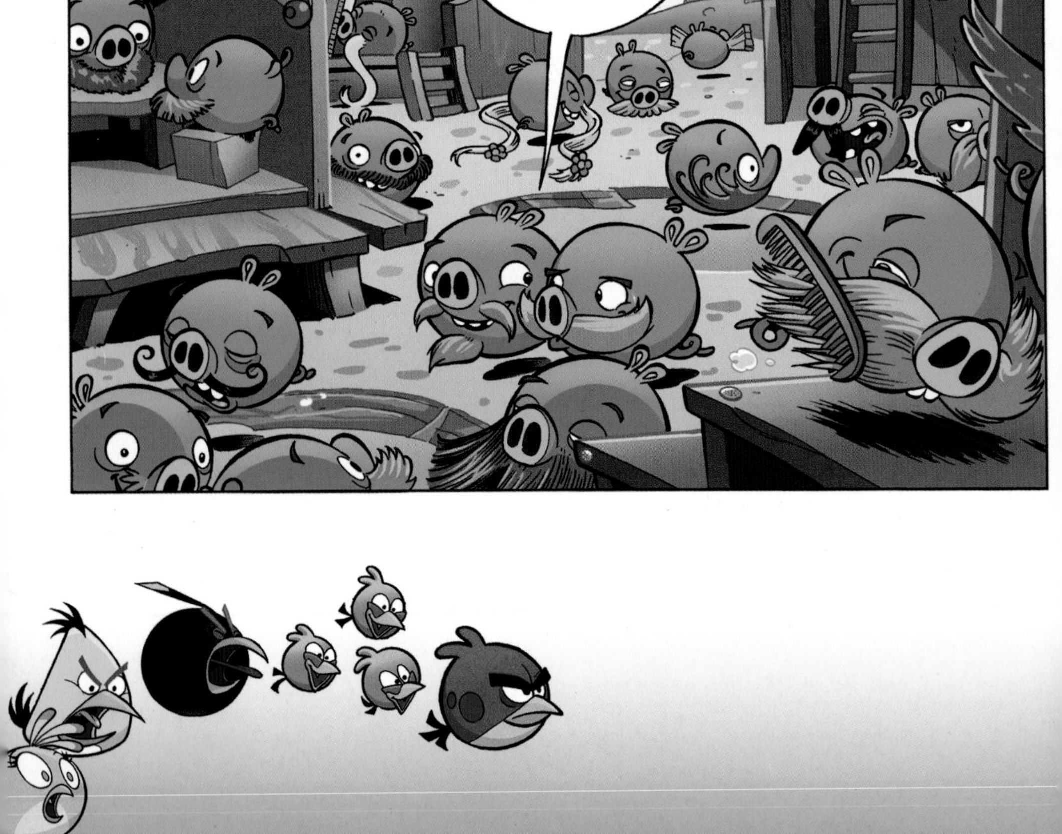

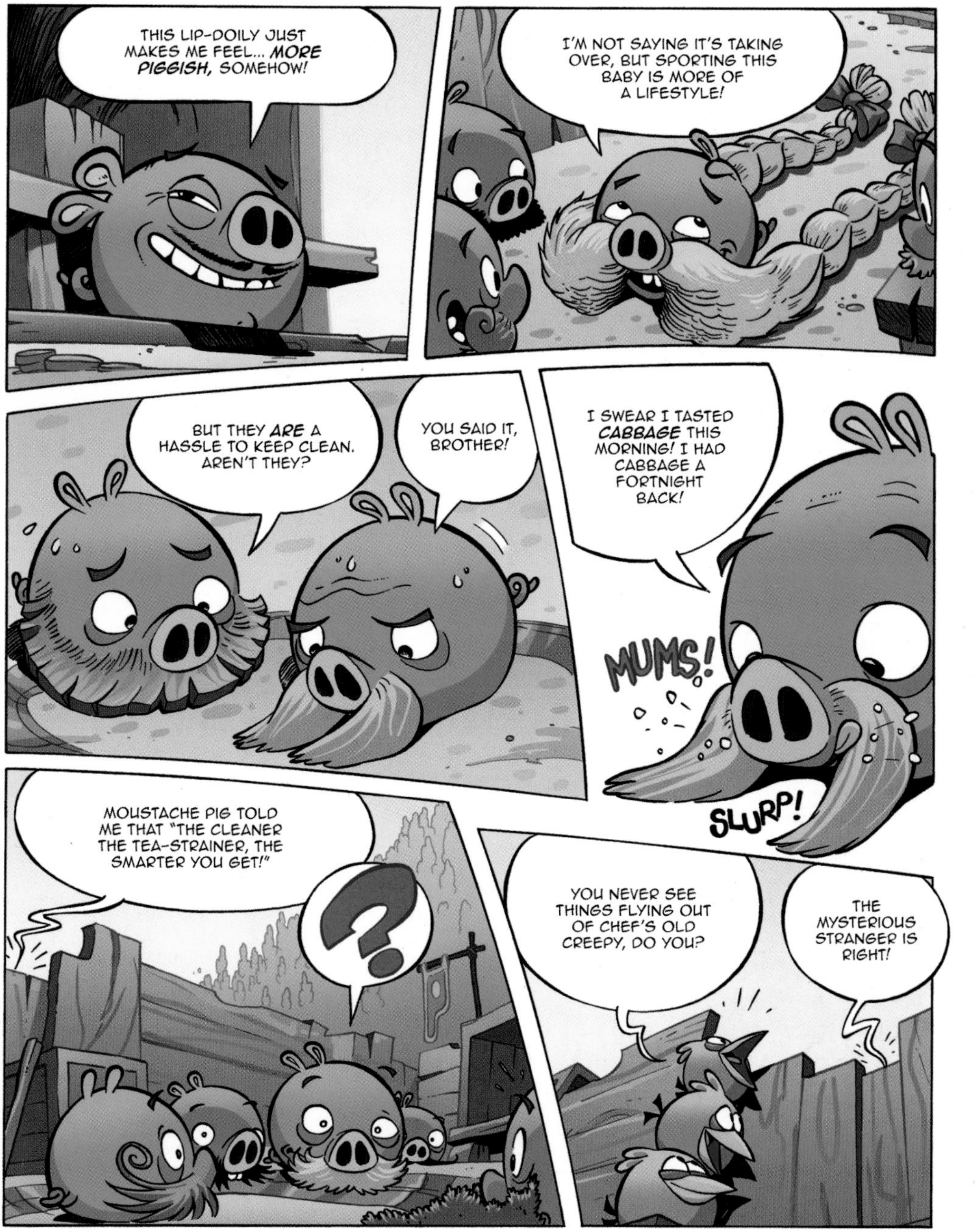
THIS LIP-DOILY JUST MAKES ME FEEL... MORE PIGGISH, SOMEHOW!
I'M NOT SAYING IT'S TAKING OVER, BUT SPORTING THIS BABY IS MORE OF A LIFESTYLE!
BUT THEY ARE A HASSLE TO KEEP CLEAN. AREN'T THEY?
YOU SAID IT, BROTHER!
I SWEAR I TASTED CABBAGE THIS MORNING! I HAD CABBAGE A FORTNIGHT BACK!
MUMS!
SLURP!
MOUSTACHE PIG TOLD ME THAT "THE CLEANER THE TEA-STRAINER, THE SMARTER YOU GET!"
?
YOU NEVER SEE THINGS FLYING OUT OF CHEF'S OLD CREEPY, DO YOU?
THE MYSTERIOUS STRANGER IS RIGHT!

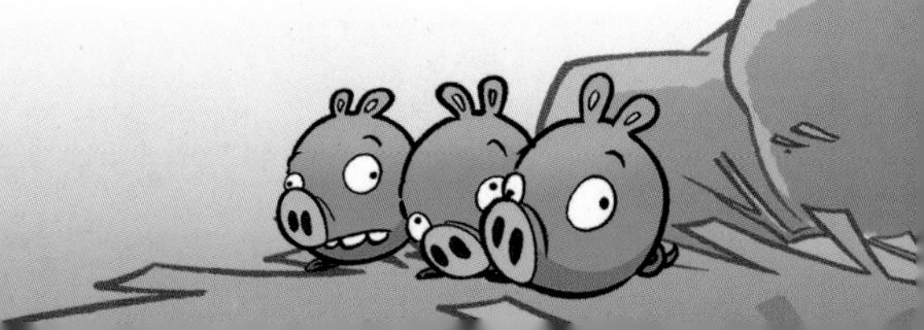

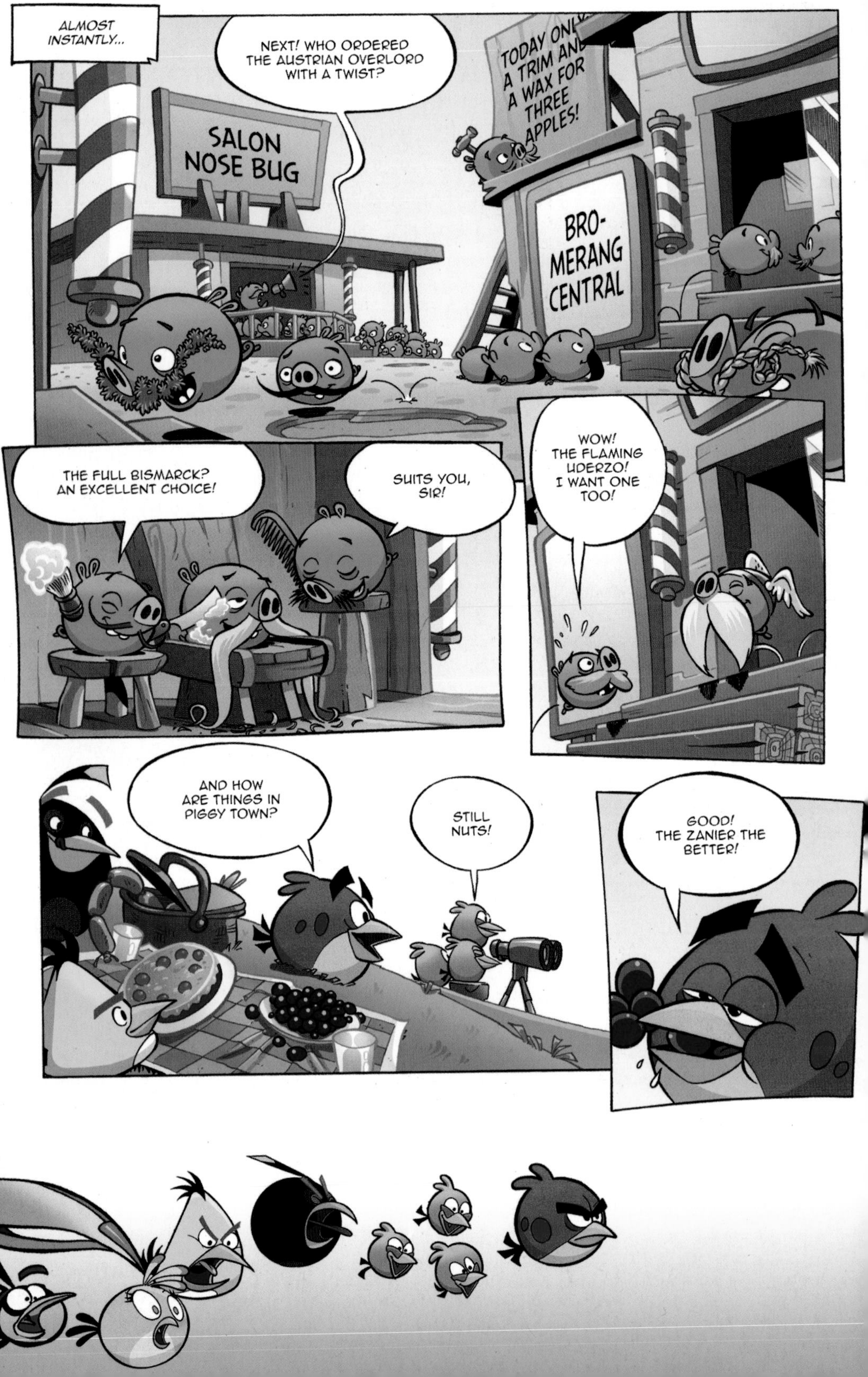
ALMOST INSTANTLY...
NEXT! WHO ORDERED THE AUSTRIAN OVERLORD WITH A TWIST?
SALON NOSE BUG
TODAY ONLY A TRIM AND A WAX FOR THREE APPLES!
BRO-MERANG CENTRAL
THE FULL BISMARCK? AN EXCELLENT CHOICE!
SUITS YOU, SIR!
WOW! THE FLAMING UDERZO! I WANT ONE TOO!
AND HOW ARE THINGS IN PIGGY TOWN?
STILL NUTS!
GOOD! THE ZANIER THE BETTER!

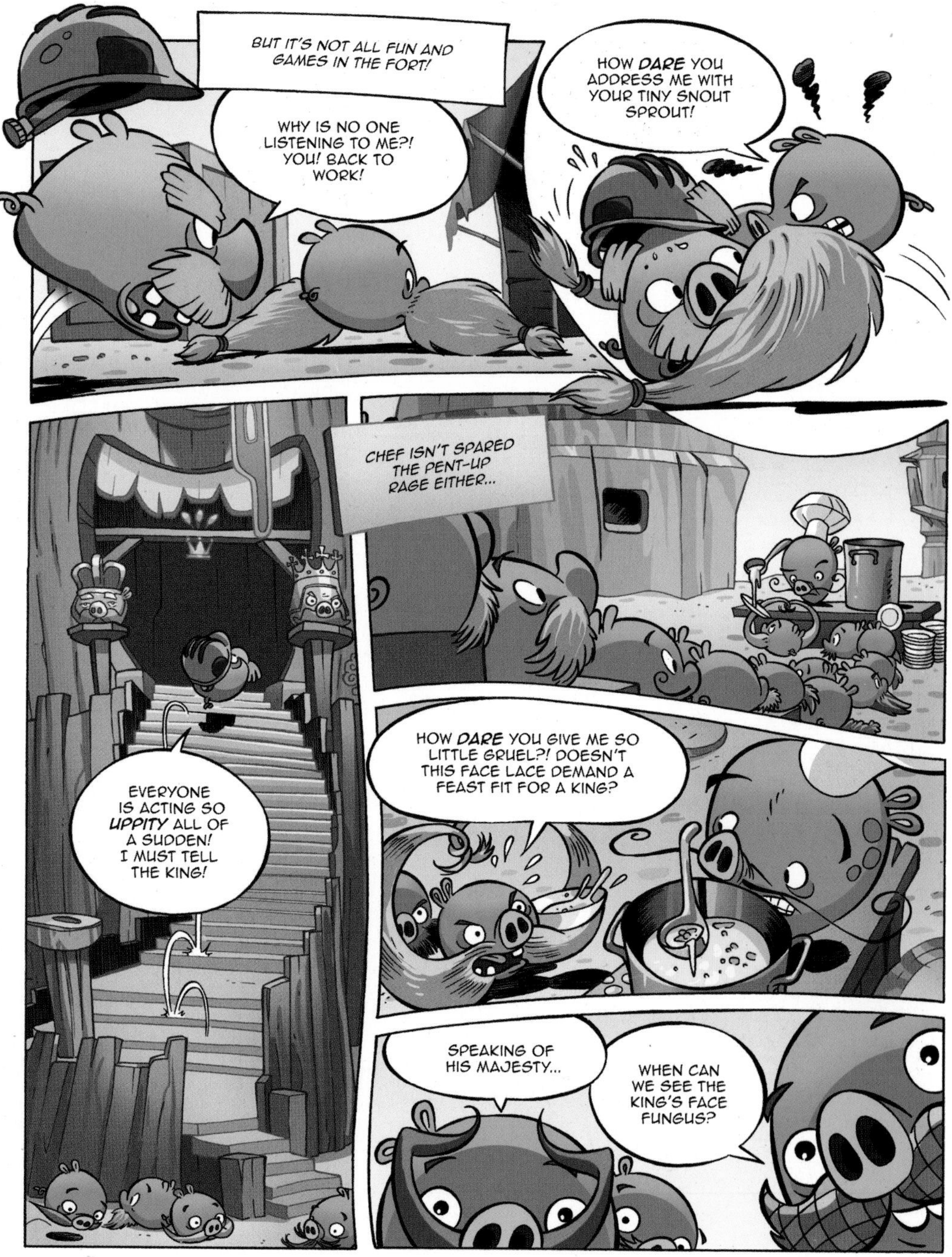
BUT IT'S NOT ALL FUN AND GAMES IN THE FORT!
WHY IS NO ONE LISTENING TO ME?! YOU! BACK TO WORK!
HOW DARE YOU ADDRESS ME WITH YOUR TINY SNOUT SPROUT!
EVERYONE IS ACTING SO UPPITY ALL OF A SUDDEN! I MUST TELL THE KING!
CHEF ISN'T SPARED THE PENT-UP RAGE EITHER...
HOW DARE YOU GIVE ME SO LITTLE GRUEL?! DOESN'T THIS FACE LACE DEMAND A FEAST FIT FOR A KING?
SPEAKING OF HIS MAJESTY...
WHEN CAN WE SEE THE KING'S FACE FUNGUS?

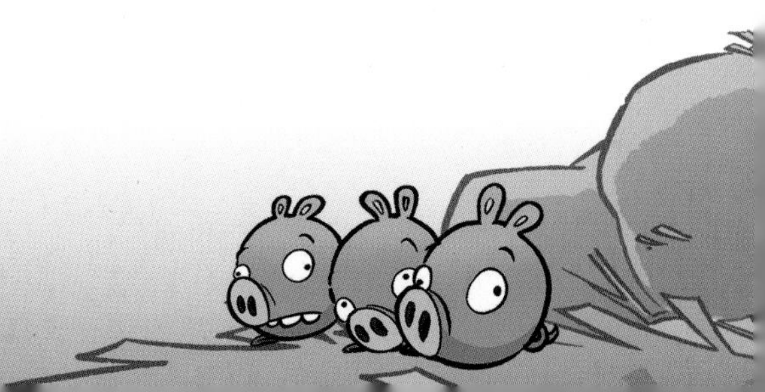

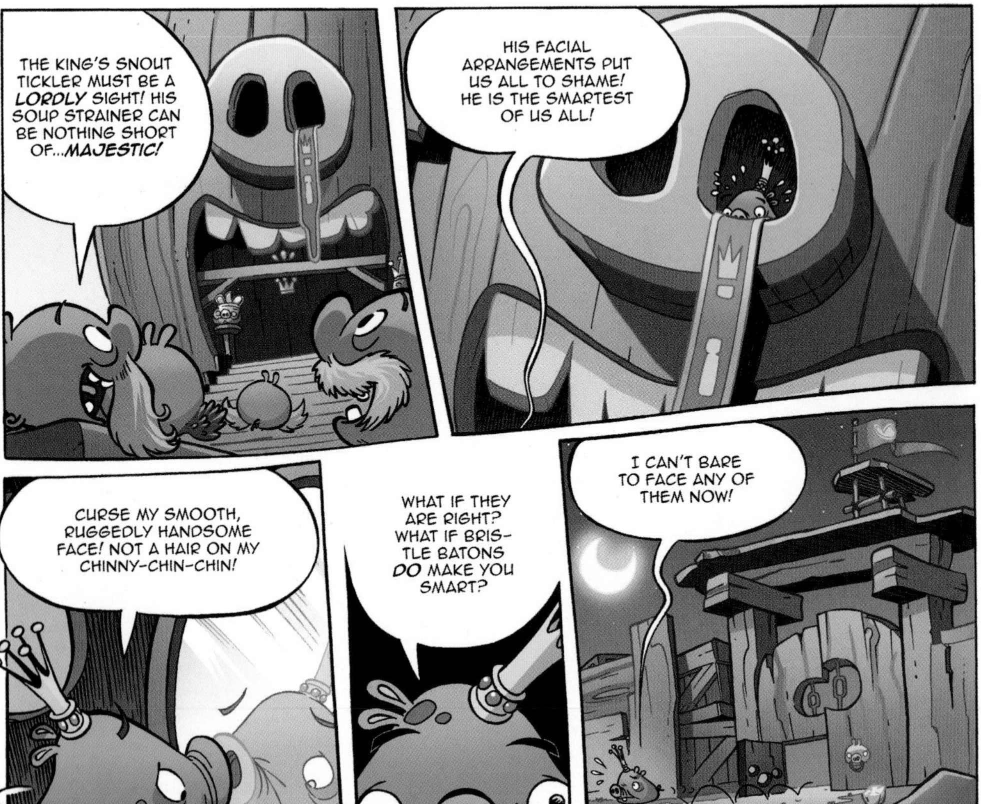
THE KING'S SNOUT TICKLER MUST BE A *LORDLY* SIGHT! HIS SOUP STRAINER CAN BE NOTHING SHORT OF... ***MAJESTIC!***
HIS FACIAL ARRANGEMENTS PUT US ALL TO SHAME! HE IS THE SMARTEST OF US ALL!
CURSE MY SMOOTH, RUGGEDLY HANDSOME FACE! NOT A HAIR ON MY CHINNY-CHIN-CHIN!
WHAT IF THEY ARE RIGHT? WHAT IF BRIS-TLE BATONS ***DO*** MAKE YOU SMART?
I CAN'T BARE TO FACE ANY OF THEM NOW!
AND SO...
WE MAY HAVE MADE A MISTAKE...
THE KING ***REFUSES*** TO SHOW HIS SNOT MOP! WHAT ARE WE TO THINK?

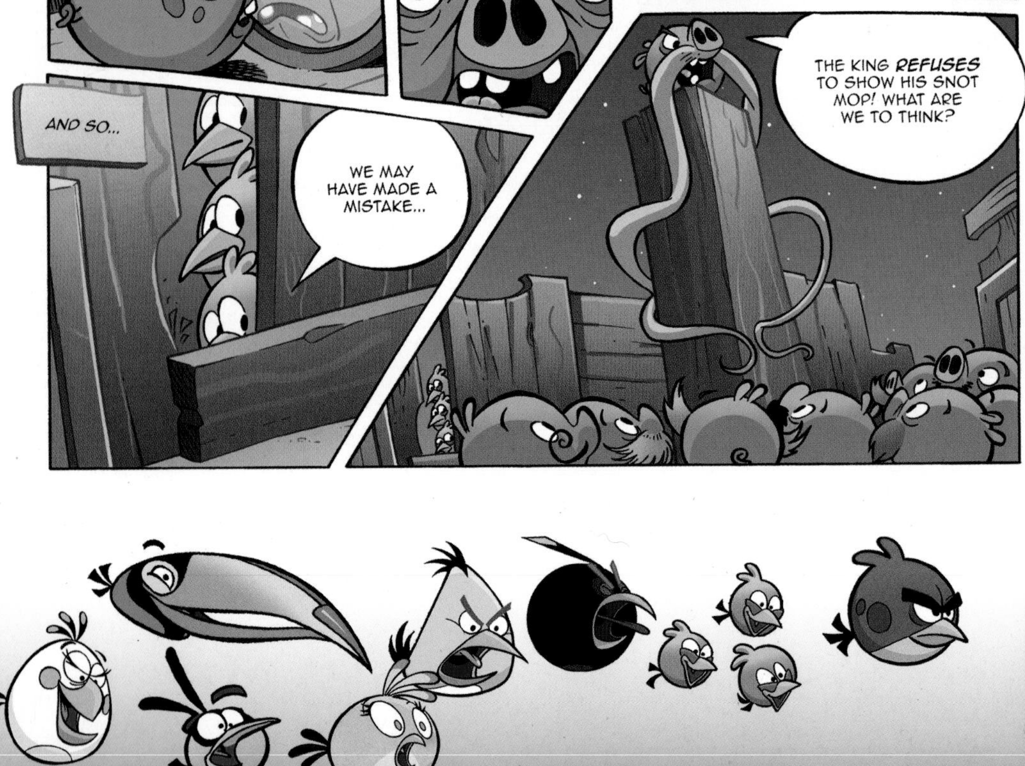

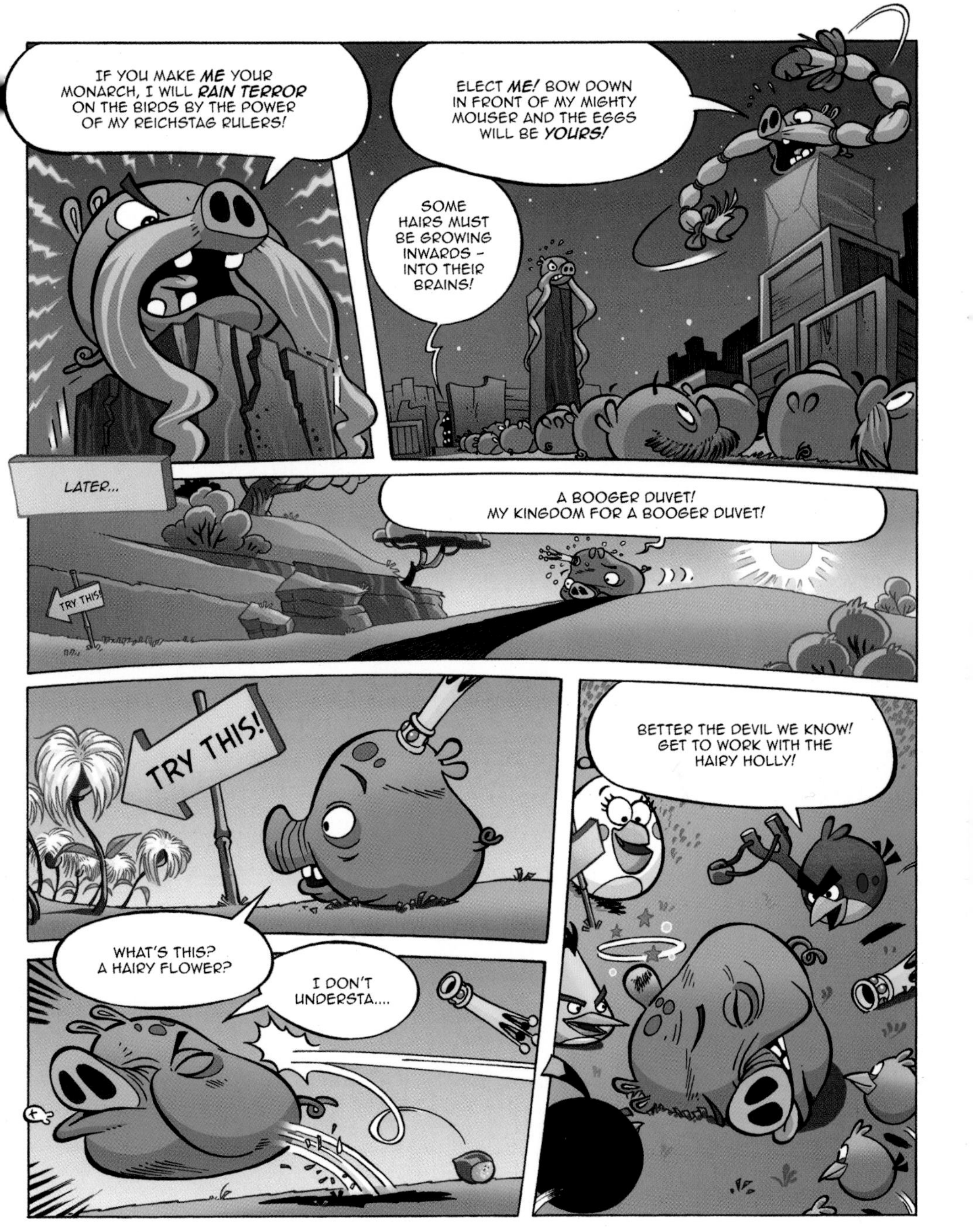
IF YOU MAKE ME YOUR MONARCH, I WILL RAIN TERROR ON THE BIRDS BY THE POWER OF MY REICHSTAG RULERS!
ELECT ME! BOW DOWN IN FRONT OF MY MIGHTY MOUSER AND THE EGGS WILL BE YOURS!
SOME HAIRS MUST BE GROWING INWARDS – INTO THEIR BRAINS!
LATER...
A BOOGER DUVET! MY KINGDOM FOR A BOOGER DUVET!
TRY THIS!
TRY THIS!
BETTER THE DEVIL WE KNOW! GET TO WORK WITH THE HAIRY HOLLY!
WHAT'S THIS? A HAIRY FLOWER?
I DON'T UNDERSTA....

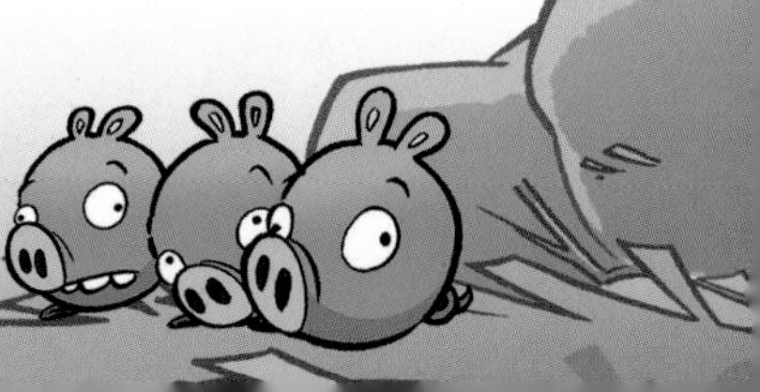

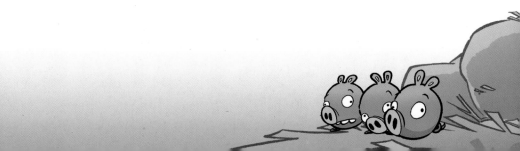

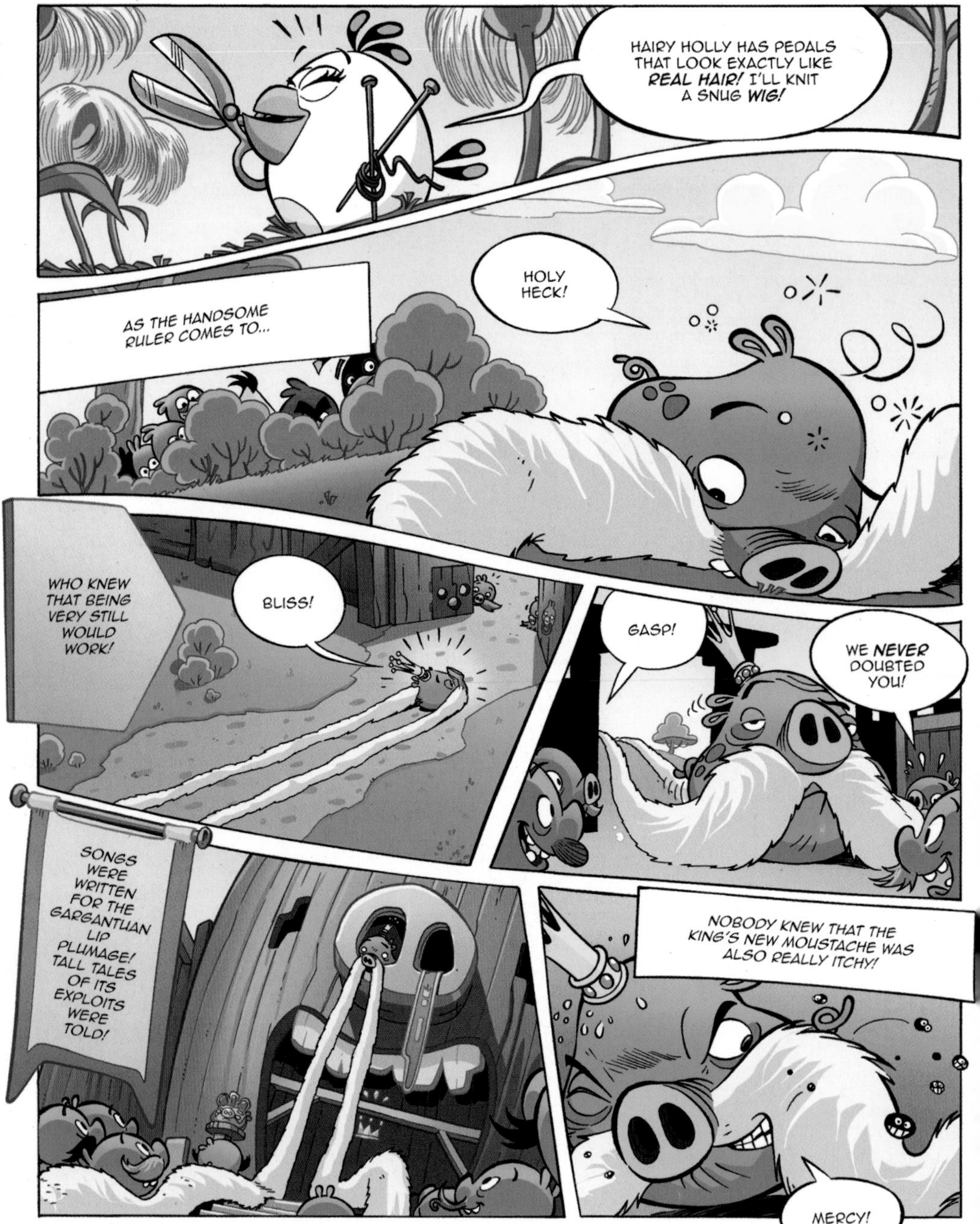
HAIRY HOLLY HAS PEDALS THAT LOOK EXACTLY LIKE **REAL HAIR!** I'LL KNIT A SNUG **WIG!**
AS THE HANDSOME RULER COMES TO...
HOLY HECK!
WHO KNEW THAT BEING VERY STILL WOULD WORK!
BLISS!
GASP!
WE **NEVER** DOUBTED YOU!
SONGS WERE WRITTEN FOR THE GARGANTUAN LIP PLUMAGE! TALL TALES OF ITS EXPLOITS WERE TOLD!
NOBODY KNEW THAT THE KING'S NEW MOUSTACHE WAS ALSO REALLY ITCHY!
MERCY!

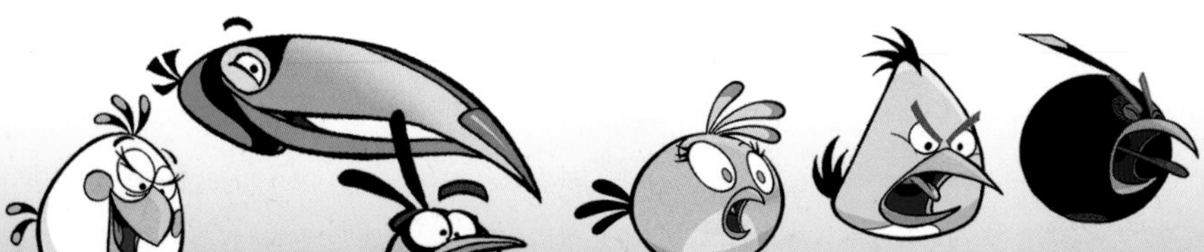

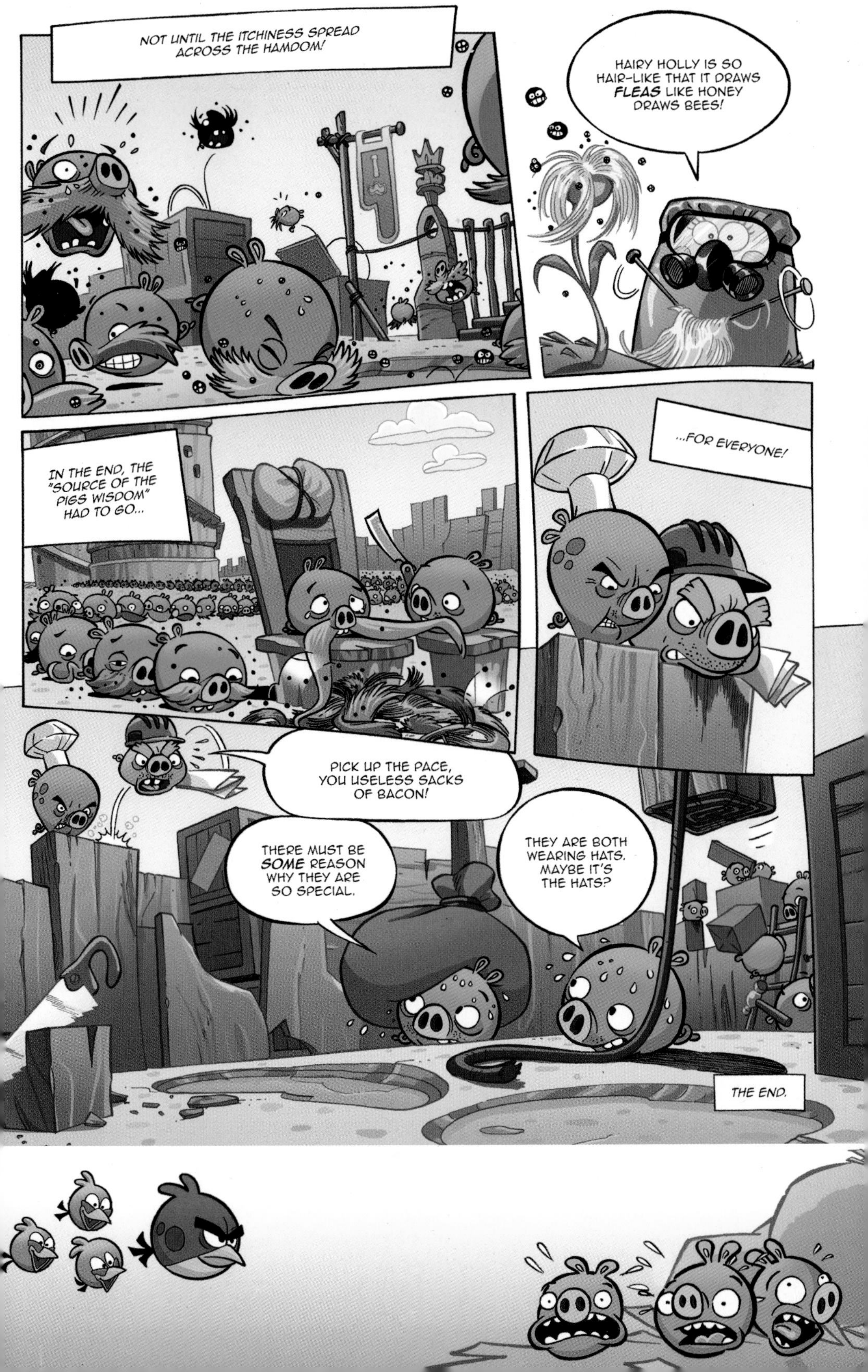
NOT UNTIL THE ITCHINESS SPREAD ACROSS THE HAMDOM!
HAIRY HOLLY IS SO HAIR-LIKE THAT IT DRAWS FLEAS LIKE HONEY DRAWS BEES!
IN THE END, THE "SOURCE OF THE PIGS WISDOM" HAD TO GO...
...FOR EVERYONE!
PICK UP THE PACE, YOU USELESS SACKS OF BACON!
THERE MUST BE SOME REASON WHY THEY ARE SO SPECIAL.
THEY ARE BOTH WEARING HATS. MAYBE IT'S THE HATS?
THE END.

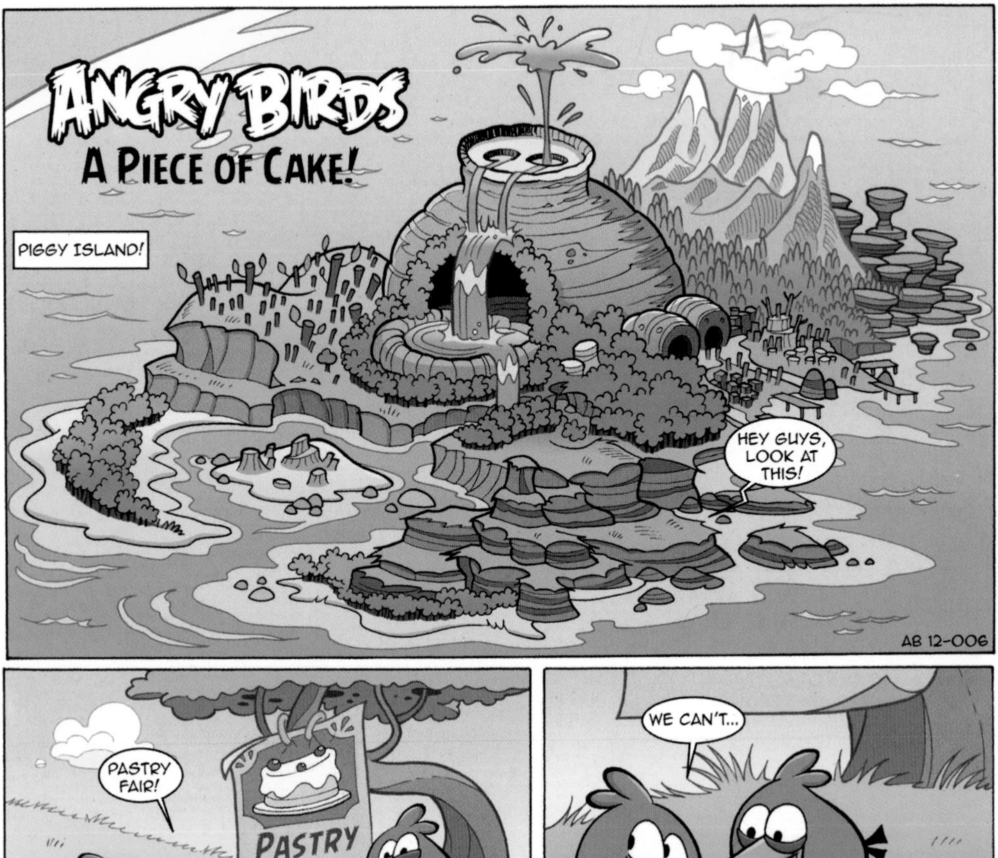
ANGRY BIRDS
A PIECE OF CAKE!
PIGGY ISLAND!
HEY GUYS, LOOK AT THIS!
AB 12-006
PASTRY FAIR!
PASTRY FAIR!
SWELL! CAN WE GO THERE?
WE CAN'T...
BUT WE CAN EAT! THERE'LL BE BILLIONS OF CAKES!
HEY! WHOA!
LET'S DO IT!

WRITTEN BY: PASCAL OOST • ART BY: OSCAR MARTIN & COMICUP STUDIO • COLORS & LETTERS BY: COMICUP STUDIO

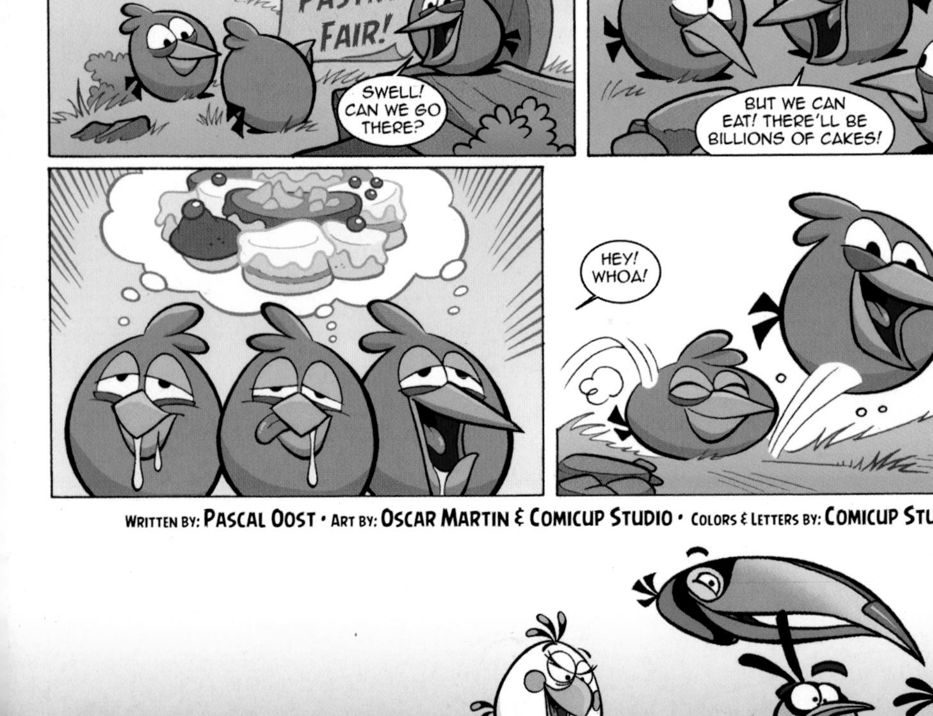

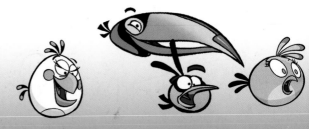

IT'S OUR TURN TO WATCH THE EGGS! WE CAN'T LEAVE 'EM BEHIND!

AWWWWWWWOW...

WE COULD TAKE THE EGGS WITH US!

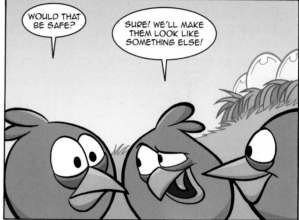

WOULD THAT BE SAFE?

SURE! WE'LL MAKE THEM LOOK LIKE SOMETHING ELSE!

LIKE?

LIKE A CAKE!

TA-DAAA!

BUT... WHAT IF SOMEBODY WANTS TO EAT THIS?

PSH! WHO'S GONNA BOTHER AN ANGRY BIRD WITH A CAKE?

OH BOY!
CAAAAAAAAAAAAAAAAAAAAAKE!
CHEF PIG!
CHEF PIG
MY GRASS-HAY-REED CAKE TURNED OUT PRETTY... ERM... INTÉRESSANT.
WHO AM I KIDDING? THIS IS A DISGRACE! I COULD BAKE THE GREATEST CAKE IN THE WORLD...
...BUT I NEED EGGS!
OH NO! THOSE DARN ANGRY BIRDS!

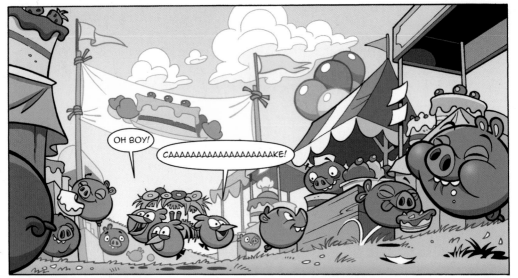

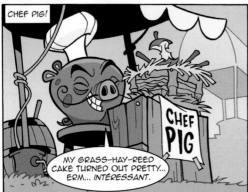

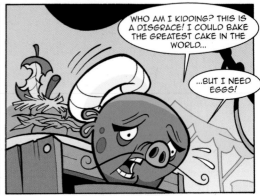

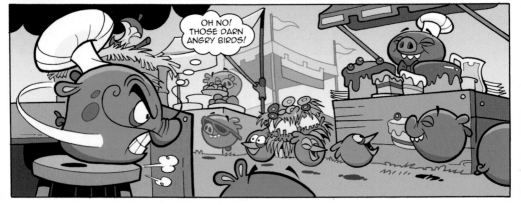

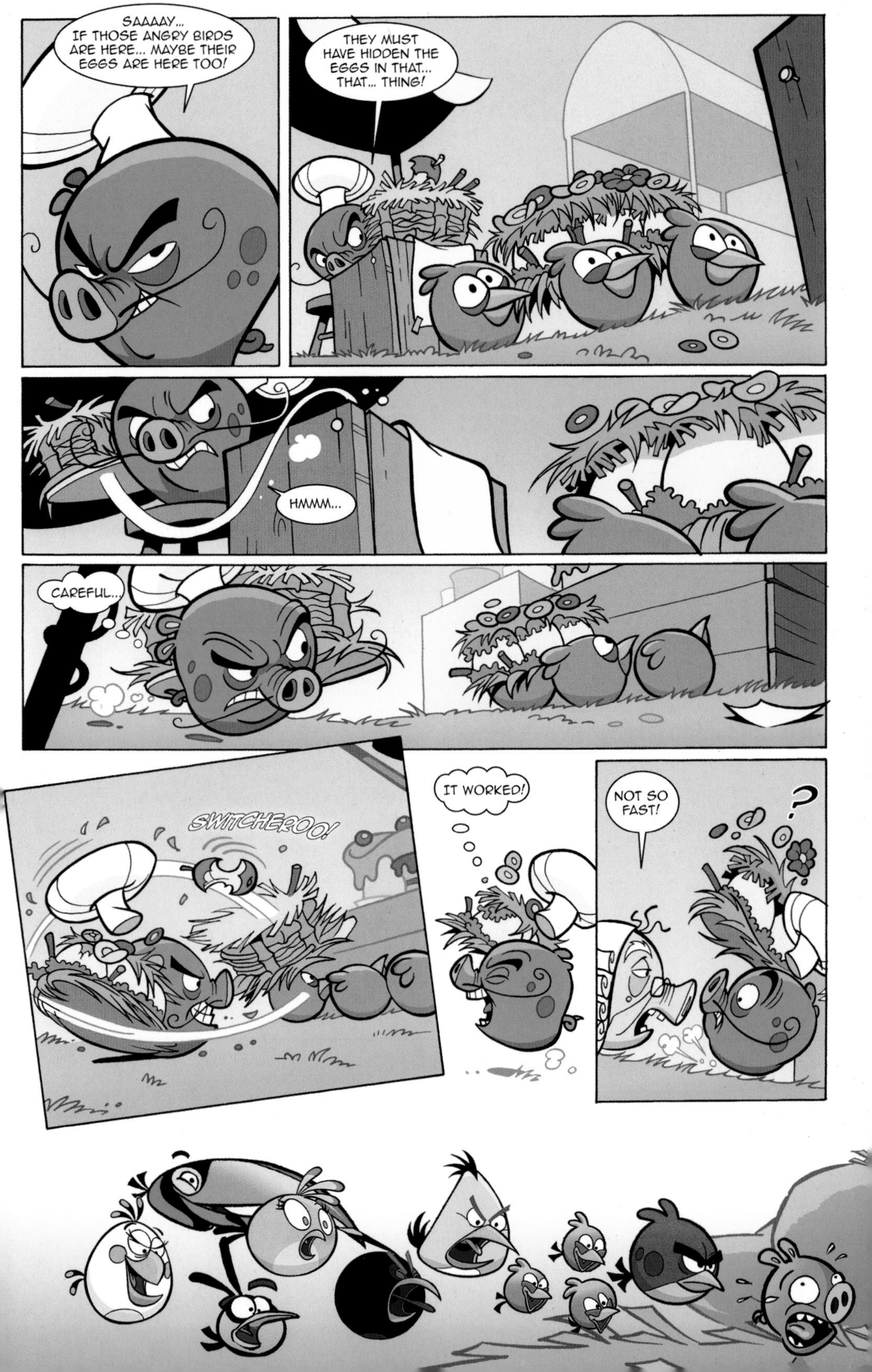
SAAAAY...
IF THOSE ANGRY BIRDS ARE HERE... MAYBE THEIR EGGS ARE HERE TOO!
THEY MUST HAVE HIDDEN THE EGGS IN THAT... THAT... THING!
HMMM...
CAREFUL...
SWITCHEROO!
IT WORKED!
NOT SO FAST!
?

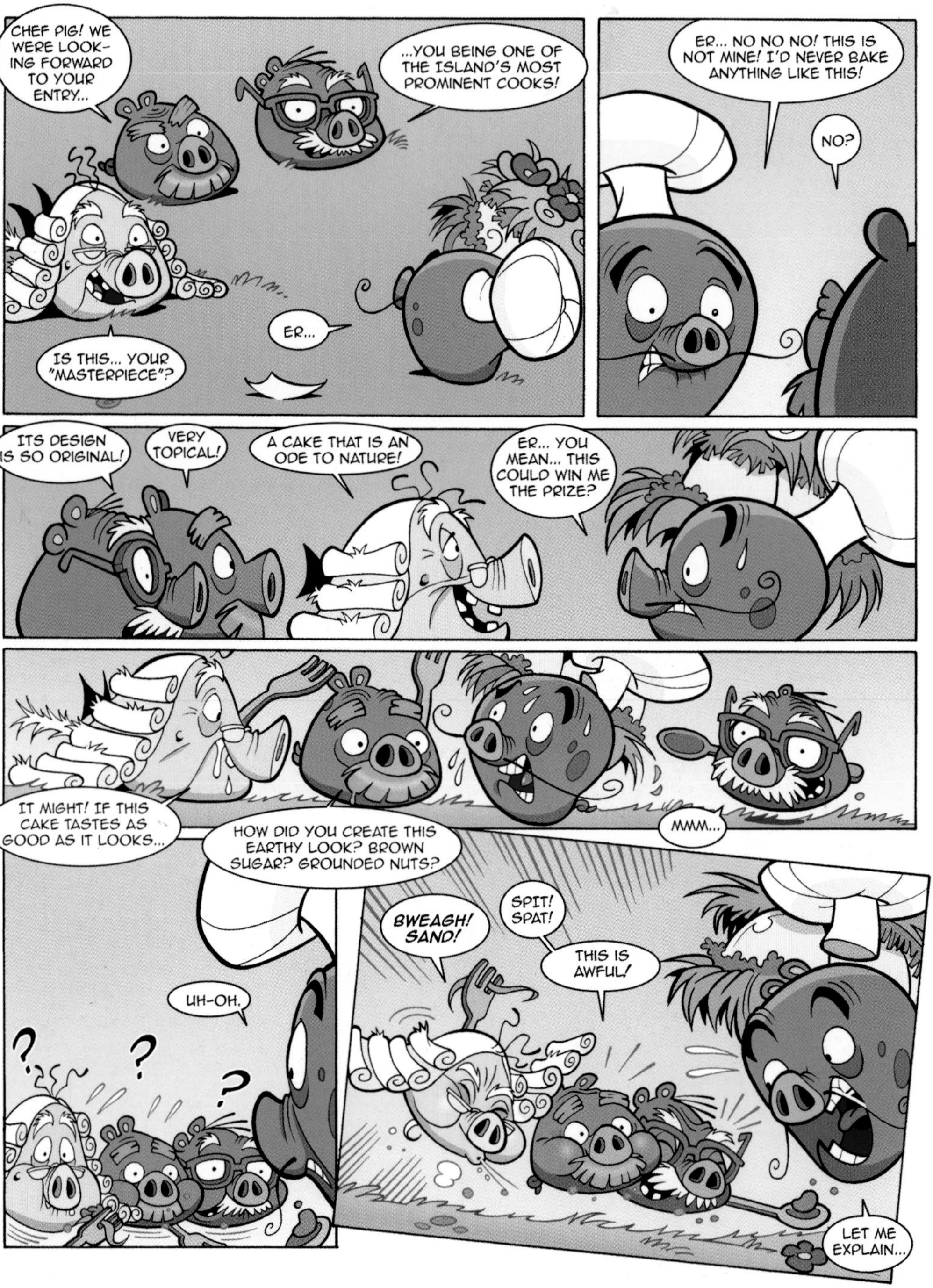
CHEF PIG! WE WERE LOOKING FORWARD TO YOUR ENTRY...
...YOU BEING ONE OF THE ISLAND'S MOST PROMINENT COOKS!
IS THIS... YOUR "MASTERPIECE"?
ER...
ER... NO NO NO! THIS IS NOT MINE! I'D NEVER BAKE ANYTHING LIKE THIS!
NO?
ITS DESIGN IS SO ORIGINAL!
VERY TOPICAL!
A CAKE THAT IS AN ODE TO NATURE!
ER... YOU MEAN... THIS COULD WIN ME THE PRIZE?
IT MIGHT! IF THIS CAKE TASTES AS GOOD AS IT LOOKS...
HOW DID YOU CREATE THIS EARTHY LOOK? BROWN SUGAR? GROUNDED NUTS?
MMM...
UH-OH.
BWEAGH! SAND!
SPIT! SPAT!
THIS IS AWFUL!
LET ME EXPLAIN...

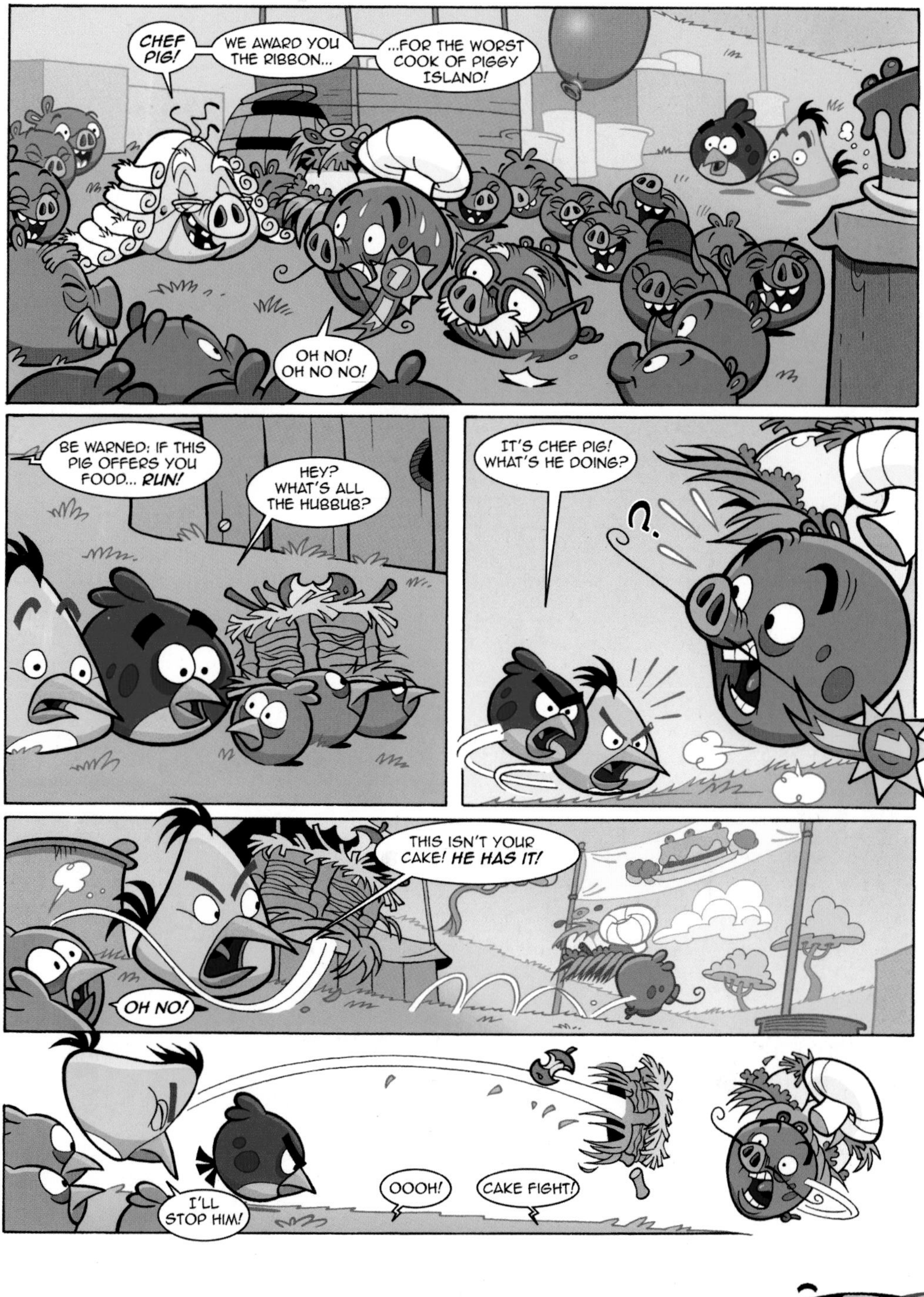
CHEF PIG!
WE AWARD YOU THE RIBBON...
...FOR THE WORST COOK OF PIGGY ISLAND!
OH NO! OH NO NO!
BE WARNED: IF THIS PIG OFFERS YOU FOOD... RUN!
HEY? WHAT'S ALL THE HUBBUB?
IT'S CHEF PIG! WHAT'S HE DOING?
THIS ISN'T YOUR CAKE! HE HAS IT!
OH NO!
I'LL STOP HIM!
OOOH!
CAKE FIGHT!

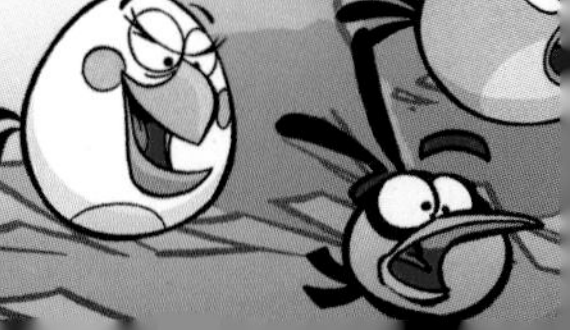

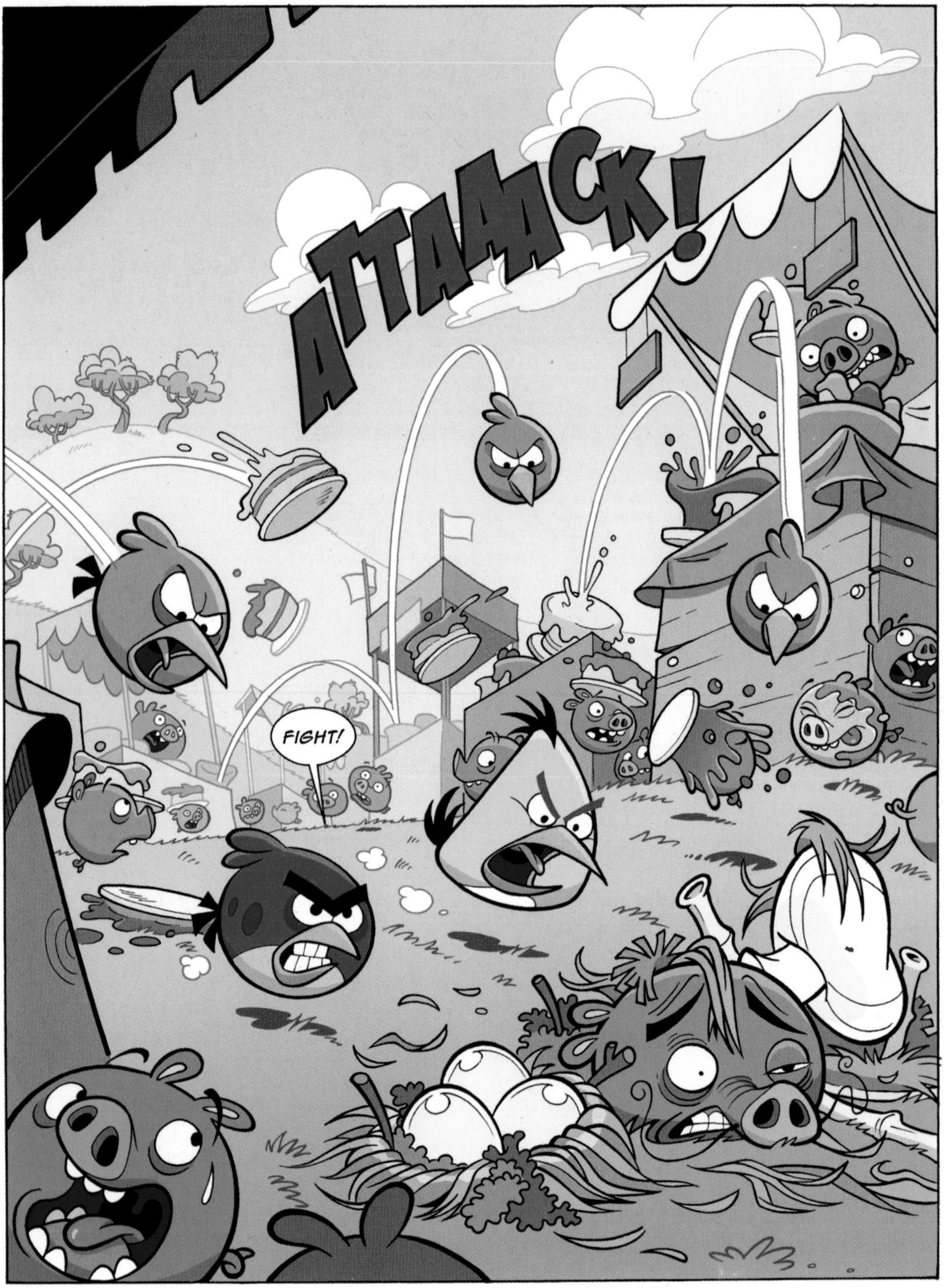
ATTAAACK!
FIGHT!

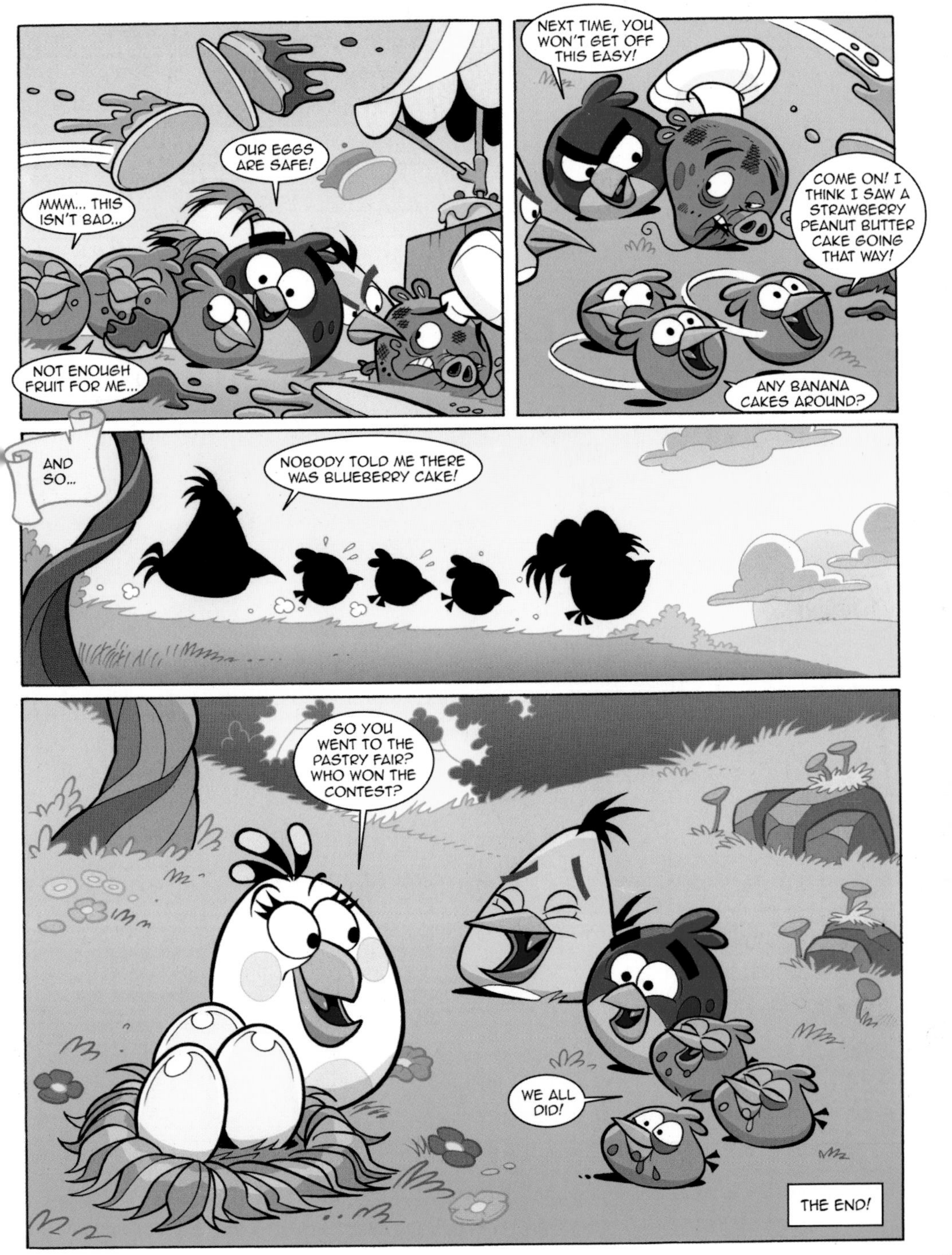
MMM... THIS ISN'T BAD...
OUR EGGS ARE SAFE!
NOT ENOUGH FRUIT FOR ME...
NEXT TIME, YOU WON'T GET OFF THIS EASY!
COME ON! I THINK I SAW A STRAWBERRY PEANUT BUTTER CAKE GOING THAT WAY!
ANY BANANA CAKES AROUND?
AND SO...
NOBODY TOLD ME THERE WAS BLUEBERRY CAKE!
SO YOU WENT TO THE PASTRY FAIR? WHO WON THE CONTEST?
WE ALL DID!
THE END!

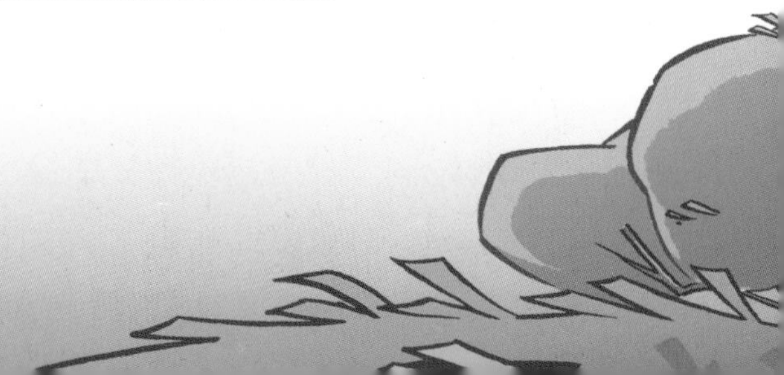

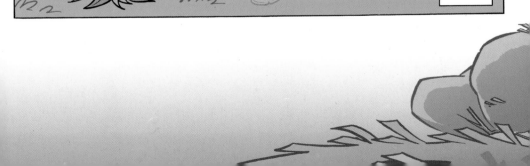

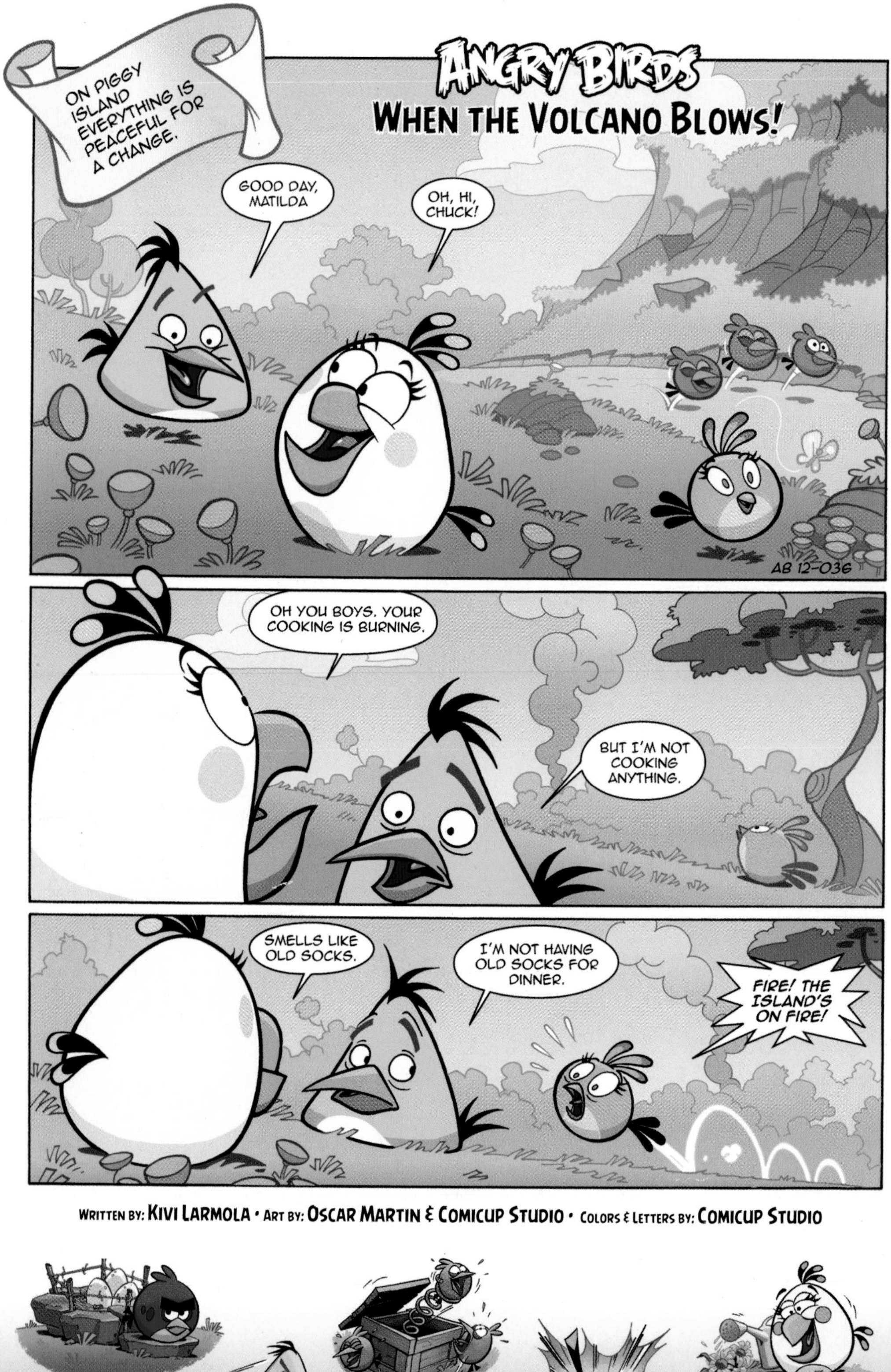
ANGRY BIRDS
WHEN THE VOLCANO BLOWS!
ON PIGGY ISLAND EVERYTHING IS PEACEFUL FOR A CHANGE.
GOOD DAY, MATILDA
OH, HI, CHUCK!
AB 12-036
OH YOU BOYS. YOUR COOKING IS BURNING.
BUT I'M NOT COOKING ANYTHING.
SMELLS LIKE OLD SOCKS.
I'M NOT HAVING OLD SOCKS FOR DINNER.
FIRE! THE ISLAND'S ON FIRE!

WRITTEN BY: KIVI LARMOLA • ART BY: OSCAR MARTIN & COMICUP STUDIO • COLORS & LETTERS BY: COMICUP STUDIO

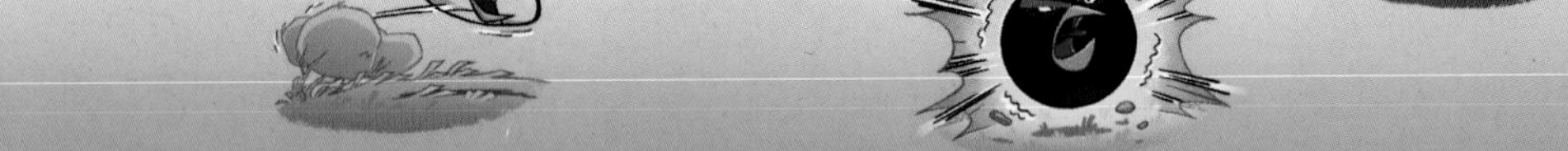

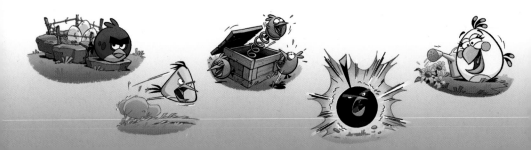

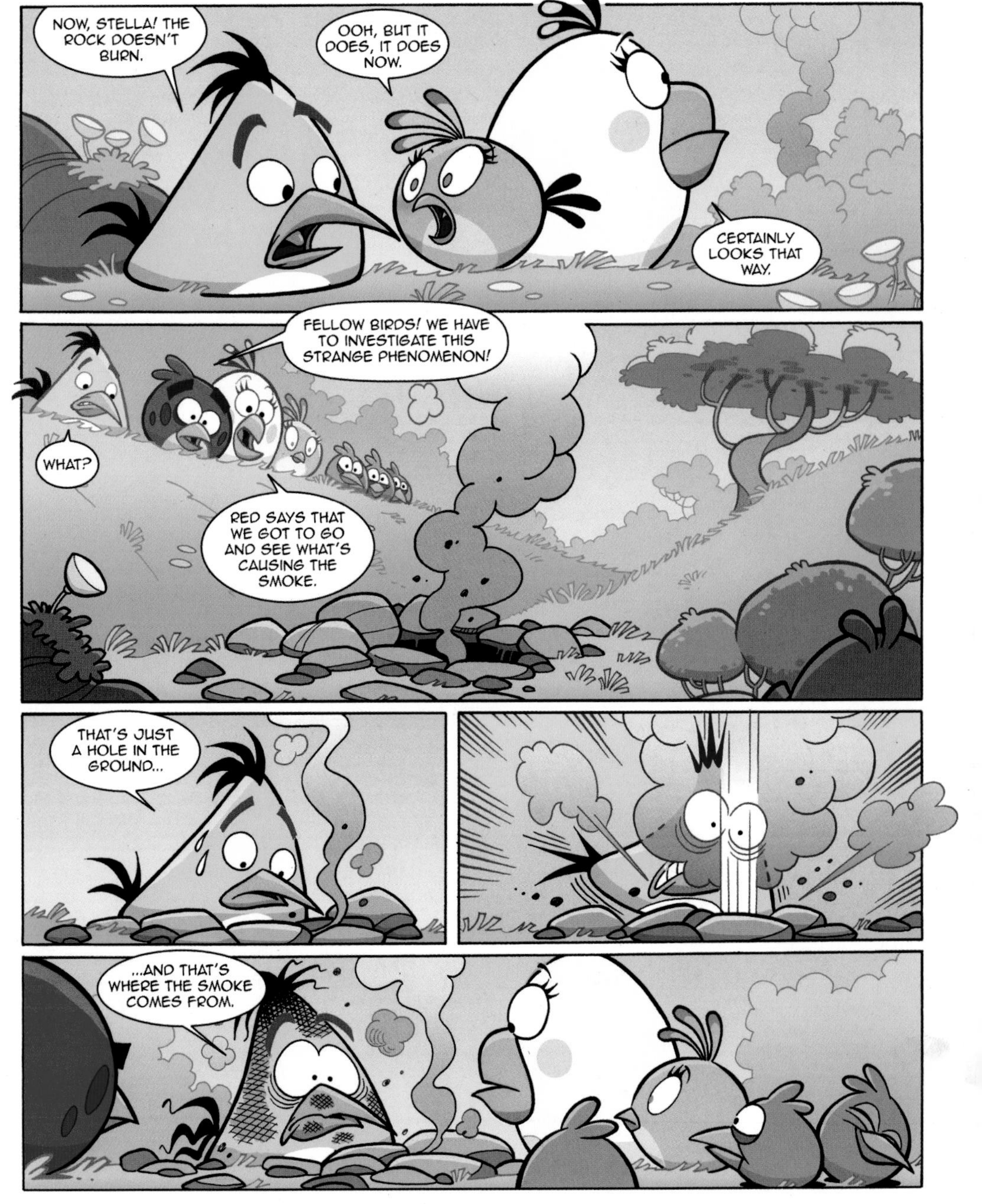
NOW, STELLA! THE ROCK DOESN'T BURN.
OOH, BUT IT DOES, IT DOES NOW.
CERTAINLY LOOKS THAT WAY.
FELLOW BIRDS! WE HAVE TO INVESTIGATE THIS STRANGE PHENOMENON!
WHAT?
RED SAYS THAT WE GOT TO GO AND SEE WHAT'S CAUSING THE SMOKE.
THAT'S JUST A HOLE IN THE GROUND...
...AND THAT'S WHERE THE SMOKE COMES FROM.

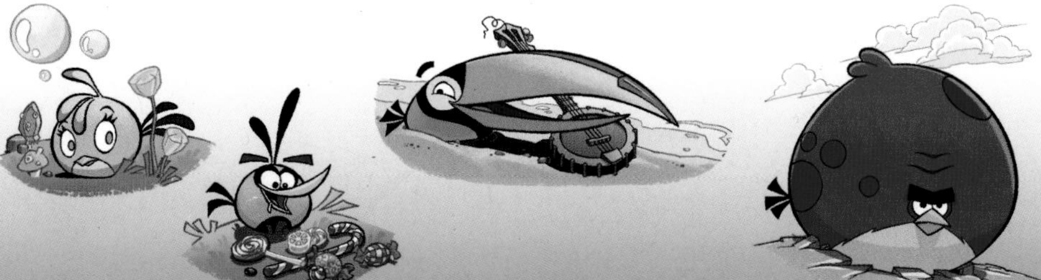

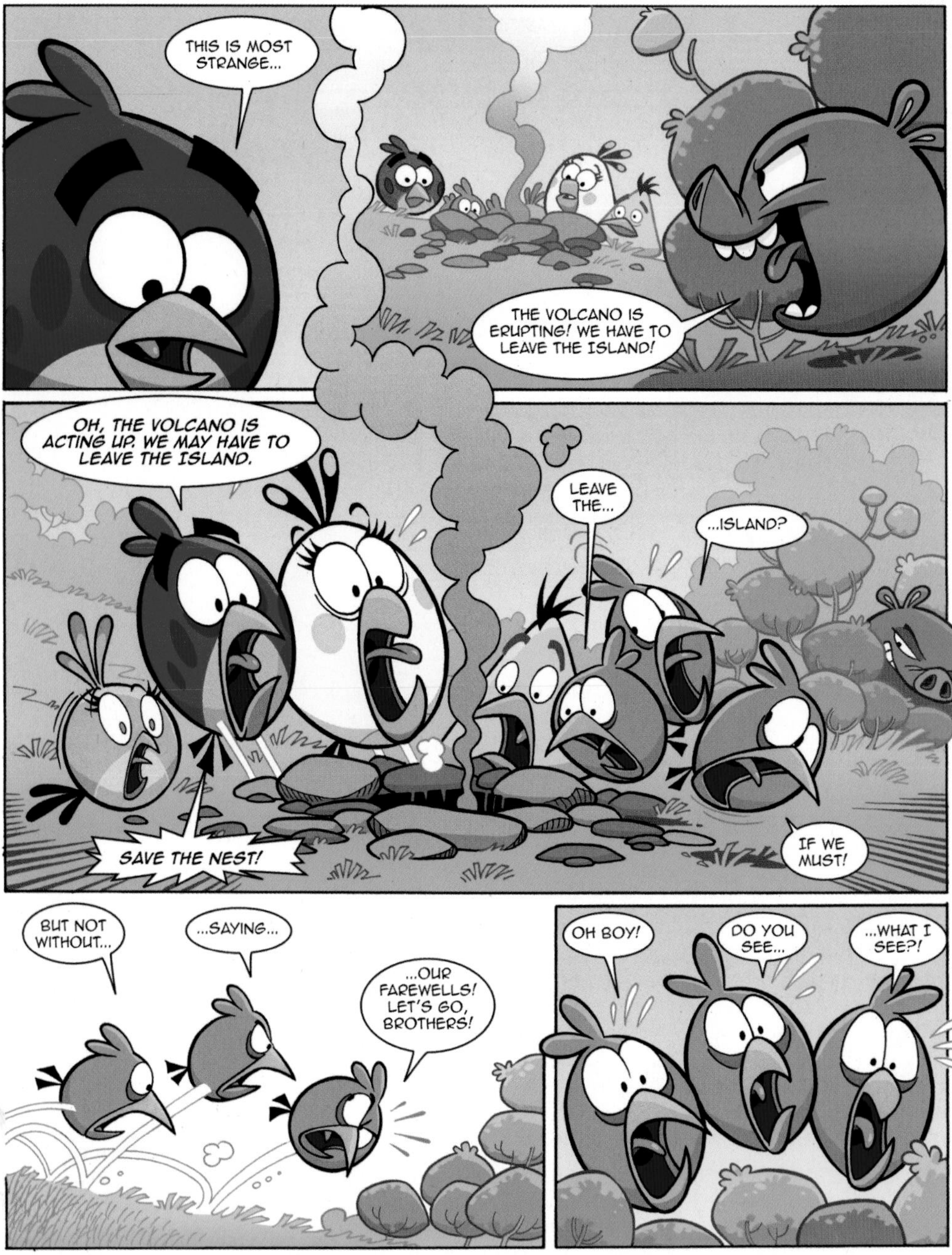
THIS IS MOST STRANGE...
THE VOLCANO IS ERUPTING! WE HAVE TO LEAVE THE ISLAND!
OH, THE VOLCANO IS ACTING UP. WE MAY HAVE TO LEAVE THE ISLAND.
LEAVE THE...
...ISLAND?
SAVE THE NEST!
IF WE MUST!
BUT NOT WITHOUT...
...SAYING...
...OUR FAREWELLS! LET'S GO, BROTHERS!
OH BOY!
DO YOU SEE...
...WHAT I SEE?!

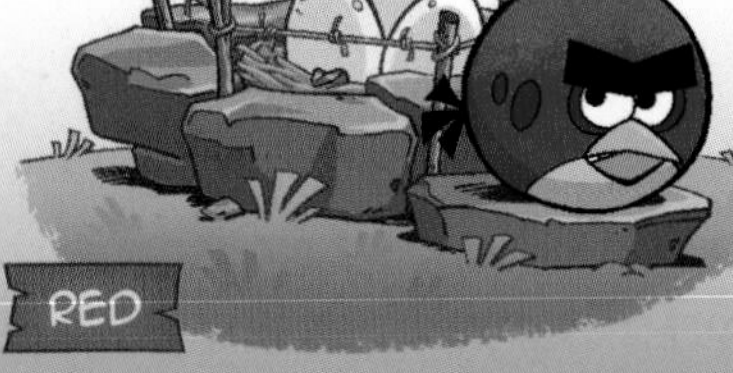
RED

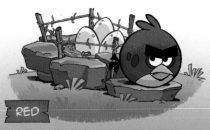

RED IS THE ANGRY BIRD – THE LEADER AND ANGRIEST OF ALL THE BIRDS. HE PROTECTS THE EGGS AT ALL COSTS.

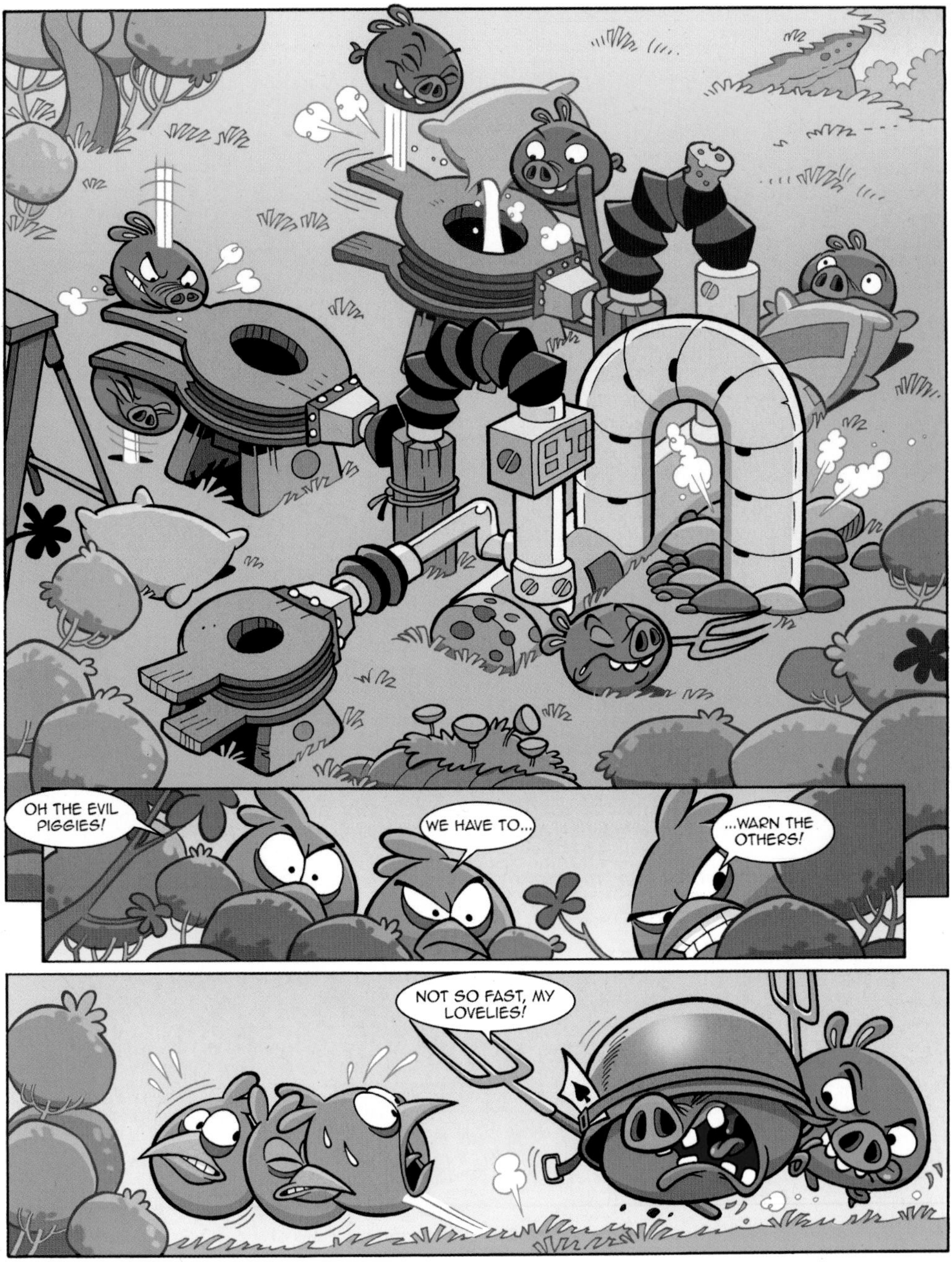
OH THE EVIL PIGGIES!
WE HAVE TO...
...WARN THE OTHERS!
NOT SO FAST, MY LOVELIES!

CHUCK IS RED'S LOYAL FRIEND AND THE FASTEST OF THE BIRDS. CHUCK ACTS BEFORE HE THINKS, AND THIS OFTEN LANDS HIM IN TROUBLE.

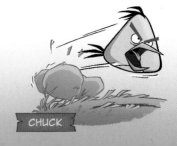

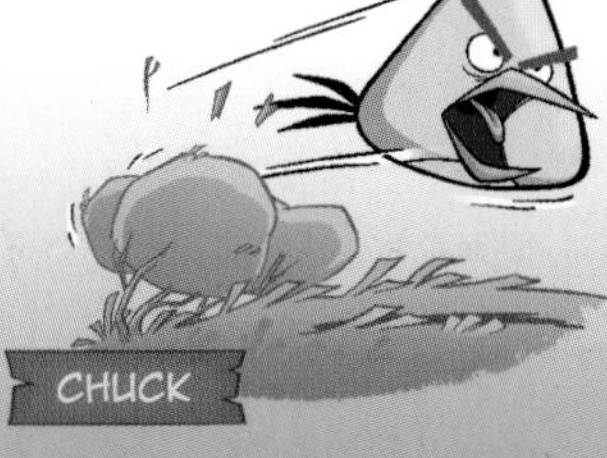
CHUCK

NOW YOU WAIT HERE NICE AND EASY, WHILE WE GO STEAL THE EGGS.
STEAL THE EGGS?!
WE GOT TO STOP THEM!
BUT HOW?
WELL, I'VE GOT AN IDEA... WHISPER...
HEY, GUARD!
WHAT?
ARE THOSE EGGS THAT YOUR PALS ARE CARRYING?
W-WHERE?
THERE!

THE BLUES

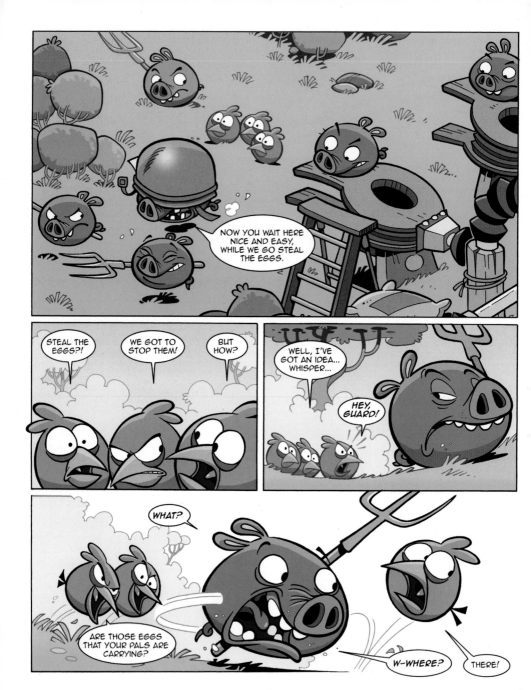

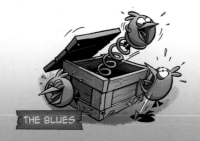

THE BLUES – JIM, JAKE & JAY – ARE THE YOUNGEST OF THE BIRDS. THEY LIKE TO PLAY PRANKS AND ARE SOMETIMES A BIT IRRESPONSIBLE.

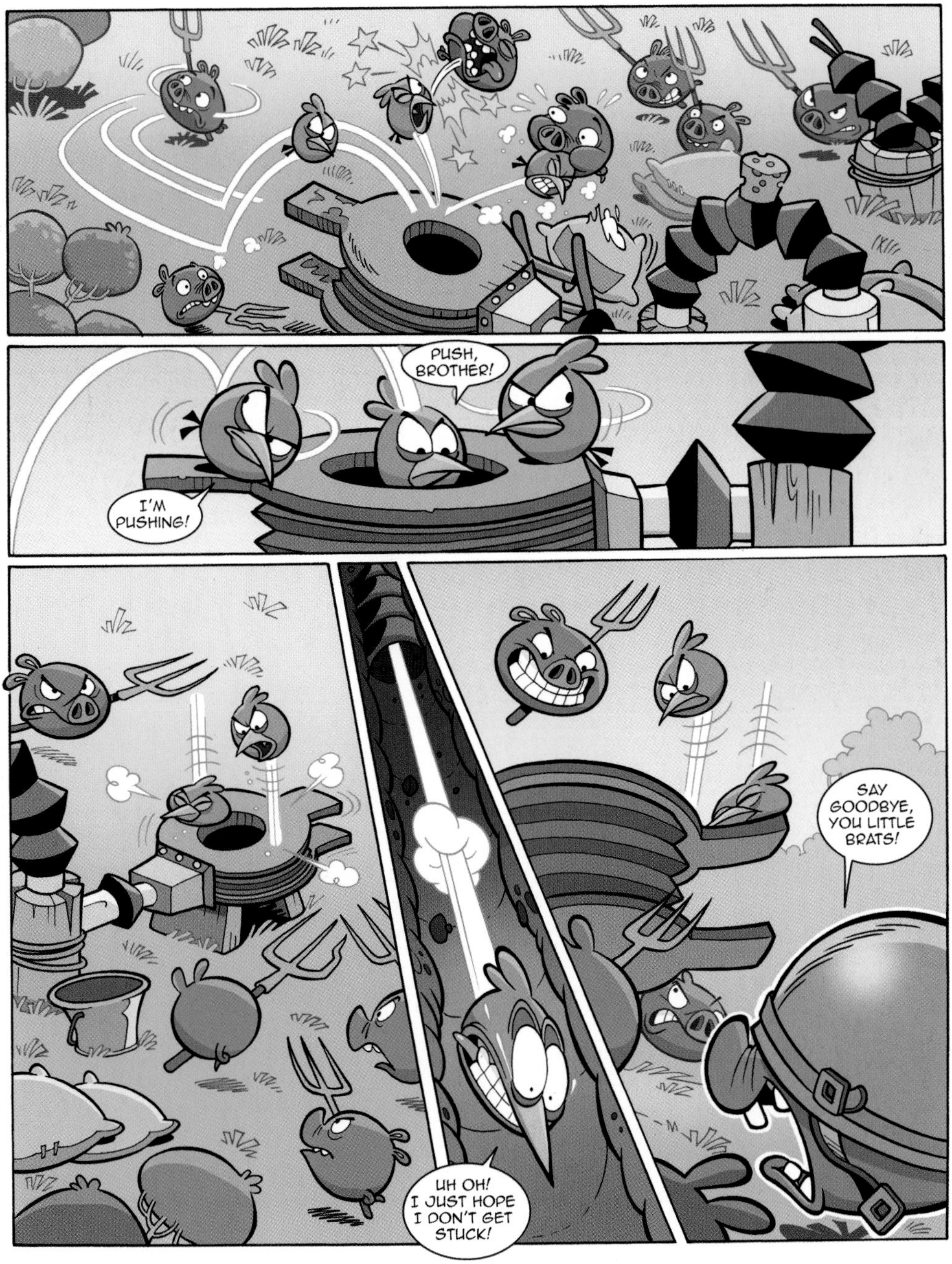
PUSH, BROTHER!
I'M PUSHING!
SAY GOODBYE, YOU LITTLE BRATS!
UH OH! I JUST HOPE I DON'T GET STUCK!

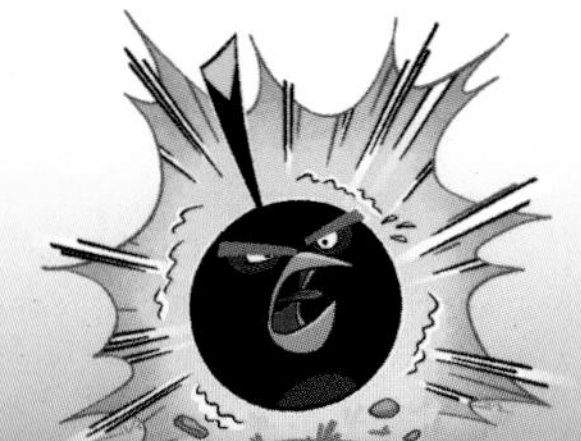
BOMB

BOMB IS ABLE TO EXPLODE AT WILL AND JUST LOVES TO BLOW THINGS UP. HOWEVER, HE IS NOT FULLY IN CONTROL OF HIS POWERS.

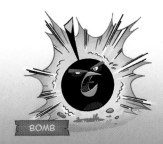

GOODBYE!
WHEE! I NEEDED THAT EXTRA PUSH!
WHAT ON EARTH WAS THAT?
I DIDN'T KNOW THERE ARE VOLCANIC BIRDS TOO. LOOK JUST LIKE...
THIS IS AN EVIL PIG PLOT!
OH, SO..!!!
UH OH!

MATILDA

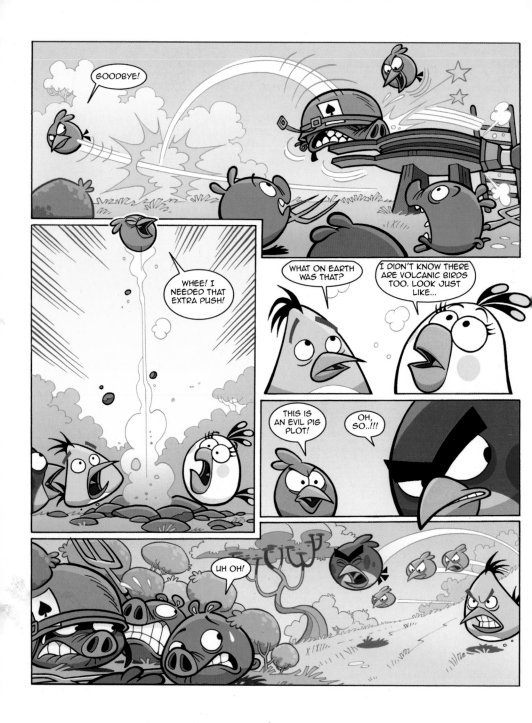

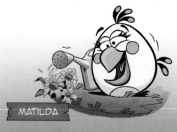

MATILDA LOVES NATURE AND TRIES TO FIND PEACEFUL SOLUTIONS TO PROBLEMS. SHE LOSES HER PEACEFUL MINDSET COMPLETELY WHEN SHE SNAPS.

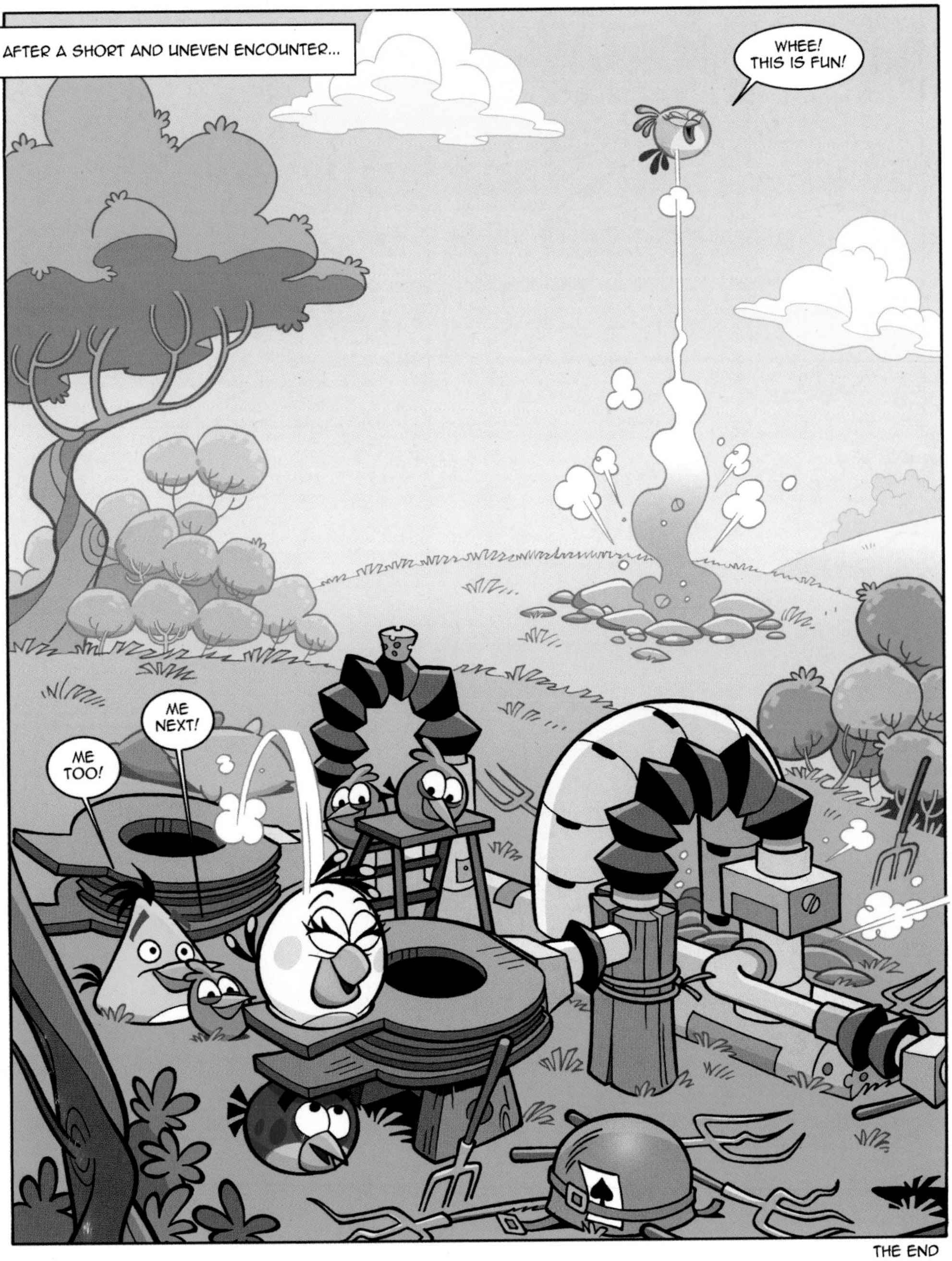
AFTER A SHORT AND UNEVEN ENCOUNTER...
WHEE! THIS IS FUN!
ME TOO!
ME NEXT!

THE END

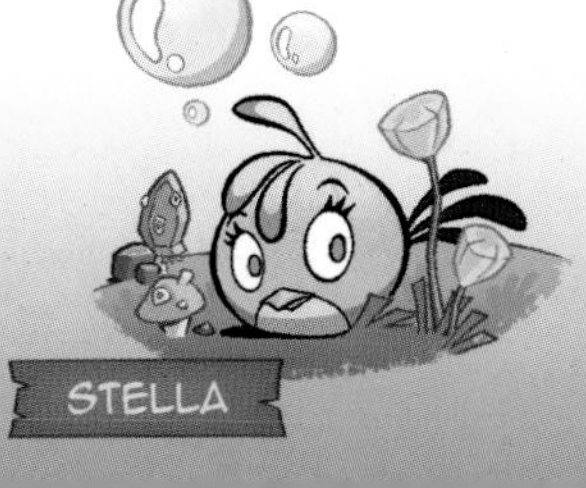
STELLA

STELLA IS A FEISTY GIRL WHO DOESN'T LISTEN TO WARNINGS. SHE LOSES HER TEMPER IF SOMEONE IS TREATED BADLY.

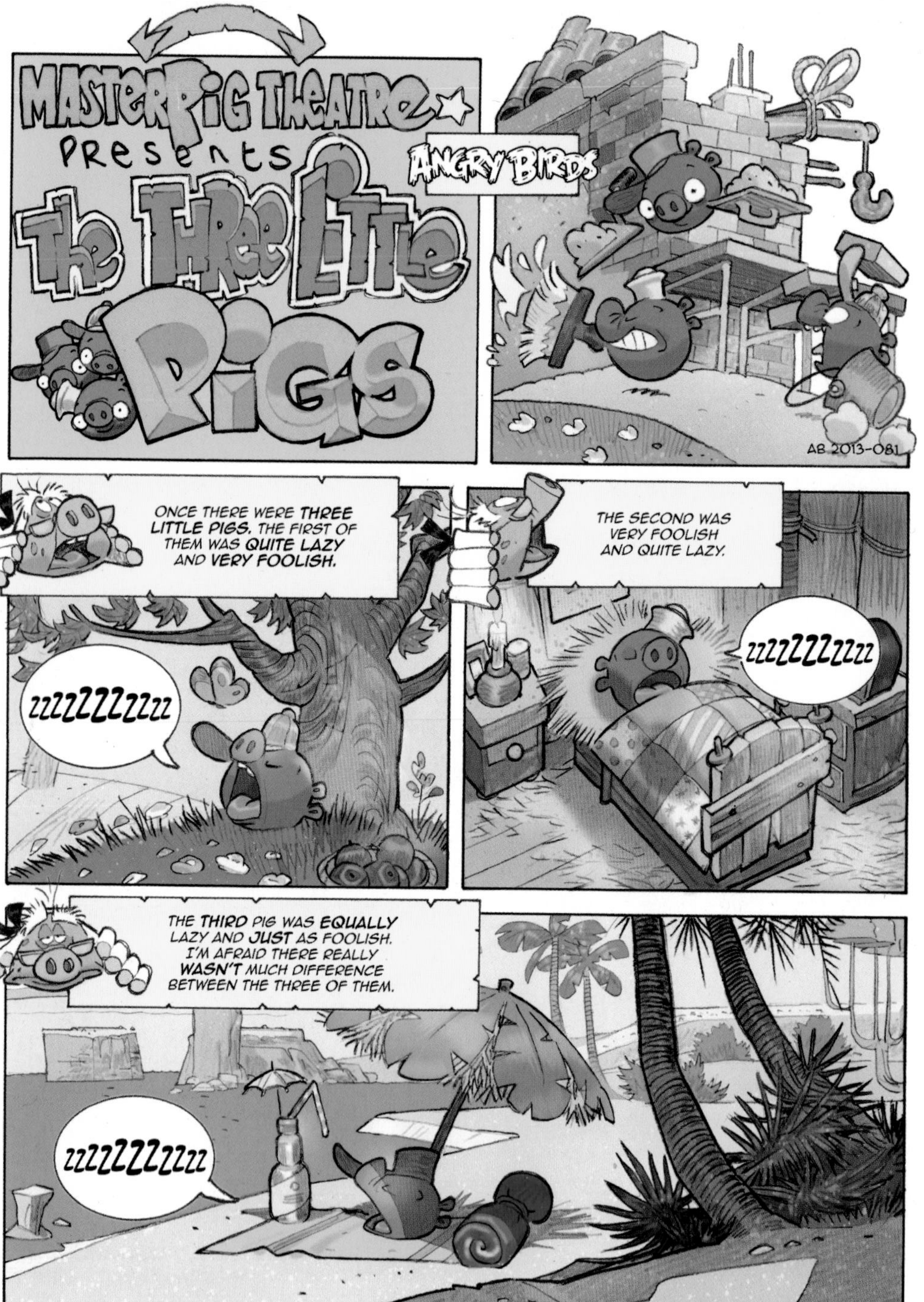
MASTERPIG THEATRE
PRESENTS
THE THREE LITTLE PIGS
ANGRY BIRDS
AB 2013-081
ONCE THERE WERE THREE LITTLE PIGS. THE FIRST OF THEM WAS QUITE LAZY AND VERY FOOLISH.
ZZZZZZZZZZZ
THE SECOND WAS VERY FOOLISH AND QUITE LAZY.
ZZZZZZZZZZZ
THE THIRD PIG WAS EQUALLY LAZY AND JUST AS FOOLISH. I'M AFRAID THERE REALLY WASN'T MUCH DIFFERENCE BETWEEN THE THREE OF THEM.
ZZZZZZZZZZZ

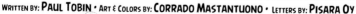

WRITTEN BY: PAUL TOBIN • ART & COLORS BY: CORRADO MASTANTUONO • LETTERS BY: PISARA OY

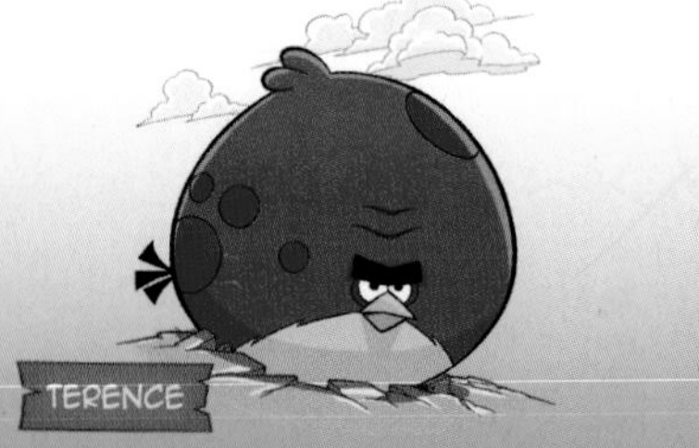
TERENCE

THE PIGS FIND TERENCE VERY FRIGHTENING. NO ONE KNOWS WHAT GOES ON IN HIS HEAD BECAUSE HE ALMOST NEVER SPEAKS.

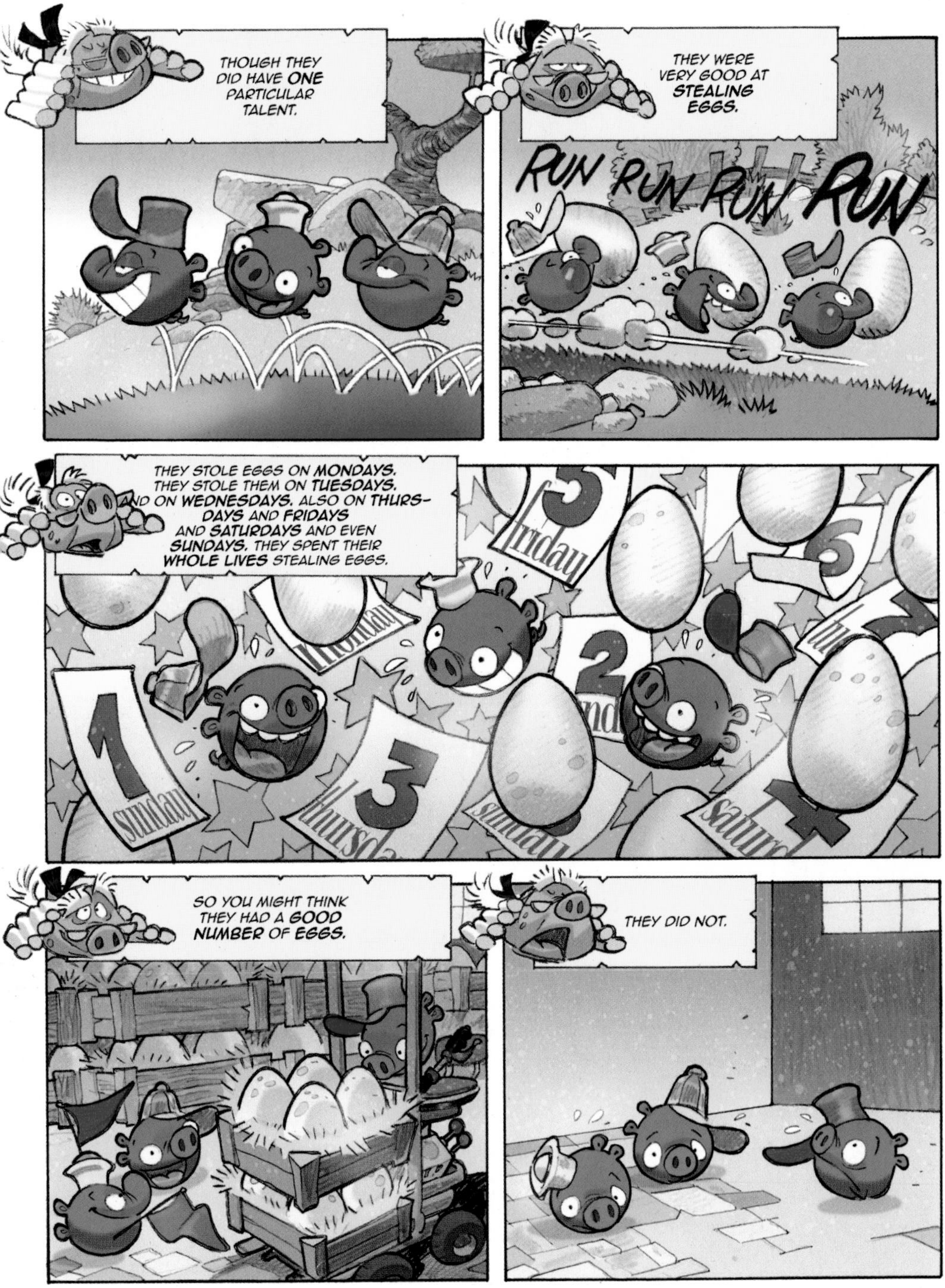
THOUGH THEY DID HAVE ONE PARTICULAR TALENT.
THEY WERE VERY GOOD AT STEALING EGGS.
RUN RUN RUN RUN
THEY STOLE EGGS ON MONDAYS. THEY STOLE THEM ON TUESDAYS. AND ON WEDNESDAYS. ALSO ON THURSDAYS AND FRIDAYS AND SATURDAYS AND EVEN SUNDAYS. THEY SPENT THEIR WHOLE LIVES STEALING EGGS.
SO YOU MIGHT THINK THEY HAD A GOOD NUMBER OF EGGS.
THEY DID NOT.

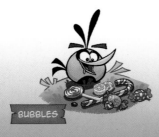

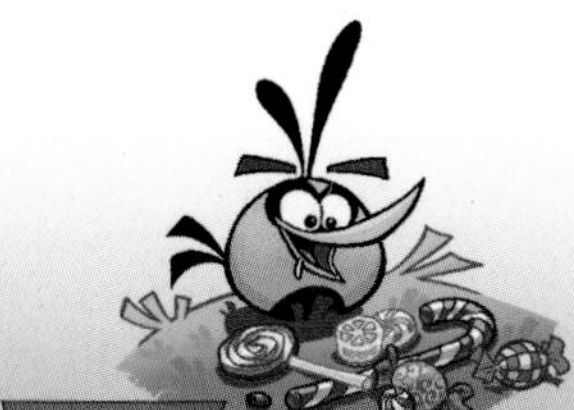
BUBBLES

THOUGH SMALL AND CUTE, BUBBLES IS ABLE TO INFLATE HIMSELF INTO A HUGE BALLOON. HE DOESN'T TALK MUCH BUT SEEMS TO LOVE SWEETS.

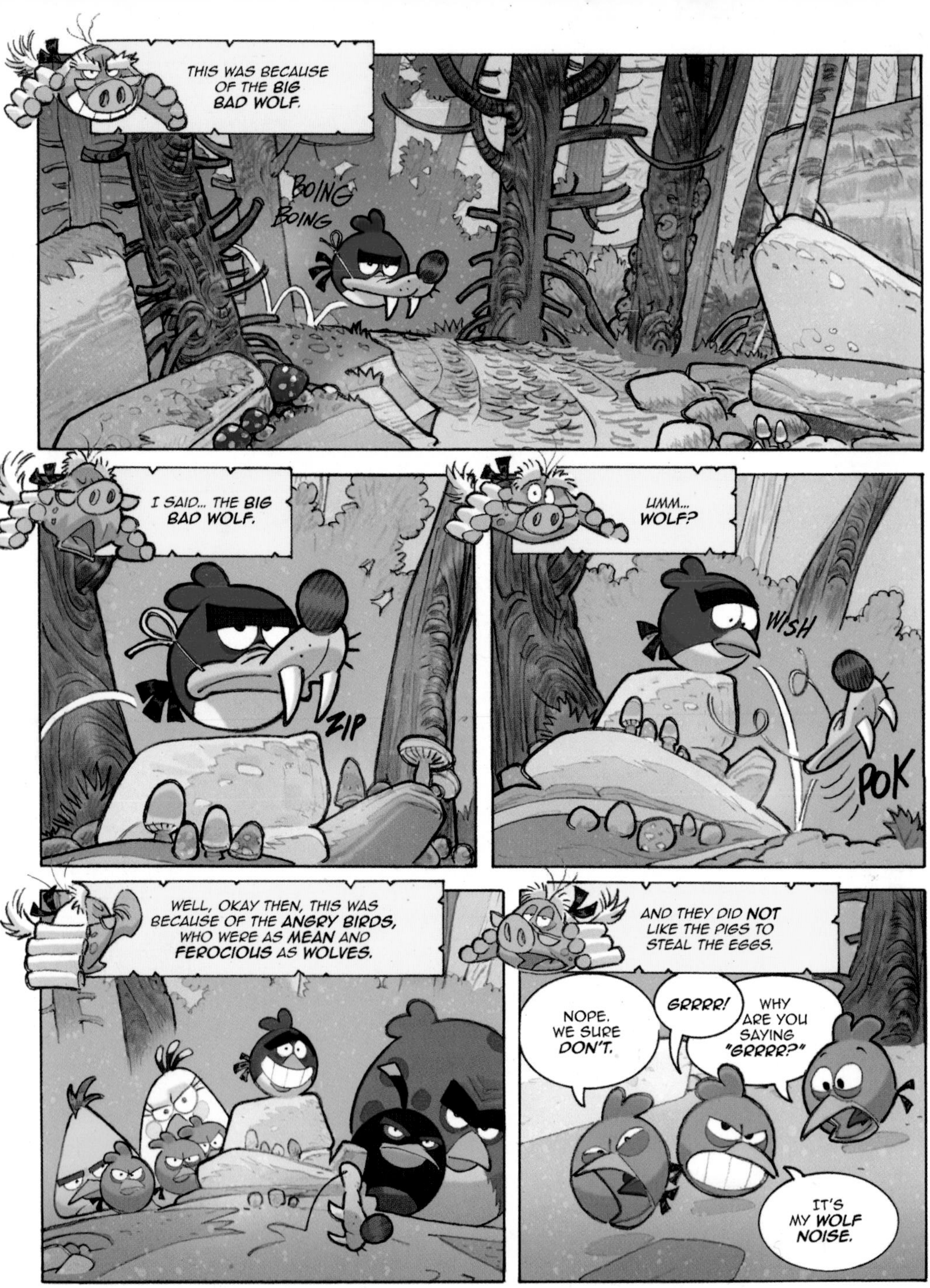

THIS WAS BECAUSE OF THE **BIG BAD WOLF**.
BOING BOING
I SAID... THE **BIG BAD WOLF**.
ZIP
UMM... **WOLF?**
WISH
POK
WELL, OKAY THEN, THIS WAS BECAUSE OF THE **ANGRY BIRDS**, WHO WERE AS **MEAN** AND **FEROCIOUS** AS **WOLVES**.
AND THEY DID **NOT** LIKE THE PIGS TO STEAL THE EGGS.
NOPE. WE SURE **DON'T**.
GRRRR!
WHY ARE YOU SAYING **"GRRRR?"**
IT'S MY **WOLF NOISE**.

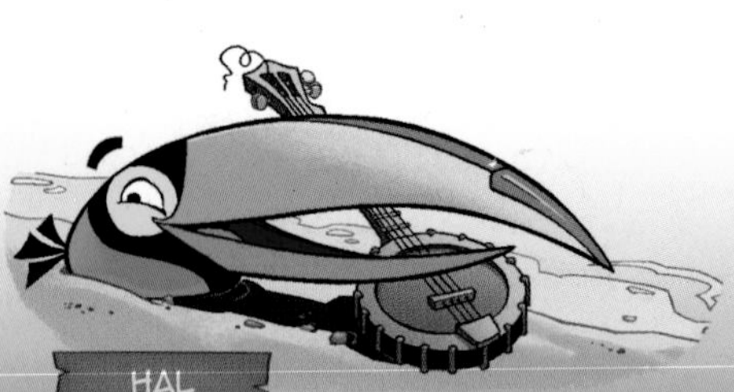

HAL

HAL IS AN ADVENTURER BIRD WHO ENJOYS PLAYING HIS BANJO ON THE SUNNY SIDE OF THE ISLAND.

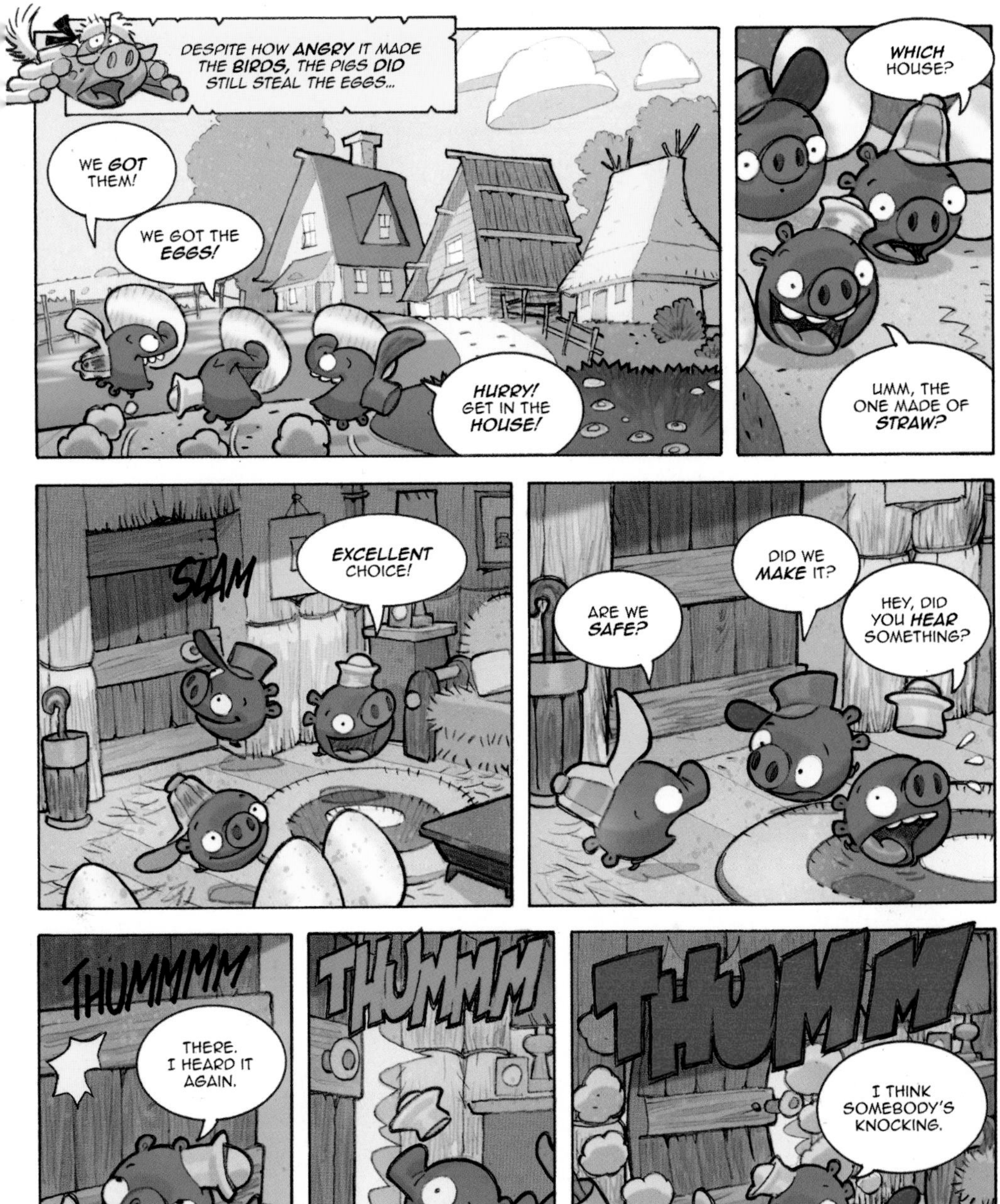
DESPITE HOW ANGRY IT MADE THE BIRDS, THE PIGS DID STILL STEAL THE EGGS...
WE GOT THEM!
WE GOT THE EGGS!
HURRY! GET IN THE HOUSE!
WHICH HOUSE?
UMM, THE ONE MADE OF STRAW?
SLAM
EXCELLENT CHOICE!
ARE WE SAFE?
DID WE MAKE IT?
HEY, DID YOU HEAR SOMETHING?
THUMMMM
THERE. I HEARD IT AGAIN.
THUMMM
ZIP
THUMM
I THINK SOMEBODY'S KNOCKING.

MINION PIGS

THE MINION PIGS ARE DOING THEIR BEST TO FIND EGGS FOR THEIR KING. THEY ARE THE LOWEST OF THE LOW IN THE PIG SOCIETY, BUT ARE STILL GENERALLY HAPPY WITH THEIR LIVES.

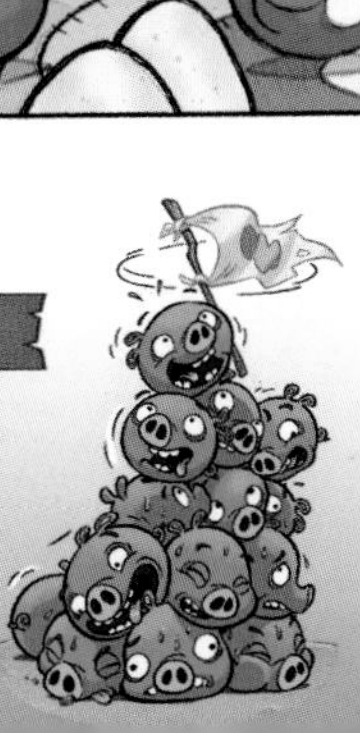

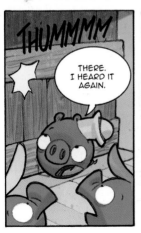

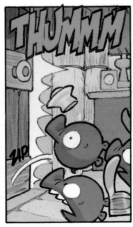

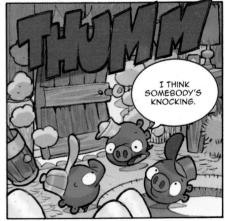

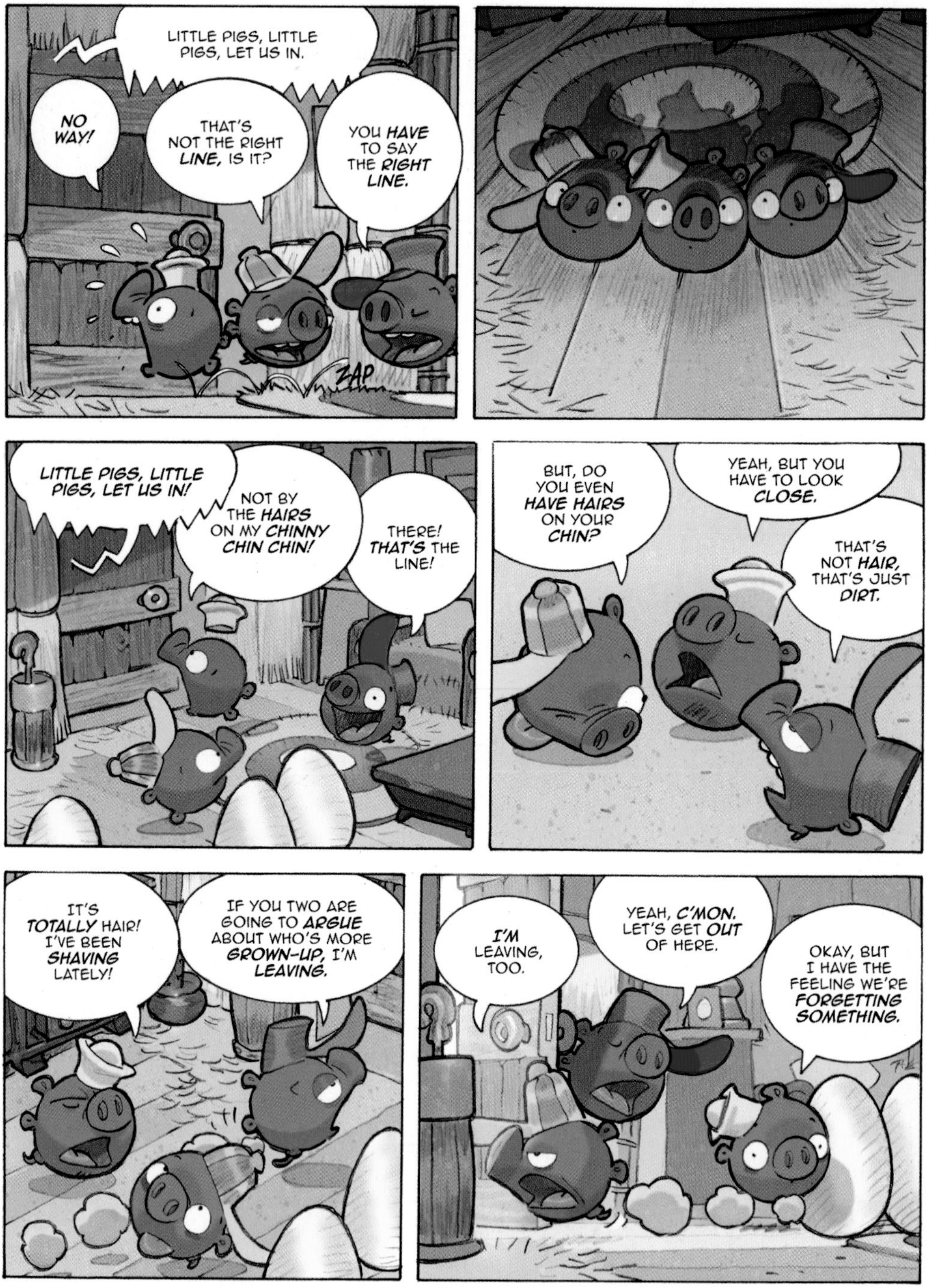
LITTLE PIGS, LITTLE PIGS, LET US IN.
NO WAY!
THAT'S NOT THE RIGHT LINE, IS IT?
YOU HAVE TO SAY THE RIGHT LINE.
ZAP
LITTLE PIGS, LITTLE PIGS, LET US IN!
NOT BY THE HAIRS ON MY CHINNY CHIN CHIN!
THERE! THAT'S THE LINE!
BUT, DO YOU EVEN HAVE HAIRS ON YOUR CHIN?
YEAH, BUT YOU HAVE TO LOOK CLOSE.
THAT'S NOT HAIR, THAT'S JUST DIRT.
IT'S TOTALLY HAIR! I'VE BEEN SHAVING LATELY!
IF YOU TWO ARE GOING TO ARGUE ABOUT WHO'S MORE GROWN-UP, I'M LEAVING.
I'M LEAVING, TOO.
YEAH, C'MON. LET'S GET OUT OF HERE.
OKAY, BUT I HAVE THE FEELING WE'RE FORGETTING SOMETHING.

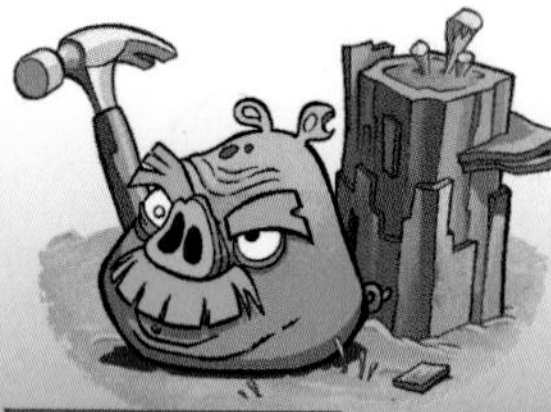

FOREMAN "BOSS" PIG

FOREMAN PIG SUPERVISES THE BUILDING OF ALL THE PIGS' CONTRAPTIONS. HE IS VERY SELF-CONFIDENT, BUT INCOMPETENT.

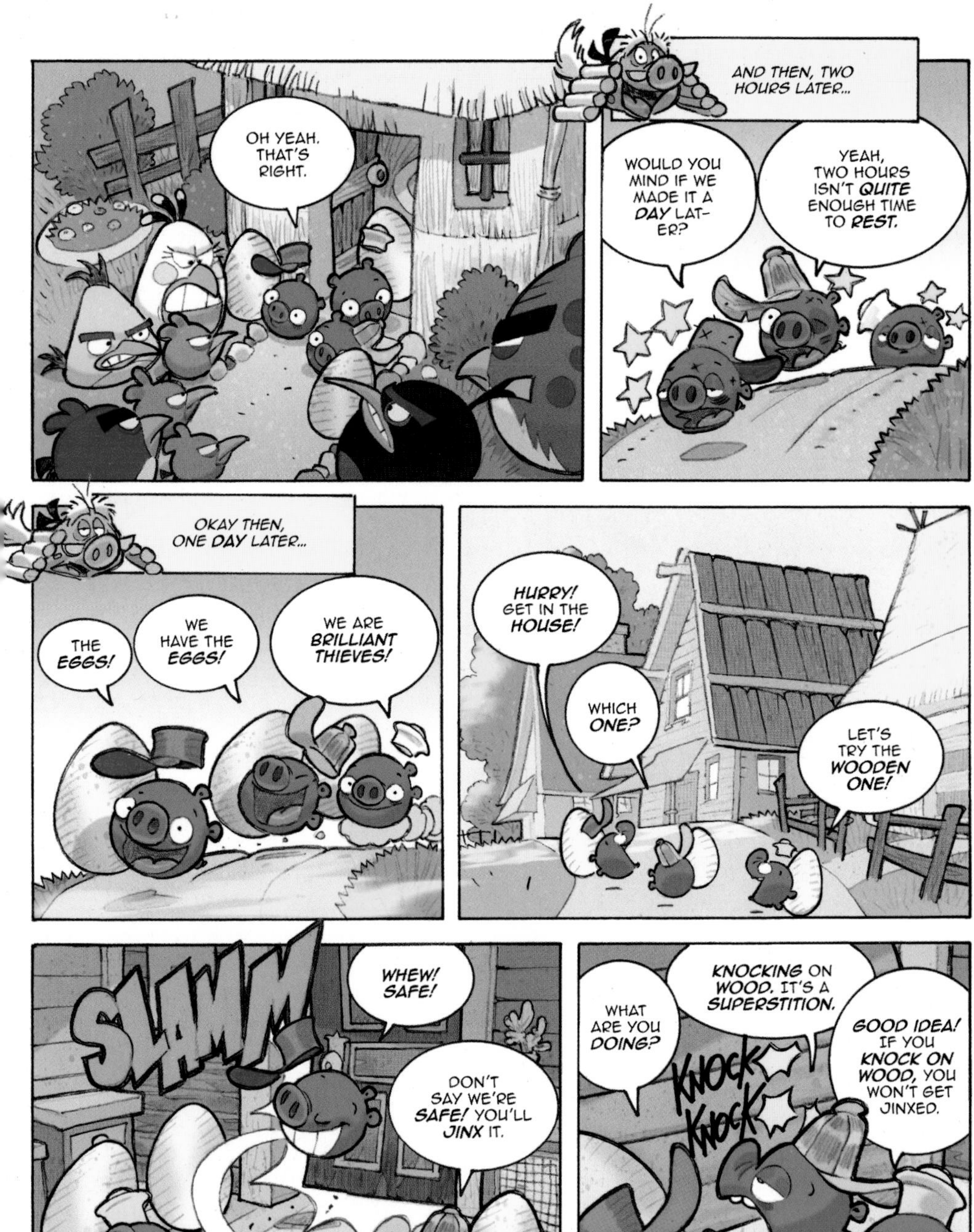
OH YEAH. THAT'S RIGHT.
AND THEN, TWO HOURS LATER...
WOULD YOU MIND IF WE MADE IT A DAY LATER?
YEAH, TWO HOURS ISN'T QUITE ENOUGH TIME TO REST.
OKAY THEN, ONE DAY LATER...
THE EGGS!
WE HAVE THE EGGS!
WE ARE BRILLIANT THIEVES!
HURRY! GET IN THE HOUSE!
WHICH ONE?
LET'S TRY THE WOODEN ONE!
SLAMM
WHEW! SAFE!
DON'T SAY WE'RE SAFE! YOU'LL JINX IT.
WHAT ARE YOU DOING?
KNOCKING ON WOOD. IT'S A SUPERSTITION.
KNOCK KNOCK
GOOD IDEA! IF YOU KNOCK ON WOOD, YOU WON'T GET JINXED.

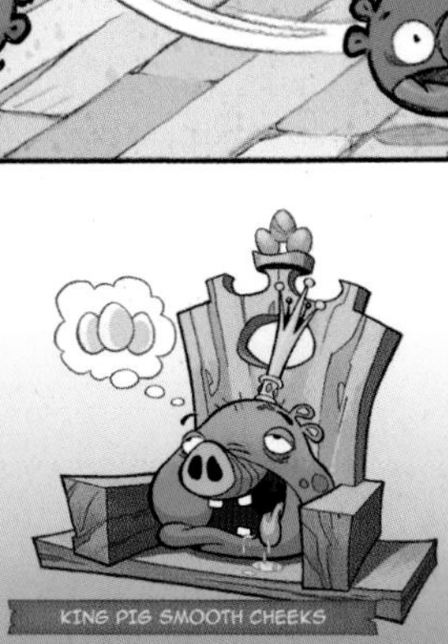
KING PIG SMOOTH CHEEKS

THE LEADER OF THE PIGS AND THE ONLY PIG WHO IS ALLOWED TO EAT EGGS. HIS BIG SECRET IS THAT HE DOESN'T HAVE ANY EGGS IN HIS TREASURE CHAMBER.

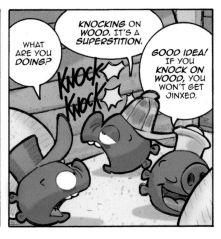

WELL, QUIT IT.
KNOCK KNOCK
I SAID, QUIT IT. THE NOISE IS TOO LOUD.
KNOCK KNOCK
I DID QUIT IT.
REALLY? THEN... WHO'S KNOCKING?
KNOCK KNOCK
LITTLE PIG, LITTLE PIG, LET ME IN.
WHAT WAS OUR LINE AGAIN?
I GOT IT. IT'S... NOT BY THE HAIR OF MY...
SMASHHH

CHEF PIG

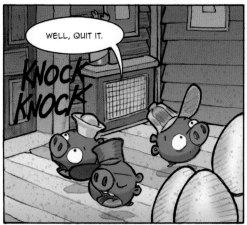

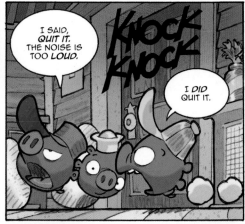

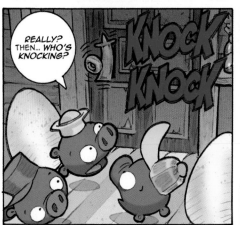

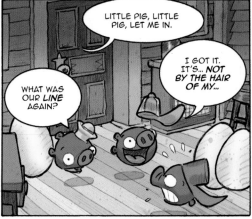

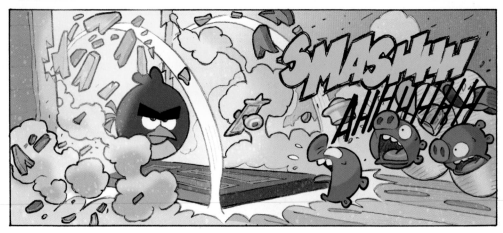

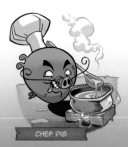

THE MOST INTELLIGENT OF THE PIGS, CHEF PIG IS ALWAYS SCHEMING TO EAT EGGS HIMSELF AND THUS BECOME KING.

OH. HELLO.

SPAKKA KRAKK SPONGI
BAMM BOOM SMAKK
OOOF

?

TWO DAYS LATER...

HEY, *GUESS WHAT?* I STOLE THE *EGGS.*

YOU STOLE THE EGGS???!

SHHHHH!

LET'S GET SOMEWHERE *SAFE.*

THIS HOUSE IS MADE OF *BRICK.*

YEAH! LET'S GO IN *HERE.*

CORPORAL PIG

CORPORAL PIG IS THE LOYAL LEADER OF THE KING'S ARMY. HE TIRELESSLY LEADS HIS TROOPS FROM FAILURE TO FAILURE.

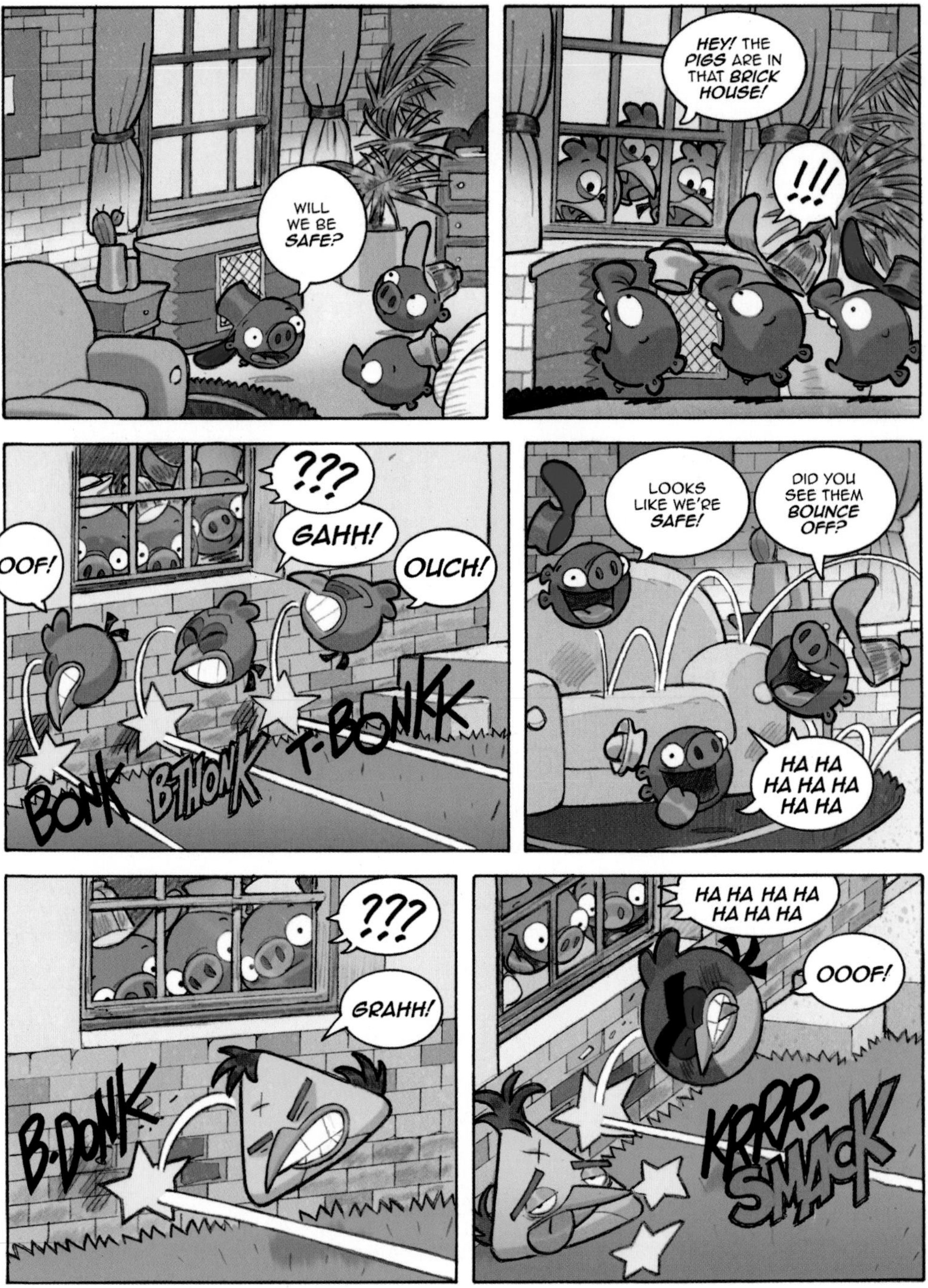
WILL WE BE SAFE?
HEY! THE PIGS ARE IN THAT BRICK HOUSE!
!!!
OOF!
???
GAHH!
OUCH!
BONK
B-THONK
T-BONKK
LOOKS LIKE WE'RE SAFE!
DID YOU SEE THEM BOUNCE OFF?
HA HA HA HA HA HA HA
???
GRAHH!
B-DONK
HA HA HA HA HA HA HA
OOOF!
KRRR-SMACK

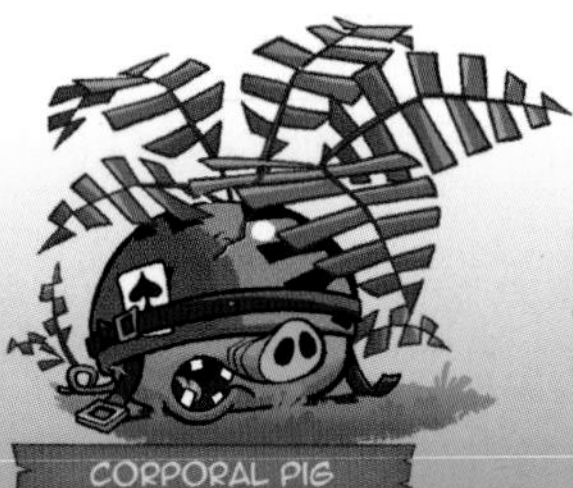

CORPORAL PIG

CORPORAL PIG IS THE LOYAL LEADER OF THE KING'S ARMY. HE TIRELESSLY LEADS HIS TROOPS FROM FAILURE TO FAILURE.

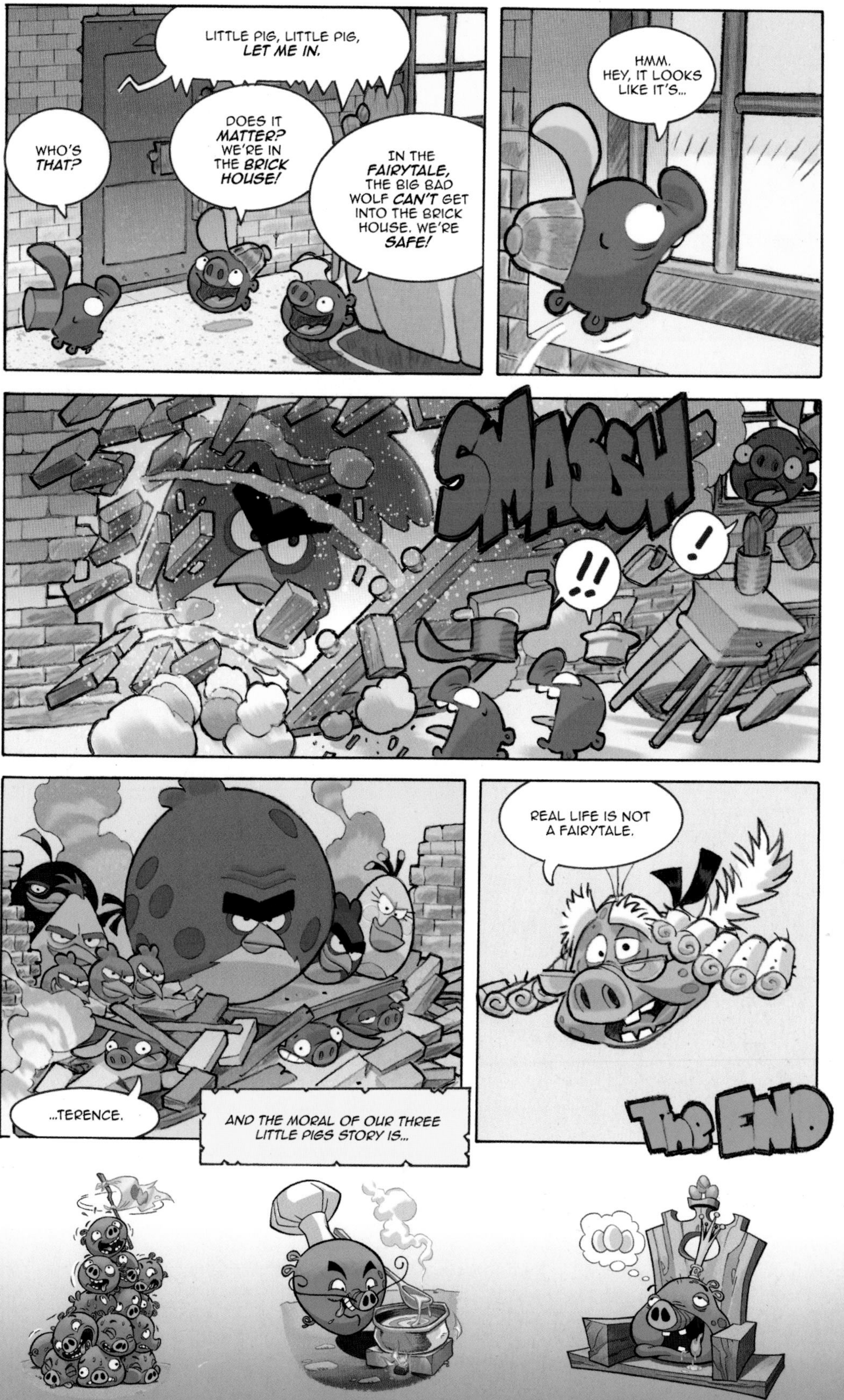
LITTLE PIG, LITTLE PIG, LET ME IN.
WHO'S THAT?
DOES IT MATTER? WE'RE IN THE BRICK HOUSE!
IN THE FAIRYTALE, THE BIG BAD WOLF CAN'T GET INTO THE BRICK HOUSE. WE'RE SAFE!
HMM. HEY, IT LOOKS LIKE IT'S...
SMASSH
!!
!
...TERENCE.
AND THE MORAL OF OUR THREE LITTLE PIGS STORY IS...
REAL LIFE IS NOT A FAIRYTALE.
The END

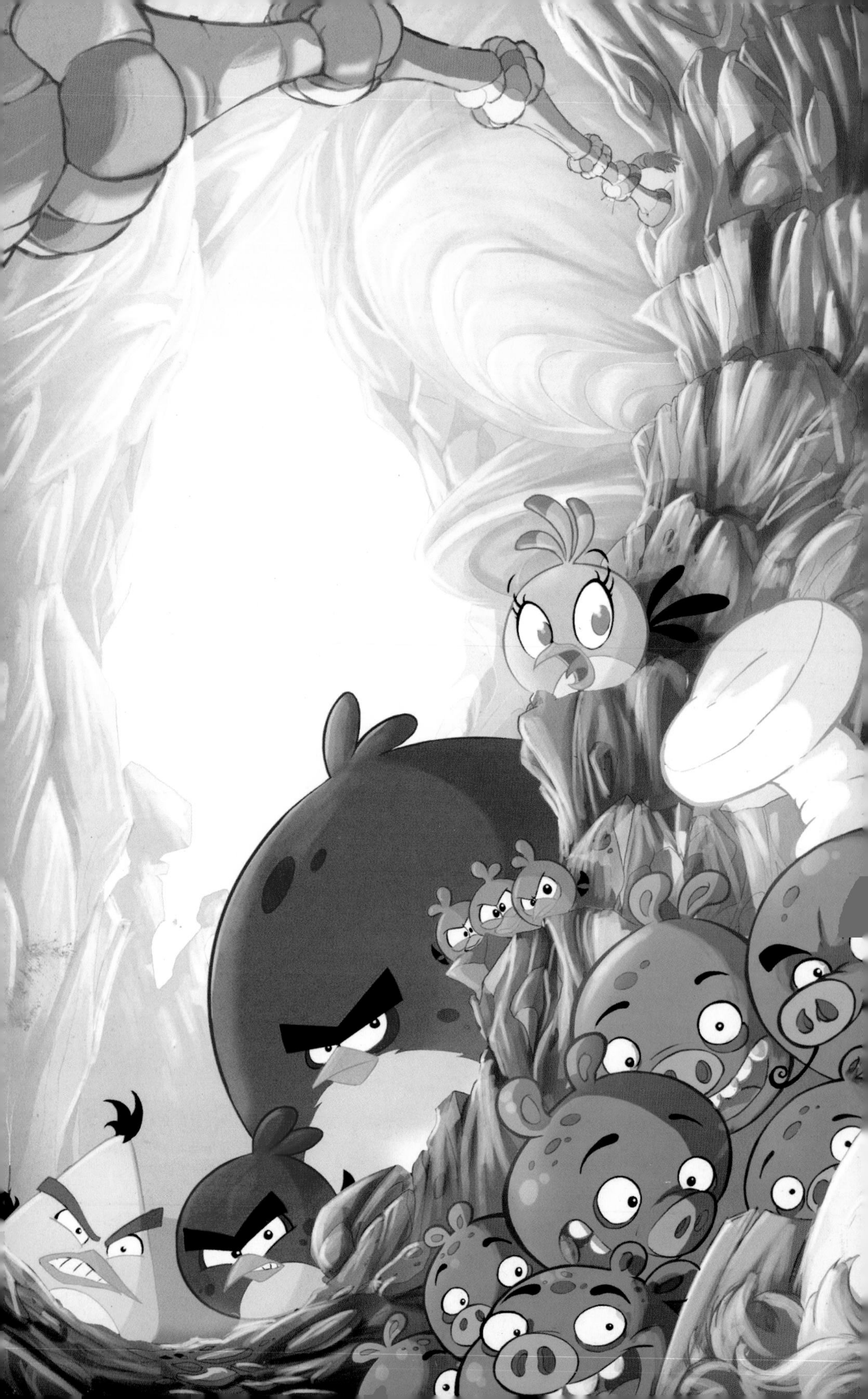

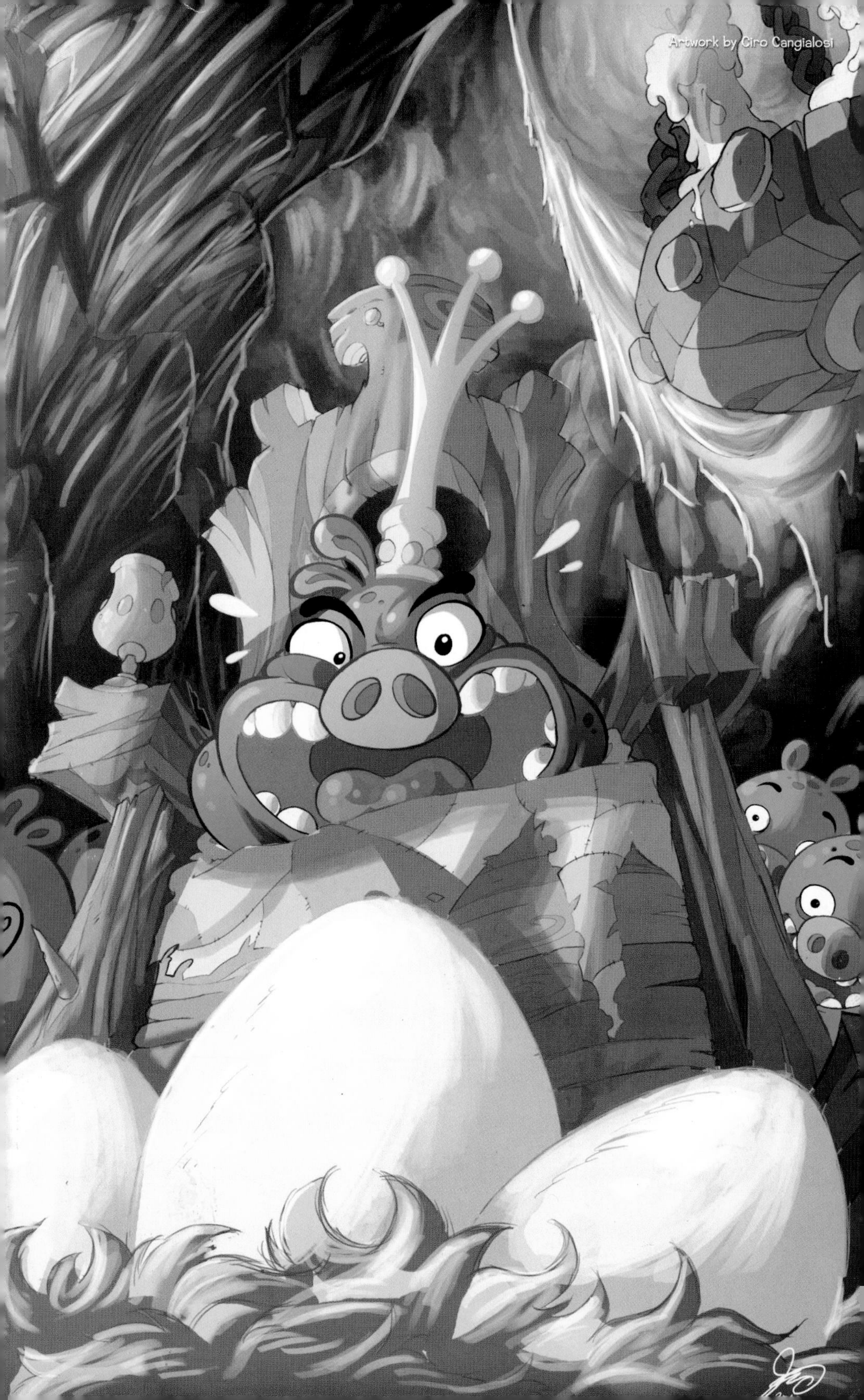

ANGRY BIRDS
COMICS

ANGRY BIRDS COMICS: WELCOME TO THE FLOCK
ISBN: 978-1-63140-090-2

ANGRY BIRDS COMICS: WHEN PIGS FLY
ISBN: 978-1-63140-248-7

Angry Birds, the world's most popular mobile game franchise, is now available in these hardcover collections of comics!

ON SALE NOW!